THE NOTHINGNESS OF BEN

BRAD BONEY

Dreamspinner Press

Published by
Dreamspinner Press
5032 Capital Circle SW
Ste 2, PMB# 279
Tallahassee, FL 32305-7886
USA
http://www.dreamspinnerpress.com/

The Nothingness of Ben

Cover Art by L.C. Chase
http://www.lcchase.com

ISBN: 978-1-62380-138-0

Printed in the United States of America
First Edition
November 2012

eBook edition available
eBook ISBN: 978-1-62380-139-7

For Stephen Nowak,
wherever you are.

ONE

SEVEN days before Christmas, Ben Walsh left his office in midtown Manhattan and began the trek across Forty-Fourth Street toward his apartment in Hell's Kitchen. He passed the St. James Theater, where *American Idiot* opened last spring. As the crowd began to gather for Thursday evening's performance, Ben thought about his latest dilemma.

A week before Christmas, and he still hadn't come up with a present for David, his boyfriend of seven weeks. David was hot, fun, and got along with his friends—Ben had no complaints. So why did he draw a blank every time he tried to think of a gift for him?

Ben had stayed late at the office again. He worked for Wilson & Mead, one of the top law firms in the city. When his iPhone vibrated in his pants pocket, he took it out and looked down at the screen. It was a text from Colin. He swiped the screen and read the text.

Meeting at M & J's place. 8p. Bring David.

Ben looked at the time. Seven thirty. He hadn't called David yet. Even though they had spent almost every night together since Thanksgiving, Ben didn't want to presume. With a touch to his phone, Ben called David, who picked up after a couple of rings. Ben grinned when he heard the deep bass voice.

"Hey, stud. I was just thinking about you."

"Oh, yeah?" Ben replied, running his fingers through his dark hair while he dodged around theatergoers. "Nasty thoughts, I hope."

"A few."

David was thirty-eight, about ten years older than Ben, and an airline pilot. A former military man, he had an effortless masculinity that everyone, including Ben, found sexy.

"Well, we've been summoned to Martin and Johnny's tonight for a Christmas thing."

"Don't your friends ever plan ahead?" David teased.

"No, never. Sorry about that. This is my last weekend in town before I head home. I think they want to kick it off early."

"Home? Oh, you mean back to Texas. You'll be here for New Year's Eve, though, right? I want to ring in 2011 with you."

"Yeah, I'll be here. Anyway, you up for a get-together tonight?"

"Of course. Definitely, I'm up for it."

"Great."

David sounded like guys do when they first start dating and don't dare say, *Look, I'm exhausted and have no patience for your friends tonight*. Ben stopped at the corner of Eighth Avenue. Something shifted. He looked up, frantic. The traffic lights were malfunctioning.

He saw yellow followed by green.

Caution. Go.

Instead of yellow followed by red.

Caution. Stop.

Were the lights turning backward? He stepped off the curb but then pulled himself back, afraid.

"Hey, Ben, you there?"

David had asked him a question. He looked up again. The lights were functioning normally, so he crossed the street.

"Yeah, I'm here. Sorry, got distracted by the throng of Green Day fans. What was the question?"

"Do you want to stop by here first or meet there?"

"Meet there. Colin's text said eight and I'm going to be late as it is."

"No problem. I'll see you there."

"Okay, thanks. See you in a few."

Ben tapped the red End button on his screen and pushed the phone back into his pocket. He could feel the cold wind start to whip through the street as he got closer to the Hudson. He hunched his shoulders toward his ears in an attempt to stay warm, but it wasn't working. He looked up and saw purple skies. Snow, maybe? He felt something shift again, the same feeling. He looked at the traffic lights when he reached Ninth Avenue. Everything seemed normal. He swallowed hard, his mouth dry. He reached into his gym bag to pull out a half-empty bottle of sports drink and took a swig.

He felt his phone buzz in his pocket again. Probably Colin, wondering where he was. He took it out and looked at the screen. It was a 512 number, Austin's area code, but he didn't recognize it. He answered immediately.

"Ben Walsh."

He took another swig of sports drink and then returned the plastic bottle to his bag. The wind blew harder now.

"Hello, Ben. This is Father Davenport. We've never met, but I'm the new priest at the University Catholic Center. I'm at Seton hospital."

Ben stood at the intersection and put his finger into his left ear so he could hear better.

"Ben, there's been an accident."

"What kind of accident?"

"It's your parents. They were coming home on the interstate and got hit by an eighteen… Ben, there's no way to make this any easier. The doctors did everything they could but… it was too much. They didn't make it, Ben. I'm so sorry, but your parents have passed. You should catch the next flight home. Your brothers need you."

The sounds of the city receded into a cavernous silence. Ben glanced up. The lights were going backward again. He heard a voice in his head, his father's voice, singing a song from when he was a little boy. Was it the Eagles? He was pretty sure it was the Eagles. "New York Minute." That was the name of the song.

Blood rushed to Ben's face and he had difficulty breathing. He could feel the earth inch forward even as he stood attached to the sidewalk. At some point he would know what to do, who to call, and where to go. Or maybe he would wake up and find that Father Davenport was just part of a really bad dream. A snowflake fell and landed on his nose. Soon the one flake turned into three, then ten, then ten thousand, until a blizzard of white engulfed him, chilling him to the bone. Through the swirl, Ben heard the disembodied voice of Father Davenport blasting its way through the tiny speaker of his phone.

"Are you there, Ben? Can you hear me? Ben? Ben?"

TWO

AT THE funeral mass two days later, Ben sat with his three brothers in the front pew of the church his parents attended every Sunday. He hadn't been to church in years. He couldn't put up with the anti-gay bullshit that came bundled with Catholicism, not to mention his healthy skepticism about the whole God thing in general. When he agreed to stay in Austin for college (as if he had a choice), leaving the church was one of the two major concessions he had wrung out of his parents. The other was that he would move out of the house and into the garage apartment in the backyard, which up until then had been rented out to a series of University of Texas grad students.

Ben glanced over at his brothers. He couldn't help but admire the consistency of his parents' gene pool. All four of them had the same dark hair, black eyes, and fair complexion as their father. They all had the same square-jawed good looks. People constantly commented on their resemblance to each other, even though Ben was ten years older than Quentin, the next in line at sixteen, followed by fourteen-year-old Jason, and Cade, the youngest at twelve. As he looked at them, Ben couldn't help but notice that Quentin needed a haircut, Jason had grown about three inches since last Christmas, and Cade kept turning around and looking in the pews behind them.

"Sit still," Ben scolded.

Quentin glared at Ben. "Leave him be. He's probably looking for Travis."

"Who's Travis?"

Quentin answered with a scowl.

Growing up, Ben had regarded his brothers as little annoyances. He had been an only child for ten years and liked it that way. Besides, he was already in high school when Quentin started kindergarten and Cade still wore diapers. As a result, the three of them were as thick as thieves, and Ben… well, he played the absent older brother very well. Travis must be a classmate or something.

After the funeral mass, the service moved to the cemetery. Ben and his brothers rode in a large black limo furnished by the funeral home. He'd had very little to do with it since his mother's sister, Julie, had made all the arrangements. At the cemetery, his parents' coffins were set up side by side over the plot they had bought years ago. Ben looked out over the huge crowd. His father was a legendary English professor at UT. The students adored William Walsh and they came out in droves, as did the faculty, English department staff, plus all of his mother's family and friends. At least three-hundred people had attended the mass and half of those came out to the cemetery. Glancing over the mourning faces, Ben noticed a man about his age standing at the back, his shock of red hair setting him apart from the sea of black suits and dresses.

Cade moved from side to side, restless. Suddenly, he tried to pull his hand away from Quentin, who didn't let go. Ben looked over and saw Jason and Quentin looking at each other as if they were communicating telepathically. Jason nodded silently and looked over at the redheaded young man. Quentin followed his gaze and his face softened in understanding, letting go of Cade's hand at the same time. Cade walked away to the other side of the coffins, toward the redhead. Father Davenport continued to recite his prayers, tossing around the clanking gold contraption that held the incense and sprinkling holy water onto the coffins.

Ben leaned over to Quentin.

"Where's he going?"

"Chillax, big brother. He's just saying hi to a friend."

Ben watched as Cade walked up to the redhead and put his hand out. The young man took it and allowed himself to be led over to where they were standing. He looked like a waiter in work boots, black polyester pants, and a white short-sleeved shirt. The mild Texas weather meant no jacket was necessary during the day. The redhead tried to smile, and Ben forced a grin in return. He looked over at Quentin for an explanation, but Quentin ignored him and kept his gaze fixed on Father Davenport instead.

When the graveside service ended, Ben reached over and offered his hand, introducing himself.

"I'm Ben Walsh."

The young man turned and shook Ben's hand. "Travis Atwood," he replied with a slow Texas drawl. "Sorry, didn't mean to butt in or nothing. I been trying to keep my distance. Give y'all some space."

"Who are you?" Ben asked, sounding more confrontational than he intended.

"Jesus, Ben," Quentin grumbled.

"It's okay, Q. He don't know me from Adam. He's just being protective."

"Wow," Quentin said. "You know less about him than he knows about you."

"I'm a neighbor," Travis explained. "I live across the street. Rent a room from old Mrs. Wright. Your family's been real kind to me."

Sounds like Dad, Ben thought. *Always taking in strays.*

"I see."

"Doubt that," Quentin muttered under his breath as they began walking back to the car, Cade dragging Travis along.

"Travis is riding back with us," Cade declared.

Ben looked at Travis, trying to signal his concern. Travis stopped and placed Cade in front of him, both hands firmly on his shoulders. He squatted down so that he was face to face with the boy. Ben looked around. As people left, several of them had one eye on the situation with Travis and Cade.

"Look, little man. I got my truck here so I'm fixin' to drive home on my own. But I'm coming back to the house, so I'll be seeing you in ten minutes, tops. Cross my heart."

Ben waited a beat before reaching out his hand to move Cade along. He didn't want to make a scene.

"Let go of me," Cade resisted.

"Cade, not now."

"Yes! Now. What happened? I don't understand how it happened?"

Sadness overwhelmed the youngest Walsh brother and he began to cry. Not the loud, wailing tears of a child, but the muffled sobs of a young boy not at all prepared to grasp the extent of his loss.

"Cade," Ben snapped, "we are not doing this here. Let's get back to the car. I've had it."

Jason stood silently, staring wide-eyed in surprise at Ben's callous reaction. Quentin shook his head as if he wasn't surprised at all.

"Jesus, big brother. On just this one day, could you not be such a dick? One day, dude. That's all we're asking for."

Quentin squatted down and took Cade into his arms. Ben could see Julie a few feet away, poised to step in if he didn't handle this quickly. He took a deep breath. They obviously had a problem here, he and Quentin, or maybe he and all three of them. But he would have to hash that out another time. *Path of least resistance*, he told himself.

"Travis, would you ride with us? Please. I'll bring you back later to pick up your truck, if it's not too much to ask. I know I haven't been around and I don't know why you matter so much, but clearly you do so... please, stay. With Cade."

Travis stood up and smiled at Ben.

"I'd be happy to, sir."

Ben laughed—for the first time since he got the phone call. He'd thought it might be months before he even smiled again. His brothers laughed with him, even Cade.

"Did you just call me *sir*?"

"Yes, sir... I mean, Ben. I called your father sir and you just... I don't know. Seem like the sir type to me."

"The sir type? I'm twenty-seven years old."

"Oh," said Travis, obviously surprised. "Geez, I didn't realize we're the same age. You were born in '83 too? You come off as much older than twenty-seven."

"It's that stick up his ass," Quentin whispered to Travis while he dug into his pocket and pulled out his phone. He smiled as he read a text. He brushed a lock of hair out of his eyes and furiously tapped away on the glass screen in response. Ben had to pause and take another deep breath. He could get into it with Quentin later.

"Shall we head back to the car?" Ben directed as he put his arm around Jason. "Cade, Travis is coming with us now, so let's start walking, okay?"

Cade didn't answer but allowed himself to be led away, sandwiched between Travis and Quentin. Julie and the rest of the crowd relaxed and continued toward their cars. They rode back to the house in silence, Ben and Travis across the seat from each other. Travis looked out the window with Cade's hand resting firmly in the palm of his own. *Handsome*, Ben thought, looking at Travis. *Really handsome*. Travis looked at him and lifted one corner of his mouth in a half smile. He had gray eyes and strawberry lashes, with about ten freckles down the front of his nose. Ben didn't consider himself tall at five eleven, but Travis was short, no taller than five seven. He always had liked shorter men. Ben looked down and saw dirt under Travis's fingernails. Or was it grease?

When they got back to the house, visitors packed the living and dining rooms. Piles of food covered every available surface in the kitchen. Ben spent the next few hours listening to stories and trying to keep an eye on his brothers, which Travis made easier. They spent the entire afternoon quietly hanging out and talking with him. At around sunset, the guests began to leave, and by seven, only the Walsh boys, Travis, and Julie remained in the house.

"I sent Robert back to Dallas with the girls," she said, referring to her husband and two children. Julie had wrapped all the various food items and packed them away into the fridge. "If it's okay with you, I'm going to stay until Monday. We have an appointment with the lawyer to go over the will. Of course, I could get a motel room, but we do need to have a discussion about... you know...."

Ben cut her off.

"Please, Julie. You're more than welcome to stay until Monday. Right now, though, I need to drive Travis back to his truck. He left it at the cemetery."

"That's fine, I'll stay here with the boys."

"Thanks. For everything."

"You're welcome, Ben." She forced a thin smile onto her face.

Ben grabbed the spare set of keys to his mom's SUV from the Peg-Board next to the fridge as he and Travis headed out to the porch. When they got to the driveway, he looked around. Of course. They had been driving the SUV during the accident.

"Shit," he said, shaking his head. "I grabbed the wrong keys. Give me one second."

He ducked back into the house and exchanged the keys for those to his father's truck. They buckled in and headed out to the cemetery. They drove in silence for awhile until finally Ben broke the ice.

"Sorry about earlier. I wasn't trying to be rude or anything. I've been out of touch these past few years."

"No worries. I get it. I'd wonder who the hell I was too, if I were you. But I ain't no cause for alarm. I moved into Mrs. Wright's place about six months ago."

"The garage apartment?"

"Nu-uh, I rent a room in her house. It's cheap and I think she likes having someone around. I met your father when I was taking out the trash one Thursday. He's a naturally friendly man."

"Yeah. I'm well aware."

"We struck up a conversation at the curb...."

"He invited you over for dinner... I know the drill."

"Yep. I spent a good amount of time in that house the past few months. They kind of took me in... like one of their own."

"I've seen it many times. They have...." Ben caught his verb tense. "Sorry. They had big hearts. My father always seemed to give the best part of himself to his students. The entire time growing up, I watched him take in one after another. It would have been nice if he had taken me under his wing like that once in a while."

"Doubt you needed it."

"Excuse me?"

"Look at you. You're Mr. Successful. Big hotshot lawyer from New York City. I reckon your dad did everything right."

They were stopped at a red light, so Ben had the chance to look over at him.

"Do you talk to everybody this way?"

"I don't talk to nobody no way. My daddy left when I was fifteen and my mama moved me all around Texas, chasing one boyfriend or another 'til she died from too much wine-in-a-box. I been on my own ever since with particularly no family whatsoever. So it's all relative, Obi-Wan. You want to whine about your shitty parents, go ahead on. I'll be sitting right here when you're finished."

There was a long pause.

"I didn't say *shitty*."

"Sorry. I didn't mean to go off on you like that. I don't know what's got me all fired up. It was strange seeing you with 'em today. I'm used to thinking of your brothers as the three musketeers. But you're like the missing fourth musketeer. What happened, anyway?"

"What do you mean?"

"Why the ten-year break between you and Quentin?"

"I was kind of a mistake," Ben explained.

"That don't sound like your mama."

"Nothing like that. They were married, just planning to wait on the kids. But the rhythm method failed, so maybe *surprise* is a better word. My mom went on the pill after I was born and then waited ten years to pop out Quentin, Jason, and Cade. Did my dad tell you he named us after the siblings in one of his favorite books?"

"*The Sound and the Fury*, right?"

"That's the one. He loved his Southern gothic."

"Yeah, he gave me a copy. I couldn't get past the first page. Didn't make no sense to me."

Travis fell silent.

"Cade seems very attached to you," Ben said as he checked the rearview mirror.

"I reckon he is. That okay?"

"I guess. More an observation, really."

"We like a lot of the same things. Did you know he plays football and baseball?"

"No. I didn't know that."

"Yep. He's gonna be too small for college football—but baseball, well, that's a horse of a different color, if you know what I mean. He's got great instincts on the diamond."

More silence.

"What's gonna happen now?" Travis asked. "With them, I mean."

"I don't know. It's been so crazy the past two days I haven't had time to think about it."

"Whatever you do, don't split them up. They can survive anything as long as they're together."

"I never talked to my parents about it. I mean, who does? Whatever they wanted, it'll be in their will, so we'll find out on Monday. Unfortunately, I know nothing about custody and estate law in Texas."

Someone cut Ben off and he honked his horn.

"Asshole. There are some terrible drivers in this town."

"Yep," said Travis, "I know."

"So—what are you studying?"

Travis looked over at Ben, silent and confused.

"You're a student, right?" Ben clarified. "I mean, you live in the neighborhood and my dad always took in UT students."

"No."

Ben raised his eyebrows, surprised. "Oh. Okay."

Travis looked out the window as he answered. "I'm a mechanic at Groovy Automotive. I fix cars for a living."

So it was grease.

"Sorry, I just assumed that... never mind. Well, you obviously know what I do for a living."

"Yep. Your daddy talked about you a lot. He was real proud. Columbia and all. I've even seen baby pictures."

"Please tell me you're kidding."

Travis smiled and turned his head. "You know your pops. I ain't kidding."

They stopped at another light. Ben looked over and saw Travis rubbing his thumbs against his fingers. "Your hands cold?" he asked, reaching across the seat to the glove compartment and unintentionally brushing against Travis's knee as he went. Travis jumped as if Ben had shocked him with a battery cable. Ben looked up at him. "Didn't mean to scare you. I was just getting you some gloves." He pulled a knit pair out of the compartment and handed them to Travis.

"No worries." Travis took the gloves but didn't put them on. The light changed and Ben continued driving toward the cemetery. "So—did you leave a girlfriend back in New York City?"

Ben paused while he waited for the oncoming traffic to file past, leaving him free to make a left-hand turn.

"My father never mentioned that I'm gay?"

He glanced over, but Travis didn't look particularly awkward.

"Nu-uh, he surely never did. Mention it, I mean."

"Classic denial," Ben said, shaking his head.

"But in that case, did you leave a boyfriend behind?"

Ben laughed. "I don't know." And that was an honest answer. He hadn't talked to David since he phoned him from the airport. "I was dating someone but it wasn't serious. My future is a bit up in the air right now. What about you? Do you have a girlfriend?"

Travis grinned. "Now just how do you know I don't have a boyfriend? I could be one of those metrosexuals Jason's told me about."

"Well, do you?"

Travis's grin got wider and he shook his head. "Nah, I'm just messing with you. I been going out with a girl I met a few months back. Nothing serious, I reckon, though doubt she sees it that way. You never know with women. They are, as my mama's last boyfriend used to say, mysterious creatures."

"What's her name?"

"My mama?"

Ben laughed. "No, your girlfriend."

"Oh. Trisha. One of the boys at the shop, Topher, hooked me up with her. She's a nice girl. Quite a looker too. I like regular, dependable sex. And in case you haven't heard, it's a lot harder for a straight man to get laid than a gay one."

"Sounds like a cliché to me," Ben protested. "Besides, I find it hard to believe you have a difficult time getting laid."

"As I was saying," continued Travis, ignoring Ben's compliment, "regular and dependable. That's what I like. You don't get that standing around some dive on Sixth Street looking for another one-night stand. The clock has run out on that game for me and my days of making lemonade are over."

"Making lemonade?"

"Making do with ugly chicks. You know, when life deals you lemons...."

"Ouch. That's harsh." Travis turned again to look out the window. "Don't take that the wrong way. I like harsh. I've been told on more than one occasion that I lack compassion. It's what makes me a great lawyer *and* a shitty brother. I didn't know that leaving Texas would make me the villain."

"It ain't that you left."

"What do you mean?"

"Quentin's not angry that you left. He's angry that you checked out. Give him some space to breathe, know what I mean? Right now he's just agger-vated. He needs a crosshair for his anger, and sure enough, that's you. Talk to him, get to know him again. He's smart. Like you, I hear."

"And you? Certainly you're not planning on being a mechanic for the rest of your life?" Travis's cheeks flushed enough that Ben could see his scarlet face in the dark cab of the truck. *Shit*, Ben thought to himself, *that's exactly what he was planning.*

"I'm sorry, really. I didn't mean to imply...."

"I don't have what you'd call ambitions to higher education, and I don't think they'd take me even if I did. I know you're probably one of those folks who thinks it's natural that everyone goes to college, but where I come from, it ain't even natural to finish high school. Being a mechanic, working with engines, it's what I'm good at. I can fix anything. And just 'cause I don't have a degree don't mean I'm stupid."

"Objection! The witness is putting words in my mouth."

That made Travis smile.

"You think you're so damn charming, don't you?"

"I think… you don't want to know what I think. Except that I really am sorry."

They had arrived back at the cemetery, and Travis pointed out his truck in the corner of the far parking lot. Ben pulled up next to it.

"So," he said. "Here we are."

"Here we are," Travis repeated.

He opened up the passenger door and stepped out. He paused for a second, as if deciding whether or not to say something, and then finally turned back.

"I'm real sorry about your parents, Ben."

"Thanks, man. And not just for the words. Thank you for looking out for my brothers today. It took a big load off my mind."

"You're welcome. Anytime you need help, or if you just want to talk, you know where to find me."

"Old Mrs. Wright's place."

"Indeed. Just knock on the side door."

Travis thrust his hand out across the seat. Ben shook it. Firm and sturdy. They said good night and Travis climbed into his truck, an old beat-up Ford Ranger. Ben backed out of the parking lot and drove away, glancing in his rearview mirror to see a pair of headlights following him. Those headlights stuck there all the way back home, until they finally broke off and headed up the driveway of the house across the street. As he was walking up the front porch steps, Ben looked behind him and saw Travis get out of his truck and walk over to the side of Mrs. Wright's house. He leaned down and grabbed some cords. He plugged them into an outlet and Christmas lights lit up all over the front yard, along the porch, and in the trees. There must have been hundreds—maybe a thousand—of the tiny white lights strung everywhere. As Travis headed back toward the side door, he looked across the street and saw Ben staring at the display, transfixed. As a boy, Ben had always wanted to cover the Walsh house with lights at Christmas, but the end of the semester was a busy time for his father and they never got around to it.

"Ben." Travis raised his voice enough so that he could be heard from across the street.

"Yeah?" Ben pulled his gaze away from the lights and looked at Travis standing on the side steps.

"Ain't nothing broken here that can't be fixed."

And then he was gone, closing the door behind him and disappearing into the back of Mrs. Wright's house.

THREE

BEN woke up Sunday morning at six. He stumbled into the kitchen and opened the fridge. He found stacks of plastic containers with everything from egg salad to fried chicken. He went to the cupboard and checked the cereal shelf. Two kinds of Cheerios (original and Apple Cinnamon), Froot Loops, Frosted Flakes, Corn Pops, some Raisin Bran, Special K, Rice Krispies, and Honey Smacks. And that was only the front row. He rummaged around behind and pulled out a box of Frosted Mini-Wheats, poured some into a bowl, and covered them with milk. He grabbed a spoon and headed for the living room, where he pulled out his iPad and started reading the *Times* and the *Journal*. He hadn't seen any news in three days.

After a few minutes, he looked up from the screen and around the room. He had to admit he loved this place—a large, two-story, five-bedroom house located north of campus on the law-school side, a few blocks from the football stadium. Built in the late 1930s, it had a one-bedroom apartment over the garage, a Depression-era feature designed to provide supplemental income. A young grad student named Betsy currently rented the apartment, but she had left for the winter break. When Ben lived there, his friends at UT called it The Ben Pad and loved sitting around on the floor talking until the wee hours of the morning. The house itself had two bedrooms upstairs, where Quentin and Jason no doubt still slept. The downstairs included Cade's room, the guest room where Julie was staying, and his parents' room, where Ben had slept. He found the arrangement more than a little creepy.

Ben stopped to listen. The house was only blocks from I-35, which provided the soothing white noise of freeway traffic at all hours of the day and night. Ben returned to his reading until, half an hour later, he heard a rustling from the guest room. He couldn't see around the corner to the hallway, but he could hear the patter of Julie's feet as she went into the bathroom and locked the door behind her. *We're all disoriented*, he thought. She came into the living room about an hour later, fully dressed and obviously ready to go somewhere. Of course, it was Sunday. It hadn't even occurred to him that they would all be going to church this morning.

"Good morning, Ben. Mass is at nine thirty. I can drive the boys if you had something else planned."

Something else planned? Did she mean whatever things homosexuals do on Sunday mornings once they stop going to Mass? His mother's family had never really accepted the whole gay thing and certainly had nothing good to say about his decision to leave the church. And they wondered why he wanted to get out of Texas. Ben decided he could use the time to himself. It was only an hour, but it would be a break from everything and he desperately needed that.

"You don't mind?"

"Of course not." Julie tried to sound reassuring, but he could see the disapproval flash across her face. She went into the kitchen and started making breakfast. "You should probably wake your brothers."

Ben bit down on his lip. He decided to broach the custody subject with Julie while his brothers were still asleep. He turned off his iPad and followed her into the kitchen. Standing in the doorway, he watched her pull out a bowl and start cracking eggs into it.

"You said last night we needed to have a discussion. Do you know what the will says about custody?"

She poured some milk in with the eggs, sprinkled a pinch of salt and cinnamon, and then started beating them with a fork.

"No. Not exactly. But I have a pretty good idea."

She pulled a skillet out of the cupboard, placed it on the stove top, and dropped a pat of butter into the middle. She flipped the knob to ignite the heat below the pan, then walked across the kitchen to the pantry, where she pulled a loaf of bread from the second shelf.

"What are the options?" he asked.

"Why don't you sit down. French toast?"

That sounded good.

"Sure, I'll take a couple slices."

Ben sat down at the large wooden table in the corner of the kitchen. Julie talked while she continued making breakfast.

"There's no one on your father's side. His brother's not fit to raise a goldfish, let alone three boys. And that, by the way, is not a criticism. Your mom and dad were in complete agreement there. Some people simply aren't meant to be parents."

Ben had a great fondness for Uncle Tommy, but he agreed with Julie. Uncle Tommy currently lived in a one-bedroom apartment in Oakland. Forty years old and never met a responsibility he couldn't dodge. He hadn't even made it to Austin for the funeral.

"All of your grandparents have been dead for years," she continued, "so that leaves me and your two uncles."

She was referring to his mother's brothers, Sam and Nick, both of whom lived in Houston. Ben thought of them as thick, emotionally distant men who nonetheless provided well for their families.

"And you," she added, almost as an afterthought.

And me, Ben thought. So there it was. He was an option, a potential guardian for his three brothers. He'd avoided the obvious for two days, but now at least it was out in the open.

"Of course."

"The only problem with us, and I think I speak for Sam and Nick as well, is that we simply don't have space for three boys. Your parents knew that. The only way to keep them together is to keep them here. With you."

"So that's it. You each take one of them and I go back to New York, or I move here and everyone stays together?"

"That's the long and short of it. Best as I can see."

"And the will? What do you think it says?"

Julie stood in front of the stove, dropping batter-coated pieces of bread into the sizzling skillet. She turned around and looked at him.

"I'm pretty sure they left it up to you." She seemed almost disappointed by this.

Ben thought about what Travis had said last night when he drove him back to his truck. *Whatever you do, don't split them up.* If he took his advice, that meant he had no choice at all. As Julie flipped the toast to brown it on the other side, his throat tightened and he had to clear it in order to continue.

"And what do you think, Julie?"

She grabbed a plate and flipped the pieces of French toast onto it, then walked over to the table where Ben sat.

"Here you go," she said, setting the plate in front of him. "I think the benefits of being raised in a traditional family setting would outweigh keeping them together."

Ben's spine stiffened.

"You'd rather split them up instead of keeping them here with their gay brother?"

"Their *single* gay brother," she said, "who will one day meet another single gay... person. And then what? Really, Ben. Do I have to paint a picture? You're not even settled down. Becoming a parent means saying good-bye to fun and independence and childish things. Are you ready for that? Don't kid yourself that this has anything to do with being their brother. This is about guardianship. Parenting. I can't believe we're even having this conversation."

Ben got up and went to the drawer for a fork and then the fridge for the maple syrup. Without saying anything else, he covered the toast with liberal amounts of the sweet goop and sat down to eat.

BEN waited in the living room until Julie returned from church with the boys.

"Cade and Jason," he said, standing up from the overstuffed chair. "Why don't you two go get changed so we can get some lunch? Quentin, do you mind if we talk outside for a minute?"

Quentin flashed a big fake grin.

"Sure, big brother. Let's go have a chat."

"I was thinking barbeque," Ben whispered to Julie as he followed Quentin to the front door. "For lunch, I mean. Unless you don't think that's traditional enough."

"Stop it," she said, looking at Ben hard.

Ben hurried Quentin out the door and onto the front porch. They were going to have this conversation no matter what, so no point putting it off. Ben had spent the hour thinking about what to say to him, but hadn't come up with anything particularly inspiring.

"So, we have a problem."

Quentin didn't look at him, but instead stared out across the street. Ben followed the line of his sight, thinking he might see Travis standing next to his beat-up old truck. But he saw neither Travis nor the truck.

"I admit there's a problem, but I don't know what you mean when you use the word *we*."

"We. You know, you and me. You're obviously pissed at me for something."

"For something? Jesus, how can one person be so clueless?" He sighed in frustration. "There is no *we*, you moron. At least not how I see it. What? You want me to act all warm and fuzzy? Is that what you're after?"

"No. But do we really need all the hostility?"

"Oh, Benjy, we need it now more than ever. You think I don't know what you're up to? You think I don't know what the options are? You're about to split us up between mom's sister and brothers, and you wonder why I'm hostile?"

"Were you listening to my conversation with Julie this morning?"

"I wasn't listening to shit. But see, I'm right. You're already talking about it. That's sweet, bro. Really, it is."

"Nothing's been decided yet."

"Bullshit. Do you honestly expect me to believe that you're going to be a part of the solution? You're going to stand there and make that argument? Since you left for law school, you come back here once a year. *Once*. I'm their big brother, Ben. They turned to me when this happened. But I'm not old enough to take care of them, so along you come and... what? Tell me. Really, I want to hear it from you. Are you actually thinking about moving back to Texas? Now's your chance. Shock the hell out of me."

Ben looked away and said nothing.

"I didn't think so. It *has* been decided, so fuck this conversation. Don't you dare try to tell me this'll be the best thing in the long run. If it was just me, I wouldn't give a shit. Really. It's a hard-knock life and all that crap. But Cade? What do you think's gonna happen to him? And if you knew anything about what Jason's going through... if you knew anything at—" Quentin stopped himself in resignation. "I might as well be talking to your voice mail." He shook his head and turned toward the front door. "I'll make you a deal. I'll dial back the hostility if you make sure we can at least spend Christmas together. Here. In the house."

Ben didn't move.

"Alright, then. I'll take that as your way of saying yes." Quentin walked to the door but then stopped. "Thanks for the chat," he said, entering the house and leaving Ben alone on the porch.

WHEN they returned from a painfully quiet lunch, Ben couldn't help but notice Travis's truck in the driveway. He needed someone to talk to and Travis had offered the night before. He thought they ended on a good note despite the obvious awkwardness of Ben's mechanic-for-the-rest-of-your-life comment.

"I'm going over to Mrs. Wright's house to talk to Travis for a minute," he announced to everyone upon entering the front door. "I won't be long."

Quentin and Jason looked at each other and wrinkled their foreheads.

"I don't know, big brother," said Quentin. "Are you sure you don't want to rethink your timing?"

Jason made no effort to contain his laughter.

"I'm just going over to say thank you again. Little brother."

Quentin grinned. "Forget I said anything."

Ben exited back out the door, then went down the porch stairs and across the street to Mrs. Wright's side door. The top half consisted of nine small panes of glass, so when Ben stood on the steps, he could see Mrs. Wright's kitchen, a sliver of her living room, and the door to the back bedroom.

He knocked on one of the glass panes. The door made a racket as it rattled in the frame. Commotion broke out behind the back bedroom door. Ben heard voices and immediately realized what he'd done, cursing himself for not listening to Quentin. He waited about five seconds too long, though, because as he was about to turn and bolt, Travis stepped out of the bedroom with nothing on but a pair of blue jeans. He was barefoot and shirtless, displaying a lean and muscled torso. He had a natural dusting of reddish-blond hair across his chest and down toward the button of his jeans. He tiptoed into the kitchen, threw back the deadbolt, and opened the door halfway.

"Ben—"

"Travis," Ben interrupted. "I'm so sorry, really, I didn't realize." Ben couldn't look at him so instead he looked down at his feet. They were perfect. Pale with beautifully shaped toes and ivory nails. Ben stood, his head lowered, hypnotized by the man's feet. What was wrong with him? Finally, he snapped out of it and looked up. "I just came by to say thank you, again. But I'll come back another time." He took a step backward and began his retreat.

Then he started to laugh.

"Oh, man, I'm so sorry. I'm having a twelve-year-old moment. I haven't interrupted anyone having sex since... I don't know. My roommate in law school, I think."

Travis cracked up too.

"You dick."

"Yes, I'm aware of that. But can you spare a minute? I know this is a total cockblock, but I desperately need to talk to someone who's not an angry relative."

Travis smiled. "I'm the one that offered. Wait for me on the back porch. I'll be out in a spell. You actually saved me from the cuddling."

"See that? I make an excellent wingman."

Travis closed the door and Ben went around to the backyard and let himself into the screened-in porch, which was furnished with the standard plastic patio table and chairs, both clean and presentable. Ben took one of the seats and waited for Travis.

When he reappeared around the corner, Travis wore a burnt orange Longhorns sweatshirt and work boots, in addition to his blue jeans. He carried two bottles of Shiner Bock. Behind him came a young woman with bleached blond hair and a pretty face. Ben stood up to greet her.

"Ben, this is Trisha."

"Nice to meet you, Trisha. I apologize for intruding like this."

She put out her hand to shake his and then started to sign.

"I'm so sorry to hear about your parents," Travis said, translating. "I wanted to go to the service but couldn't get off work. I only met 'em once but they seemed like good people."

"Thank you." Ben looked at the two bottles of beer. "Aren't you going to stay?"

She shook her head and continued signing.

"No. It was time for me to leave anyway. Sunday night is girls' night and I'm hosting this week. Need to clean the apartment. But I hope I'll be seeing you again real soon."

"Me too."

Travis put the two bottles down on the table and escorted Trisha around the corner. After a couple of minutes, he returned and took a seat on one of the adjacent plastic chairs.

"Cheers." Travis raised his bottle.

"Salute." Ben clinked the neck of his own bottle against it. "When did you learn sign language?"

"As a boy, growing up in Lubbock. My next door neighbor and only friend at the time was deaf. Jamie Johnson. My mama always said I talked with my hands, so that's why it came natural, I reckon."

"Well, I'm sorry about my bad timing. Really."

"You apologize a lot, Ben."

"I like to keep my bases covered. Catholic guilt, and all."

They drank for a moment in silence.

"Mrs. Wright is gone most of the day on Sunday, with church activities and her ladies auxiliaries and a whole bunch of other things I don't dare ask about."

"And you use the time wisely."

"Indeed I do. Quentin and Jason know better than to come around knocking on a Sunday afternoon. I'm surprised they didn't warn you."

"They did. That was my fault. I have a listening problem."

Ben heard a car start up and then drive away.

"She seems like a nice girl."

Travis shrugged. "What else you gonna say? But yeah, she is. So, what's up?"

Ben took another swig of his beer and let the icy sensation slide down his throat. "I need to make a decision."

"You're in a bad way, Obi-Wan, if you're coming to me for advice."

"Somehow I doubt that."

Ben decided he liked Travis's nickname for him, an obvious but still clever *Star Wars* side reference to Ben's name.

"This about custody?"

"Of course. My Aunt Julie thinks I'm in no shape to be a parent. She thinks they should be raised in a more *traditional* setting, even if it means splitting them up."

Travis rubbed the top of his head with his right hand, scratched behind his ear, and then matted down his short red hair in a petting motion.

"What do *you* think?" Travis asked.

Ben looked at him. "I don't know. This is serious shit. If I fuck it up, then I'm fucking up three lives. And I don't know if I can do it. I have a life back in New York. I'm supposed to walk away from all that?"

"I don't know."

"But you said yesterday, *don't split them up*. You have an opinion."

"Of course I have an opinion. Is *all that* really more important than your brothers? They need you right now, and you may not know it yet, but you need them too. Your parents died, Ben, and those three boys are the only other people on the planet who know exactly what you're going through. How do you think that splitting them up and you hightailing it back to New York is gonna do anybody any good? Dressing it up with excuses ain't gonna change what you're doing. You can put your boots in the oven, but that don't make 'em biscuits."

"Me being a failure as a parent isn't going to make them biscuits either."

"Making a few mistakes here and there is a hell of a lot better than living with that kind of regret. I'm telling you, Ben, if you leave 'em behind now, they ain't never gonna forgive you. In fact, Quentin may never speak to you again. And no matter how successful you become or how much money you make, you'll never be able to come back to this moment and fix it. Your aunt is two sandwiches short of a picnic, and I would tell her so to her face."

"I don't think that'll be necessary. Besides, Julie is only half the problem. Quentin is just so...." Ben paused. "He hates me."

Travis shrugged again, a gesture that suited him.

"Can you blame him? He's a smart boy—he knows what's going on. If you're thinking about splitting them up, then I'm sure he knows it."

"Oh, he knows."

"And besides, he don't hate you. He hates your absence. There's a difference."

"I'm not sure he even wants me here."

"Well, now you're just being silly. He misses you like crazy. Take it from your replacement."

Ben was stunned. It had never occurred to him that his absence had left a void in his brothers' lives—or that someone else could fill it.

"Any advice?"

"All you got to do is be there. They don't need you to be the perfect brother. Ninety percent of life is showing up. I think somebody famous said that."

"Woody Allen."

"Really?"

"I think so."

Ben took another swig of his beer and looked around the brown backyard, some raked leaves still in a pile next to the chain-link fence. The neighborhood grew silent again, like the night before, except for the rumblings of nearby freeway traffic. Ben could feel Christmas approaching. He put his hands over his face and took a deep breath.

"What if it's too much?"

"Christ. Stop being so dramatic."

"Don't underestimate how selfish I can be."

Travis reached over and pulled Ben's hands away from his face.

"Then let it be too much."

"What does that mean?"

"Whatever comes your way, accept it. Accept what you can't change. Let it rain. That's what they used to say in Al-Anon."

Ben looked into his eyes, remembering something. Why did Travis seem so familiar? For a moment he thought he might lean over and kiss him, but then he realized how crazy that sounded and panicked.

"I should go," Ben said, getting out of his chair. "I told them I wouldn't be gone long."

Travis stood up and sighed, looking disappointed, as if nothing he said had sunk in.

"Thanks for talking to me. I heard you. Really."

Ben turned to go, but then stopped and asked, "What are you doing for Christmas?"

Travis grinned. "Your father had already invited me to spend it with your family. Now, I think I'll just stay in and watch some movies or something."

"If you're watching movies, then you should definitely come over, because that's what we'll be doing too. I know that much about my brothers. Maybe we'll do a theme—things blowing up, saving the world, that kind of stuff. A real testosterone fest."

"*Armageddon?*"

"That's what I'm talking about. And *Deep Impact.*"

"*The Day After Tomorrow.*"

"Always room for Jake. And *Speed*, of course."

"It does sound like fun. Count me in."

Ben said good-bye and left Travis on the back porch to finish his beer. He crossed the street to his house and bounced up the front stairs. He felt better, that was for sure. Talking to Travis had gone a long way toward clearing his head. He went into the house, hoping to find his brothers hanging out in the living room, but there was no one. *Must be upstairs*, he thought. *No rush.* He felt confident about tomorrow and the meeting with the lawyer, and because of that, he knew there would be plenty of time to get to know them.

He heard something splattering against the window and looked out to investigate. It had started to rain. And for some reason that he couldn't explain, that made Ben smile.

FOUR

ON MONDAY afternoon, Julie explained that she was returning to Dallas directly from the lawyer's office, so she would be driving on her own. When Ben arrived for the appointment at three in the afternoon, Sam and Nick, Julie's brothers, surprised him. He hadn't even known they were driving over from Houston.

They all said hello and then went inside to meet with Russ Hardwick, his parents' attorney. He had two copies of the will, which he handed to Ben and Nick. They sat down, and Ben started reading while Sam and Julie huddled on each side of Nick, scanning the first page of the document.

After a few minutes, Hardwick began. "First, let me say I'm terribly sorry for your loss. Ben, I've known you since you were a boy. I never thought I'd be sitting here having to do this."

"Thanks, Russ. Worst-case scenario."

Hardwick forced a weak smile. He referred down to the will.

"There's nothing of great surprise here. The estate and all its assets are distributed equally among the four children. The house is paid for. Your father set up an account to cover the taxes and insurance. In addition to the life and supplemental life payments, he also set up college funds for each of the remaining three boys. As for the matter of custody, you, Ben, are named as the sole guardian to your brothers. They did, however, add an addendum last year when you took the job in New York. Should you decline custody, which they specifically detailed as an option for you, guardianship would pass to Mrs. Walsh's siblings. You three."

Hardwick stopped and waited.

"Ben, do you accept or decline custody?"

Ben looked at Julie. Things had turned out exactly as she'd predicted. But why hadn't she told him that Sam and Nick would be at this meeting?

"I accept."

"Mr. Hardwick," said Nick, still looking down at the document. "What are our legal options? Regarding custody, I mean?"

Ben looked at him, shocked.

Hardwick continued. "When they added the addendum, there was no indication that they intended your custody clause to supersede Ben's. Suing for custody is always an option if you believe—"

Nick interrupted him. "We believe the boys would be better served in a more traditional family environment."

Ben scoffed at the suggestion. *This is an ambush*, he thought.

"Are you serious, Uncle Nick?" Ben kept his voice calm as he spoke. "And I'm not talking about your *traditional family* bullshit. You're going to take me on in court? Really? Do you know who I work for?"

"That's a New York firm," said Sam. "This is Texas."

"I know I'm not supposed to talk to you this way, Sam, but you're an idiot. Julie, talk some sense into your brothers. Seriously, I can't believe we're even having this conversation."

"You pretentious little prick," Sam sneered. "The sun don't come up just to hear you crow. You're gonna take those boys down the road to ruin."

Ben didn't blink.

"Well, isn't the Thompson clan just full of pithy bon mots today? Your contempt in the face of my mother's death is truly comforting. So, let me break it down for you. Do you mind, Russ?"

Hardwick nodded, both flustered and proud at the same time.

"First of all, Sam, *bon mot* means a clever saying or witticism, or more literally, *good word*. It's French. How's that for pretentious? Second, if you're going to sue me for custody then you'll need to lawyer up, because I will be heavily armed. And I will drag this out and cost you so much money that you'll be filing Chapter Thirteen before it's even close to being settled. By then Cade will be graduating from high school and the whole thing will have been for nothing. Whatever you're thinking, don't. It will not change the outcome and it will only destroy your lives."

Ben stood up and offered his hand to Hardwick.

"Thank you, Russ. I assume we're done here. If there's anything that needs a signature, please send it to the house. And tell Susan I said Merry Christmas and I hope everything stays safe and sound for your family."

Hardwick got up and shook Ben's hand.

"If you or the boys need anything, Ben, I want you to call me. You hear?"

"I hear." Ben turned to Julie and her brothers. "I think we're going to spend Christmas in Austin this year. On our own. No further explanation necessary. Merry Christmas, Julie." He bent over to give her a hug. "Merry Christmas, Nick. Sam," he said, shaking both their hands and enjoying the dumbstruck looks on their collective faces. He exited the office and made his way back to his father's truck. He drove home knowing full well what the next step was. There were a lot of decisions that had to be made, but all that could wait until later.

Right now, it was time he and his brothers had a talk.

ALL three of them were in the living room when he got back to the house. Quentin and Cade were watching something on ESPN. His nose firmly planted in a book, Jason sat sideways in the overstuffed chair, his legs dangling over one arm. Ben looked down and read the cover. *Lord of the Flies*. Excellent choice.

"I hate to interrupt your doing nothing, but there are a few things we need to talk about. The four of us. Quentin, would you turn off the television? Let's all move into the dining room. We should sit at a table for this."

Quentin reached for the remote and turned off the TV, then looked up at Ben with disdain in his eyes.

Ben decided not to sit at the head of the table. Instead, they sat where they always did—Ben and Jason on one side, Quentin and Cade on the other. Simple and familiar, except for the empty chairs at each end.

Ben began.

"So, our parents are dead. I'm sure you've noticed the way people like to dance around that fact. They're dead and it sucks. I don't know about you, but I'm not happy about it. They're gone, and we'll be damaged for a while without them, no matter what we do. That's just a plain and simple fact. Still, I know you have a lot of questions."

Quentin stiffened against the back of his chair.

"I met with the lawyer today about the estate. And custody."

"Custody of what?" Cade asked.

"Not what, moron," said Quentin. "Who. Custody of who."

"I'm not a moron," Cade protested.

Ben looked across the table in disbelief.

"Really? And you call me a dick? For God's sake, don't call your brother a moron."

"Don't tell me what to do," Quentin said, his black eyes ablaze.

Ben turned toward Cade.

"You and your brothers are still minors. Legally, you'll need a guardian to take care of you. Since Mom and Dad are gone now."

"But you're gonna come home, right?" Cade asked. "You're gonna come back here and take care of us."

Ben looked at Quentin. He wanted to see his face when, maybe, he didn't disappoint him for a change.

"Yes. Of course that's what's going to happen."

Quentin raised his brows and widened his eyes. Jason sat up and looked sideways at Ben, smiling and sighing with relief as he placed his forehead on Ben's arm. Ben reached around and patted the back of Jason's head.

"Thank you," Jason whispered.

"Congratulations, big brother. You stepped up."

"I'm glad you see it that way, because now it's your turn. You have to help me. All three of you. I know I disappeared five years ago. I understand I hardly know you. Just, please, don't be angry with me. I'm here now and, like it or not, the four of us are in this together."

"So," Cade said, raising his hand, "you're gonna be, like, the dad now?"

"Sometimes." Ben nodded. Then he shook his head. "No. I'm not sure. Something like that."

"What about Travis?" asked Cade.

"What about him?"

"He eats dinner here all the time," Quentin explained.

Cade nodded and laughed. "He'll probably starve if we don't feed him."

"No," Quentin said, "*we'll* probably starve. He helped Mom a lot in the kitchen. He likes to cook and we need someone like that. He's our only hope for feeding ourselves."

"Then good thing I invited him over for Christmas. Hope you don't mind, but he and I have already discussed a theme. We'll be watching movies in which large things blow up and someone saves the world. Or at least a bus."

"You're such a dork sometimes," said Quentin, laughing. "You and your themes. Is that a gay thing?"

"Like *Independence Day*?" Jason suggested.

Ben smiled, ignoring Quentin.

"Can't believe we didn't think of that one. Would you two give me and Quentin a minute alone now?"

"Sure. Come on, Cade, let's go wrap some presents."

The two left the dining room and went upstairs.

"I was kidding about the gay thing!" Quentin protested defensively, certain that he had pushed it too far.

"Relax," said Ben. "I couldn't care less about that. So we're good? You and me?"

Quentin smiled at him.

"Yeah, we're good. I didn't think…. Sorry, I underestimated you."

"Let's put it behind us. I want to talk to you about Jason. He's been so quiet, even for him. And then you said something yesterday, if I knew what he was going through… what were you talking about?"

"It's not really my place."

"I'm making it your place. The rules have changed, Q. You've got to catch me up. I'm suspending your attorney/client privilege."

Quentin eyed him with suspicion.

"After school started, back in October, Mom walked in on him. He was up in his room."

"Jacking off?"

"No. He wasn't alone."

"A girl?"

Quentin was silent.

"A boy?"

He nodded. "Nothing was going on. Not really. He told me they were just making out a bit. Had their clothes on and everything. Still, Mom kind of freaked and threw the kid out. She loves you and all, but really, two in one family? Isn't that a little much for one Catholic mother to bear?"

"He talks to you about that kind of stuff?"

"Of course. Mom sure as hell didn't tell me. You've really missed out, Ben. Having brothers is cool. Jason and I talk about everything.

We're totally different—he's all intellectual and I'm...." Quentin stopped.

"You're sixteen years old. I know you have a girlfriend."

"How do you...."

"I've seen that look on your face when she texts you. Gay or straight, all guys get the same look. You're using condoms?"

"We're not...."

"First house rule. No pregnancies. Ever. Use a condom every time, I'm begging you. This is going to be tough enough without asking me for varsity-level parenting."

"That was an old house rule. No sex, remember?"

"Right, I do remember. Except that I broke that rule and someday you will too, if you haven't already, so let's throw it out and replace it with a new one, shall we? No pregnancies. Condoms every time. Please."

Quentin looked down at his hands.

"This is going to be weird, isn't it? Not having Mom and Dad around?"

"Yeah, it is. I'm a terrible Plan B."

"No, you're alright. Sucks about having to leave New York, though. Can you get a job in Austin?"

"I'll need to take the Texas Bar Exam, which I thought I had put behind me. But yes, I can work here."

"Sweet. I'm glad you're home, Ben. Sorry I blamed you for not being around lately."

That was when Ben realized they had gotten sidetracked.

"Wait a minute. We were talking about Jason kissing some boy. Did he come out to Mom and Dad after that?"

"Yeah. They tried to be supportive. He talks to me about it sometimes, but what do I know? He needs someone like you around."

"So why didn't they call me when this happened?"

"Didn't want to bother you, I guess."

"Then why didn't Jason call me?"

"I don't know, Ben. Ask him. But you weren't around. We're not used to thinking of you as someone we can depend on."

"Shit, I'm the worst brother ever. And what about Cade? Anything I should know about him?"

"Nah, he's low maintenance. He's gonna be the jock in the family. Took them four tries but Dad finally got an athlete. He plays football and baseball. Already bleeds orange. Loves Longhorn anything. He's at that age. For the past four months, every Saturday, Texas football, he and Dad and Travis."

"You like Travis?"

"Sure. He's a good guy. Didn't have much growing up. He fits in here, you'll see. Even Mom said so and she was wary at...."

A knock on the front door interrupted Quentin.

"Speak of the devil...."

"Travis?" asked Ben.

Quentin nodded.

"Go answer it, big brother."

Ben got up and walked to the front door. When he pulled it open, Travis stood in front of him on the porch.

"Were your ears burning?"

"What?"

"We were just talking about you. Come in."

Travis walked in and nodded a greeting when he saw Quentin sitting at the dining room table.

"Hey, Q-Ball. Everything okay?"

"Hey, Trav. Everything's dandy."

"Hmm," grunted Travis, looking back to Ben. "Usually when he uses the word *dandy* it's cut with a hell of a lot more snark than that. This mean you decided to move back home?"

Ben smiled. "That's exactly what it means."

"Well, then, welcome to the neighborhood. Or back to the neighborhood, I reckon I should say."

Travis thrust out his hand. Ben looked down and shook it. Firm and sturdy.

"Thank you. I was about to drag Quentin into the kitchen. We're having leftovers for dinner. You staying?"

Travis looked at the floor.

"Quentin, would you mind giving me and your brother a few minutes to talk?"

"I'll be in the kitchen. Sorting leftovers."

Quentin left them alone.

"What's up?" asked Ben.

"I was thinking about your invitation to Christmas. Don't you think it's best if I stay away for a while? You're here now. You need time with 'em."

Ben scoffed. "No. I don't think it's best at all. In fact, I think it's the worst idea I've ever heard. They love you, man. Especially Cade. I saw that on Saturday. More than anything right now, they need comfort and consistency. And I need help. If you're a second big brother in their lives, then that's fucking fantastic. You were there for them before this happened, so please be there now when they really need you. Seriously. Come over for Christmas and stay tonight for leftovers."

"Well, when you put it like that...."

"Will you go upstairs and get Jason and Cade? They're wrapping presents."

"You betcha."

Ben went into the kitchen, where Quentin had already started to unload plastic containers from the fridge. In a few moments, Jason and Cade broke through the door with Travis on their heels.

"Aunt Harriet brought some delicious mac and cheese," said Jason.

"Mmmm," Cade growled, rubbing his stomach. "Mac and cheese good."

"There's also another whole turkey defrosting in the bottom rack," added Travis.

"How do you know that?" asked Quentin.

"I saw it on Saturday. Talked to your Aunt Julie about it."

"Do you know anything about roasting a turkey?" Ben asked him.

"Nu-uh, but I know something about frying a turkey. What kinda Southern boy don't know how to fry a turkey?"

"Our kind," Ben and Quentin answered simultaneously.

"You boys are all hat and no cattle. I swear."

"Then you are in charge of frying the turkey," said Ben. "Whatever that means. For Christmas."

"I can do that."

"Can we just start Christmas now?" asked Cade.

Everyone looked at him. It was a great idea.

"Yes, Cade," said Ben. "Christmas officially starts now."

FIVE

CHRISTMAS began that night with a hefty meal of leftovers and a double feature of *Armageddon* and *Deep Impact*, with a young Elijah Wood, pre-Frodo Baggins. The five of them sat in the living room on the large, L-shaped double sofa, with Jason in the overstuffed chair. Travis had to work on Tuesday, so the Walsh boys watched the entire first season, all six episodes, of *The Walking Dead*. Ben thought it was a perfect way to spend the afternoon because, frankly, Rick Grimes and his family had it much worse.

On Tuesday evening, Travis returned and suggested a trip to the grocery store. Ben knew he should have thought of that. The leftovers were obviously not going to last forever. Eventually, Ben would need to address the daily basics of a household. Three boys ate a lot of food and produced a lot of dirty laundry. And how would the kitchen run?

Stop, Ben thought.

All that would have to wait. Right now, Ben needed to focus on getting through the holidays. The boys were off from school until after the New Year, so he had two weeks to adjust to all this, and then he would think about long-term solutions to things like food and laundry.

So far, Ben had avoided Colin and David, his one absolute friend and the guy he had spent every night with before all this happened. He just couldn't bring himself to call anyone right now. He knew his boss, one of the managing partners at Wilson & Mead, had already flown to Aspen and didn't expect to hear from Ben until after the holidays. Christmas would arrive, without his parents, in only two days. Things would slowly shut down and come to a stop. Ben was looking forward to it. He could relax for a while and get reacquainted with his brothers. This Christmas didn't have to be a complete disaster.

Travis and Ben left the boys behind and headed to the neighborhood grocery store. As they strolled up and down the long aisles, Travis seemed to have a plan—specific meals and recipes in his head—while Ben grabbed anything off the shelf that looked good. When he was in college, he used to get stoned with his friends at The Ben Pad and then walk over to this very store, wandering the aisles in a hemp haze. He quit smoking in law school, but a bong hit sounded pretty good right about now.

"Do you know anyone who sells weed?" asked Ben.

Travis looked at him, surprised.

"You smoke pot? Aren't you an officer of the court or something?"

"Please. Austin is the San Francisco of the Southwest. Besides, I'm not going to keep it around the house or anything. I'm just saying if someone was thinking about what they wanted to get me for Christmas—hint, hint—a joint would be an excellent option. I promise to be very discreet."

"You? Stoned? This I gotta see."

"No observation without participation."

"You saying we're gonna get high together?"

Ben pulled a box of Cap'n Crunch off the shelf and changed the subject. "I need to say thank you again. I'm leaving a whole lot of slack in my wake and you're turning into a lifesaver."

"Stop, Ben. Really. I can't take all this gratitude."

"I mean it. You obviously came here with a meal plan. You know how you're going to feed all five of us for the next week, don't you? I wouldn't even know where to start."

"Look, my mama didn't do her job. So I learned how to put meals on the table. Ain't no big deal."

"Well, it's a big deal to me."

"You asked for my help, so… here we are."

"Here we are," Ben repeated.

"You're grateful. I get it. Now let's move on."

Ben looked over at Travis, who opened up one of the refrigerated sections and pulled out a gallon of milk. On the one hand, Ben couldn't deny certain facts. Travis looked sexy in a pair of red gym shorts and a black thermal shirt. He might find this whole *friendship* thing difficult after all. On the other hand, he couldn't have anything blowing up in his face. If he did something to make Travis uncomfortable and he stopped coming around, his brothers would never forgive him.

"Then let me put it another way. Instead of saying thank you, I'll just say it was cool last night. Having you around. And I'm glad you decided to come back."

Travis looked up from the cart, smiling.

"I'm glad you feel that way. I miss your folks something awful too. They were like the Cohens to me."

"The Cohens? You mean Kirsten and Sandy?"

"Yep."

"You're like an onion, aren't you? First the sign language and now *The O.C.*"

"I got layers you ain't never dreamed of, Obi-Wan."

Is he flirting with me? Ben thought.

That night, Travis served up his first real meal to the Walsh brothers—fried chicken and waffles—and afterward they enjoyed another high-octane double feature.

ON WEDNESDAY, Travis still had to work, even though it was Christmas Eve. After that, the shop would be closed until Monday. Ben had the afternoon to come up with a present for him. He at least had the forethought to grab all the gifts for his brothers while he'd scrambled to get to the airport the previous week. He and Quentin found their parents' stash in one of the storage closets behind the garage. Quentin knew what belonged to whom, so he took care of wrapping and labeling everything.

"What do I put on the *From* part?" he asked Ben.

Ben thought about it. "Let's go with, *Santa*. Hey, any ideas about a present for Travis?"

"He likes to fish. We went in together and got him a new rod and reel."

"Fish?"

"And cook."

"Nah," Ben said, rejecting the idea. "I don't want to get him a frying pan."

"He talks about Alaska a lot. Says he wants to see a place where the sun never sets."

"That's perfect."

Ben knew exactly what to get him.

He went out and made it back in time to wrap the present and stash it under the tree. That evening, Travis made dinner again, followed by another double feature. Cade had already fallen asleep by the time the credits rolled on the second movie. Travis put him to bed while Quentin and Jason headed upstairs.

"You're welcome to stick around for a while," Ben offered when he returned.

Travis smiled. "What time is it?"

Ben pulled his phone out of his pocket and tapped the home button. "Eleven forty-eight."

"Almost midnight. Close enough. Would you like to open your Christmas present?"

Ben sat upright when he heard the question. "Are you kidding me?"

Travis walked over to the front door, where his jacket was hanging. He reached into one of the pockets and pulled out a small box wrapped in green paper with gold wreaths. He waved the box and grinned. Ben got up and went over to the tree in the corner. He bent down and pulled out his gift for Travis.

"Shall we head out to the backyard?" asked Ben.

"Probably a good idea."

They grabbed their jackets and went outside, heading to the backyard, where two nicely padded lounge chairs sat parallel to each other, with a small table between them.

"We forgot beverages. I'll be right back."

Ben ducked into the house and grabbed two bottles of water from the fridge. When he returned, Ben watched Travis kicking back on one of the chairs. *Still sexy*, he thought. He placed the two bottles on the table and sat down on the opposite chair, holding out his gift.

"For you."

They exchanged boxes.

"You first," said Travis.

"The suspense is killing me."

Ben tore off the wrapping. Underneath he found a Kmart box. He removed the lid and smiled. He took the fat joint in his fingers and rolled it around before lifting it to his nose and inhaling deeply.

"Good shit?"

"So I's told."

Travis reached into his pocket and produced a lighter. "What about Betsy?" he asked.

Ben wondered how well Travis knew the tenant in the garage apartment. "She went back to Pittsburgh for the holidays. It's cool."

Travis handed the lighter to Ben, who sparked up the doobie and then passed it. The two men did some coughing and laughing before Ben felt the familiar buzz overtake him. They sat in silence for a few minutes, basking in the glow of the half-baked moon.

"So," said Ben, "you referenced *The O.C.* Didn't see that coming."

"You imagine I don't watch TV?"

"No. Of course not. I just imagine you watch sports channels or something like that."

"So you imagine me?" Travis teased.

Ben felt his face flush. "I don't imagine you. I have an impression of you. Which, by the way, has turned out to be wrong."

"Nu-uh. I do watch a lot of sports. But I also love me a good teen soap. I remember when I was a freshman in high school, watching that first episode of *Dawson's Creek*. Damn, I loved that show. You think my mama ever bought me an Xbox? Hell, no. So I watched a lot of TV. One day I discovered the original *90210* in repeats on SOAPnet. I watched every episode, all the way up to Kelly Taylor's classic 'I choose me' speech. But frankly, I was happier than a pig on a spit when Joey finally picked Pacey. I was a huge Pacey fan. Joey and Pacey forever."

"Wow. You turn into quite a Chatty Cathy when you're stoned."

Travis laughed. "Now, why you trying to make me feel all self-conscious like that?"

"Sorry, I don't understand half the things that come out of my mouth sometimes."

"That's okay. I bet you don't understand half the things that go into it either."

Ben started laughing uncontrollably. "Damn, boy, you are good."

Travis smiled in the moonlight.

"I liked *The O.C.*," Ben continued. "But I always thought Ryan and Seth should've ended up banging each other."

"Then it wouldn't have been a bromance, now would it? So, tell me something about yourself. Tell me something I would never in a million years have guessed."

Ben thought it over.

"Would you have ever guessed I smoke pot?"

"Never. And something tells me you don't anymore, so I would have been right."

"He said as he waved the joint around."

"Something else."

"Let's see…." Ben, with a little help from the weed, decided to be bold. "I have a foot fetish."

Travis looked over at him, his eyes wide.

"Really? Well, we ain't holding back, now are we? But I got to admit, that's a good one. Would have never guessed that in a million years."

"I can surprise you. I led a spectacularly average life until I was twenty-two. And I think most people assume I still do. When they first meet me, I mean. But my life has been anything but average. A foot fetish only scratches the surface of my bad-boy charm."

Travis snorted.

"There ain't no such thing as a bad boy with clean fingernails. What happened when you were twenty-two?"

"I was a senior at UT and decided to take the LSAT."

"That a test?"

"Yeah. It's what law schools use to decide admissions. I scored a 176."

"Is that good?"

"That's write-your-own-ticket good. I got into Harvard but it wasn't for me, so I went to Columbia instead. I wanted to live in New York."

"Harvard? What was that like? People noticing you, I mean, paying attention like that."

Ben paused.

"It was a head rush. Turns out the law is the one thing I do better than almost anyone else. I graduated top of my class. Had all the big firms in Manhattan trying to hire me. And at the same time, I was hanging out with Colin Mead."

"He the guy you're dating?"

"No, that's David. Colin was one of the first people I met when I moved to New York. He was first-year law at Columbia too. One day, he sat next to me in Civil Procedure, spilled coffee all over my bag, and then brought me a much nicer one the next day as an apology. He comes from old-school, Upper East Side money. His grandfather is one of the founding partners of the firm where I work. By the time we graduated, I was like a member of the family, so it was a natural fit. They're grooming me to be Manhattan's next great litigator."

"So you were like Lonely Boy on *Gossip Girl*."

Ben cracked up.

"Yes, that's exactly who I was like. I was the scholarship student from Brooklyn."

"Or in your case, Texas. *Thrust into a world of wealth and power.* Good premise for a TV show."

Ben laughed. "Like I said, anything but average. So, where all have you lived?"

"Me? Oh, gosh. Exotic places. Born in Round Rock actually, moved to Lubbock when I was eight. We lived there 'til my daddy left us. I was a freshman in high school at the time. Mama got a job in Houston, of all places. I hate Houston. That didn't last but six months before she up and followed a guy to San Marcos. We lived there for a spell. That was okay, I reckon. I graduated from San Marcos High. Go Rattlers. I stuck around there for a few years 'til Mama died. I'd just turned twenty-one, I think."

"When's your birthday?"

"July 22."

"Seriously?"

"Yeah, why?"

"Because that's my birthday too—1983?"

"Yeah."

"We were born on the same day?"

"Looks that way."

"I'm on the Leo side."

Travis laughed. "I'm on the Cancer side. Had my chart done a few years ago."

"Isn't that crazy?"

"It's a little bit strange," Travis admitted, sitting up. "So, tell me about David."

"Not much to tell. We met at a Halloween party. Been seeing each other ever since. He's hot. Nice guy. I had nothing to complain about."

"Wow. What a ringing endorsement."

"Sorry."

"Is something wrong?"

Ben laughed. "Is it that obvious? Yes, something's wrong, or maybe I'm just bad at it. It's always been this way, though, ever since Matt McKay in high school. He was my big crush. I thought I was in love with him. I felt it. But I was a coward, and it didn't matter anyway because he was straight. Once I started dating guys who wanted to have real, live sex with me, I never mustered that feeling again. I can't seem to put the feeling together with the sex."

"Sounds like you're still ahead of me."

"Why's that?"

They both leaned back in their chairs, looking up at the night sky.

"I don't understand a damn thing about women. I don't know what they want, and I sure as hell don't know what they want from me. I'm just awful at talking to 'em. I've been in lust plenty of times, believe you me. I'm good at the 'little less conversation, little more action' part."

Ben laughed.

"I hear you, Elvis. I'm the same way."

"But after that, I'm a piss-poor excuse for a boyfriend. And Trisha and I are getting to that point. I can feel it around the next bend. One of these days I'm gonna disappoint her and she's gonna know that I don't really care enough."

"Dude, that's harsh."

"I know, dude!" Travis sat up so he could face Ben. "So what am I doing? I ask you, as my new friend, what in the fuck am I doing?"

"You're enjoying regular and dependable sex."

"Yes! That's the good ol' boy answer. But here's another question for you."

He paused for effect.

"What are *you* doing?"

"You mean existentially or right now in this moment?"

"Don't get all deep on me. I mean, when was the last time you talked to David?"

Ben looked over at him and snarled. "When I was at the airport."

"You mean, when you were at the airport *five days ago*? Equally harsh, dude, that's all I'm saying. Equally harsh."

"Fuck, you're right. I'm a douche bag. But I know he's going to ask me when I'm coming back to New York. And I'm going to tell him that I'm not. Then there's going to be the inevitable, and the worst part is, I know he's already figured it out. He knows I'm not coming back. He knows there's no one else to take care of them. He knows I'm not leaning on him."

"Still gotta make that call."

"And you need to shit or get off the pot."

Travis started laughing hysterically. "You said *pot*, dude." Ben joined in with his own laughter. Finally, after they'd settled down, the two men lay back again and returned their gaze to the stars.

"Favorite stoner movie?" Travis asked.

"Oh, man, tough one. Never got into the Cheech & Chong thing. Too old school for me. You looking for movies about pot smoking or good movies to watch stoned?"

"The question don't come with rules, Ben."

"Okay, okay. It's an important distinction. Personally, I'd go with *Bill & Ted* as the classic to watch stoned. After that, *Dude, Where's My Car?* Hard to beat Ashton Kutcher and Seann William Scott making out. *Harold & Kumar* scores points for the Neil Patrick Harris bit, but they're not as hot as Ashton and Seann, and they don't make out, and frankly, that movie is kind of a buzz kill, so…."

"Love *Bill & Ted*."

"'What's your favorite number?'"

"Sixty-nine, dude!" they said together, playing an air-guitar riff.

"Christ," Travis said. "You're alright, you know that, Obi-Wan?"

"'Fess up. You thought I was going to be an asshole. Mr. Hotshot Lawyer from New York City."

"Nu-uh, I never thought that. But when I met you at the cemetery, you did intimidate the hell out of me. Right down to the way your suit fit."

"Are you serious?"

"One hundred and ten percent serious. Thank God Cade threw that hissy fit. I could see you were about ready to kick my sorry ass to the curb."

"I wasn't...."

"Don't lie to me."

"Okay, I was. But consider the circumstances."

"That's what I was doing. I was trying to be polite, but then Cade started crying and I thought, well, it wouldn't be a Southern funeral if someone didn't make a scene. I'm glad you invited me along."

"Cade didn't give me much of a choice. For the record, though, I'm glad I invited you along too. But enough of that. Continue your life story. What happened after your mom died?"

Travis looked confused. "Oh. I went to the Gulf. Biloxi. Worked on oil rigs and tankers for a few years. Learned everything I could about engines. Saved a lot of money. Got tired of working for evil oil companies and wanted to come home to Texas. I thought about going back to San Marcos but decided to give Austin a shot instead. I got an apartment up on Anderson Mill the first year."

"Damn. That's north."

"Yeah. Might as well be in Williamson County at that point. And I didn't like living alone. So when I was just about ready to kill myself from boredom, I decided to look for a place in central Austin. Got the job, moved into Mrs. Wright's place, met your dad and your awesome family, met a nice girl. I'm thinking life ain't too bad for a change. And then...."

Silence.

"That part I understand."

"So when did you know you were gay?"

Ben thought for a moment. "Depends on how you define *know*."

"Sounds like something a lawyer would say. Did you ever date or fool around with girls?"

"Sure. Did you ever date or fool around with guys?"

Travis laughed nervously. "No."

"Did you ever *want* to date or fool around with guys?"

"Wait a minute, am I on the witness stand or something?"

"Sorry about that. Bad habit. I tend to favor an aggressive line of questioning. Let's see. Like I told you, I was in love with my debate partner, Matt McKay, in high school..."

"Debate? What a nerd."

Ben flipped him the middle finger. "... so I had to know something was up then. But I was okay dating girls at that point. After college, it was all guys. That's when I came out to my parents. They say you always know, but college was when I *knew* knew."

"Hmm."

"What?"

"Nothing."

"Don't ask me if it hurts. Another stupid cliché. Besides, I wouldn't know."

"Really? So you're the man in bed?"

"You did not just say that."

"Only to get a rise out of you."

"It's called the top, not the man. And yes, I'm the top. Don't think that all gay guys like to bottom. There are some guys that respond to the butt sex and some that don't. Doesn't matter if you're gay or straight."

"I'm sorry, but that dog don't hunt."

"You're wrong. Lots of straight guys discover they like ass play. It's a known fact. Doesn't make them gay. Me, I don't like anyone going near my rear end. Doesn't make me straight. Top and bottom, gay and straight—the two have nothing to do with each other. It's all about anatomy."

"So David's the bottom?"

"You mean the guy I'm dating?"

"Yeah."

"The guy I haven't called in five days?"

"That one."

"Power bottom. Only happy when my dick is in his ass. His words, not mine."

Travis blushed and then laughed to cover it.

"You're such a moron."

"And you've been hanging around Quentin too long, using that word."

"So, you think I'm a top or a bottom?"

Ben snickered. "Look at you, all curious and shit. I suppose there's only one way to find out. I bet Trisha would strap one on if you asked her."

"No!" Travis yelled, laughing. "I ain't never gonna be able to get that image out of my head, thank you."

"Sorry, my bad. But you asked the question, and yes, I will go there when I'm stoned."

Travis moved his hands and looked back at Ben. "So you're saying some guys like it and some guys don't? No matter if you're gay or straight?"

"That's what I'm saying. There's a dude on this gay-for-pay porn site that is totally straight. I'm the first one to be suspicious of that, but even I believe him. Says he'll never kiss a guy, ever, but loves a dick up his ass. Has no problem admitting that—just the way he's built, he says. And when he gets fucked, his eyes literally roll back into his head. Me, I'm pretty gay, but on the few occasions that I've tried it, there was no eye rolling."

"So you have tried it? Getting poked in the butt?"

"Of course I tried it. You think I'm uptight or something? You have to try things out to know whether you like them or not. You have to be a little adventurous. Like you, man. You've never tried it with a guy?"

"Nope."

"Well, I tried it with several women and it didn't float my boat. Even if I were a perfect Kinsey six—I'm more of a five, really—I would still have tried it with at least one girl just to see what it was like. Personally, I think every guy who calls himself straight should take a hike on the gay Appalachian Trail at least once in his life."

Travis didn't say anything and Ben squirmed in his chair. "But what do I know?" he said, sitting up. "How about we dig out *Bill & Ted*. Watch that before we crash. You should stay in the guest room tonight. That way you can be here when the brothers wake up. Can't miss the best part."

"Do I get to open my present?"

"Oh shit, I forgot. Of course. It's nothing big."

Travis unwrapped and opened the box. A broad smile spread out across his face. He held up a folded Rand McNally map of Alaska.

"Quentin said you wanted to go."

"Thanks. Yeah, I do. In the summer."

"This summer?"

"Yeah, I've been looking into it."

"Cool. Well, now you can plan your day trips."

Ben sat back again. There was a long pause. "It hasn't happened yet."

"What do you mean?" asked Travis.

"I mean, they haven't died yet. It's not real."

"Give it time. This part don't last forever."

"Both your parents are gone?"

"Yep. My daddy died last year. So we got something in common."

"Why am I not sad? I feel… nothing. Just numb."

Travis sat up and faced him.

"Give it time, Obi-Wan. It's coming. Trust me when I say that in no uncertain terms. It's coming."

SIX

CHRISTMAS morning arrived without any of the usual fanfare. Cade didn't wake up at the crack of dawn and there was no running through the house calling at the top of his lungs. Instead, at nine thirty, the five of them shuffled out of their rooms and into the kitchen.

"You moving in, Trav?" joked Quentin, pouring himself a glass of orange juice.

"It was late. We watched *Bill & Ted* after y'all went to bed."

"Hey, royal ugly dudes!" Cade quoted as he high-fived Travis.

"Too late to cross the street?" Quentin continued.

"Ben thought...."

"Relax," said Ben. "He's just busting your balls."

Quentin flashed his eyebrows at Ben.

"Merry Christmas, big brother."

"Wipe that smirk off your face."

"Can we have pancakes?" Cade asked.

Ben looked at Travis. "Is that in your arsenal?"

Travis scoffed at the suggestion that it might not be. "I got you covered."

So Travis started making pancakes for breakfast.

"We should eat in the living room," Jason said. "And watch a movie. We can call it Pancake Cinema."

"That's a stupid name," complained Quentin.

"It's an awesome name. You're the one that's stupid."

"Why does it even need to have a name? It's just breakfast while we watch a movie."

"Really?" Ben interrupted. "On Christmas morning?"

"Just like any other day of the year," said Quentin. "You know what Dad used to say."

"Don't start quoting my father to me."

"He was my father too."

"What did he used to say?" asked Travis as he measured flour, milk, and eggs into a bowl.

Ben and Quentin remained silent, so Jason spoke up.

"As long as everyone's alive, we're doing just fine."

An awkward silence fell over the kitchen. Jason looked around and realized what he had said.

"Jesus," said Quentin, "let's not get all morose every time someone mentions death."

"He wasn't talking about himself," Ben explained to Travis. "He was referring to Cain and Abel, the first brothers. Dad always expected four boys to fight. In fact, he kind of encouraged it. As long as we didn't spill any blood, he gave us a long leash when it came to how we talked to each other."

"No one would ever guess," Travis muttered under his breath.

"That's all I'm saying," said Quentin. "No use acting all Disney Channel just because it's Christmas."

"Speaking of which," Ben said, "let's move on and exchange some gifts."

ALTHOUGH left unspoken, the Walsh brothers observed the absence of their parents with a casual air, as if they had gone out of town for a long weekend, leaving the boys to fend for themselves. A few more days and they'd return. Then everything would go back to normal, except the Walsh brothers understood that would never happen.

The next few days passed in something of a fog. The boys came to a stop with an emotional thud. Travis produced meals at regular intervals, and they watched movies continually in the living room. On Monday, Travis went back to work but returned for dinner, and their routine continued unabated. Some nights Travis crossed the street to Mrs. Wright's house, but mostly he crashed in the guest room if it got too late. The five of them said little to each other. They would occasionally discuss the better films or become overly invested in a particular character. They huddled together in the warm house, absorbing one story after another, mourning.

They slept. They ate. They watched movies.

And they did this for days.

"YOU should invite Trisha over for dinner."

Ben suggested this to Travis one night in the kitchen as Travis stripped meat off a chicken carcass.

"She'd probably like that."

"Tomorrow night's New Year's Eve. What do you think?"

"I think she's planning a trip down to Sixth Street. For the two of us, I mean. With some friends of hers."

"Sounds perfect. We can have dinner at eight, and then you two can head downtown around eleven."

Travis hesitated, taking a deep breath through his nose. "I don't want to set up any expectations." Travis lowered his voice. "In her head, you know?"

"She's been here before, right? I mean, my mom and dad certainly invited her over."

"Yeah. I mean, no… yes, she met them once. And your daddy had been pestering me to bring her over for dinner."

"And you were able to put him off all this time?"

"Yep."

"Impressive. But you're making a mountain out of a molehill. Really. It's dinner, not a marriage proposal. Invite her, already."

"Okay, okay. I'll call her."

Instead of a movie that night, Travis taught them some basic sign language and then the English alphabet. "Sign it if you can," he explained, "spell it if you can't, and if all else fails, write it down. It takes longer to say stuff, but that'll frustrate her more than you."

"Great," said Ben, not enthusiastic about the clumsiness with which his hands moved. "But you were interpreting for me when I met her last week. Why can't you do that again?"

"Because I can't interpret a conversation with six people."

"I suck at this," Ben said in surrender. "I look like an idiot."

"Finally," Quentin agreed.

SINCE Travis was making dinner and couldn't pick her up, Trisha arrived at the Walsh house on Wednesday evening, a few minutes after eight. Ben had been practicing his greeting all day. He opened the door and smiled.

"Good evening," he signed. "Travis is in the kitchen. Come into the living room and meet my brothers."

Trisha forced a polite look onto her face. Either she found his level of effort below average or she didn't like him very much.

"Thank you." Ben knew he got that part right. She signed something else which he translated as, "I've heard so much about them."

He introduced her to Quentin, Jason, and Cade. They immediately started signing all at once, so Trisha sat down and put her hands on theirs to quiet them.

"One at a time," she signed.

Ben excused himself and headed into the kitchen to check on Travis.

"You should come say hi to your girlfriend."

"I'm fixin' to put the dumplings in just as soon as this comes to a boil. I'll be out then."

"Smells great, by the way."

"My grannie's chicken and dumplings recipe. I ain't never seen no one else attempt it, but since I'm the last of the Atwoods, I don't reckon it much matters."

"What are we having with it?"

"Nothing. We're talking white trash cooking here, Ben Jovi. There ain't no salad or side vegetable. The dumplings stretch the meal so that one chicken feeds six people. Everything you need is in the pot. Except peas. I don't much like peas, so I leave 'em out."

"White trash cooking, eh?"

Travis grinned wide and flashed his red eyebrows.

"Welcome to my trailer park, Hotshot."

They muddled through dinner as best they could. Since Ben adamantly refused to sit at the head of the table, the Walsh boys sat in their customary configuration: Quentin and Cade on one side, Ben and Jason on the other. Travis sat at the one end between Quentin and Ben. Trisha sat at the other, facing him. Everyone tried to sign everything they said, but that produced a slow and difficult conversation. At one point, Ben tried to stretch his legs out under the table. He looked over at Travis and their eyes locked.

That's when he felt it.

For the past week and a half, whenever they bothered to sit at the table for a meal, Travis had sat at the other end, between Jason and Cade. Now, Ben could feel Travis's knee resting against his own. He wasn't rubbing it or anything obvious, just resting it there. Travis turned his gaze away from Ben and watched Cade attempt to spell something for Trisha, seemingly oblivious to Ben's concerns. If they were alone, Ben would definitely speak up. But they weren't alone, and

Ben didn't pull his knee away. He kept it there for Travis to lean against.

At about ten thirty, Trisha signaled that they should be going. Everyone said good night as they headed down the front steps and out toward Travis's pickup. After they left, an eerie silence settled over the house. As his brothers each went to their rooms, Ben ducked into the kitchen to clean up.

About an hour later, after he had finished with the dishes and moved to the living room, Ben heard a knock on the door. When he opened it, Travis stood there, frowning.

"What are you doing here?"

Travis didn't speak.

"Oh, shit. Come on in."

Travis followed Ben into the living room and plopped down on one of the sofas. Ben stretched out on the other, propping himself up on his elbow.

"What happened?"

"She told me that if I didn't want to go out, I should have said so."

"But you did want to go out."

"Nu-uh, I didn't."

Ben looked at him, surprised.

"Oh. Then she's probably right. She'll get over it."

"I don't think so."

It took a second for Ben to realize what that meant.

"Wait a minute. She broke up with you?"

"Something like that."

"Seems a little extreme, don't you think?"

"She told me she felt like you and me were on a date tonight. Instead of me and her. That's when I… she said it ain't working out and maybe we should see other people for a spell."

"You and me? On a date?"

"Is that a crazy idea?"

The suggestion disquieted Ben, but he decided to ignore it. He pulled out his phone and looked at the time.

"Four minutes 'til midnight."

"Well, ain't we a sorry pair of pups?" Travis exclaimed, talking a little louder than he probably intended. "Two good-looking guys sitting at home on New Year's Eve with no one to kiss but each other."

Ben sat up. Now he had to say something.

"What's going on with you tonight?"

"What do you mean?"

"'No one to kiss but each other'? You do remember I'm gay, don't you?"

"It was a joke."

"Don't do that. Don't come on to me like a clumsy teenager and then call it a joke."

"Come on to you?"

"Yes. I mean, really, what was that stuff under the table tonight?"

"What are you talking about?"

"Tonight. At dinner. You were resting your knee against mine."

Travis paused as his face turned red. "You're crazy," he said softly. "I may have knocked against you, but it's a small goddamned table."

"Bullshit. You had your knee against mine. I could feel it."

Travis sat up with a huff.

"You should talk."

"What is that supposed to mean?"

"Don't think I forgot about your little hint the other night."

"What are you talking about?"

"'Every straight fella should take a hike down the gay Appalachian Trail.' Christ, Ben, why didn't you just volunteer?"

Ben felt the sting of embarrassment slap him in the face. "Okay, fair enough. But me being stoned and gay explains my bad behavior. What's your excuse?" Travis didn't answer and Ben pressed on. "Are you attracted to me?"

"I suppose that depends on how you define *attracted*."

"What's wrong with you? Are you drunk?"

"I had one shot."

"Then answer my question."

"I just said you're a good-looking guy."

"That's not what I asked."

"I know it's not what you asked. But chill out. Seriously. There ain't nothing going on here, period. I didn't come back so I could kiss you at midnight, Ben. Give me a fucking break. My girl just broke up with me thirty minutes ago, so excuse me if I crack a few bad jokes. And if I bumped your knee at dinner...."

"It was more than a bump."

"What the fuck ever. Excuse me for that too. I wasn't trying to give you a boner, for Christ's sake. Do you got to make a fucking federal case out of something like that? Geez Louise, you faggots are all alike."

Ben rolled his head back and sighed. Travis stiffened up, knowing full well that he had crossed a line.

"I'm sorry, Ben. I don't know what's going on here...."

"Well, I suppose that's just the redneck in you coming out. Travis, I have no other choice but to ask you to leave."

"I said I was sorry. I don't know why I...."

"Stop, it's okay. My skin isn't that thin, and I don't think you're a bad person who hates gay people. But you should sleep at your place tonight. Come back tomorrow and we'll pretend this whole conversation never happened."

"I can't crash in the guest room?"

Ben shook his head.

"No. I don't think that's a good idea."

Travis paused, like he was wondering what he should do. Finally, he stood up and clapped his hands together. "I reckon I'll be going, then. Happy New Year."

Ben didn't get up. "Happy New Year," he grumbled. "Lord knows, it's got to be better than the last one."

"I hope so," Travis said. He turned toward the front door and then stopped. "I'm sorry, Ben. Really." When Ben didn't respond, Travis continued out the door, down the porch steps, and across the street to Mrs. Wright's house.

As he lay in bed that night, Ben thought he felt something he hadn't felt in years. *This can't be happening*, he told himself. He covered his head with a pillow and tried to wish it away, until the same eerie silence settled over the Walsh house again and Ben reluctantly fell asleep.

SEVEN

WHEN he woke up the next morning, Ben decided to call Colin.

"Finally. Your parents get killed in a car accident and I do not hear from you for two weeks. Unacceptable, Walsh."

"Happy New Year to you too."

No response.

"I've been texting you," added Ben.

"Not the same thing."

"How long are you going to be upset with me? Don't be a prick and make this all about you."

Silence.

"Okay," Colin finally said, the anger draining from his voice. "You're right. How are you doing?"

"Where do I even begin?"

"Did you get custody of your brothers?"

"Yes."

"Brilliant. So what's next?"

"What do you mean what's next? New York is over. I'm moving back to Austin to take care of them."

"What are you talking about? New York is never over."

"Well, it is for me. I don't have options, Colin. They'll split them up if I don't come back."

"They'll split them up if you don't take guardianship."

"What's the difference?"

"Who says you have to take care of them in Austin?"

Ben was silent for a few seconds. Then he said, "You mean move them to New York?"

"Yes, I mean move them to New York."

"I could never afford that. Raising three teenage boys in the city? And besides, they live here. They go to school here. Their friends are here."

"You're not looking at the big picture. They have schools in New York, Ben. Better schools. And they'll make new friends. Families move where the job is. That's how the world works. If you're going to be of any use to those boys, you need to be happy. What kind of role model are you going to be wasting away in Texas? You're not going to be any kind of role model at all because you'll be miserable." Colin paused for a second. "And I already talked to my grandfather about the money issue."

"Tell me you didn't do that. Please."

"He's setting up a trust to cover a bigger place to live and private schools in the city. For all three of them."

"I can't accept that."

Ben heard Colin sigh. Familiar.

"Play the hand you're dealt, Walsh. Life is painful right now, I understand that. But you're not going to make the situation any better by clinging to your pride. You're one of us now, and we take care of our own. I've told you a thousand times…."

"I know."

"No one is batting an eyelash at the money except you. Promise me you'll think about it. It's the best option. And don't assume your brothers won't like the idea. Give them a chance, at least. New York can be an exciting place for a teenage boy."

"You should know."

"Exactly. I do know. What makes you think the same thing won't happen to them that happened to you? You came alive when you moved here. Maybe they will too."

Ben smiled at the new possibility.

"Okay, I'll think about it."

"And you'll talk to them?"

"Yes, of course. I'll talk to them today."

"Brilliant. So when do you plan on calling David?"

"He's on my list."

"You need to dance as fast as you can if you want to keep that door open. I am not saying it's over, but he doesn't understand why you're not reaching out to him."

"I'm not a reacher."

"I tried to explain that to him."

"You two get your nails done together or something?"

"He called me."

"I can always play the dead-parents card."

"Once. You can play that card once."

"I'll call him."

A pause.

"So how are you holding up?" Colin asked.

"Honestly, it hasn't hit me yet. I'm still waiting for my *Steel Magnolias* moment."

"What's that?"

"Never mind. There's this guy across the street who's been helping out. Travis. Straight guy, except…."

"Is he hot?"

"That's always your first question, isn't it? Yes, he's hot. I thought something was going on, but turns out it was nothing. At least, he claims it was nothing. Still, it was weird. I mean, I thought we were just friends, but then last night at dinner he starts knocking up against my knee under the table."

"What does he look like?"

"He's a ginger."

"Have you seen him with his shirt off?"

"Oddly enough, I have. I dropped by while he was having sex with his girlfriend. Except that she's now his ex-girlfriend. As of last night. Anyway, he answered the door in nothing but a pair of blue jeans."

"Sexy. So what is this *last night* you keep referring to?"

"Let's drop it."

"Let's not."

"Well, he goes downtown with his girlfriend last night and then shows up at the house an hour later. Tells me they broke up. Some things were said, and we got into this really uncomfortable argument about... I don't even know what it was about."

"What does he do?"

Ben cleared his throat.

"He goes to school," he lied.

"A college boy?"

"No, he's our age. Grad student."

Ben felt bad, but he really didn't want to think about it right now. Over the years, he had learned that there were some things Colin didn't need to know. Telling the truth would only bring out a nasty 'grease monkey' comment.

"Grad student, eh? So what happened after the argument? You didn't cheat on your boyfriend, did you, Walsh?"

"No. Nothing happened. He claimed it was all a misunderstanding, but something was going on with him." Ben paused for a moment. "Let's forget about it. I'm probably just hypersensitive right now. It was nothing, really. I'm sorry I mentioned it."

A pause.

"When are you coming back to New York? You have to bring your brothers up to visit so that they can see how brilliant living here will be."

"This is why I didn't want to call you. You've opened up a whole new can of worms now. I thought everything was settled."

"Settled for the worse, maybe."

"Give me a couple of days to think things through."

"Of course. Now, please, call David. And forget about this Travis person."

Ben hung up the phone but didn't call David. Colin had presented a real alternative. If he had a bigger apartment, it might work. Cade would be thirteen soon and even he didn't need constant supervision anymore. If Ben settled the money issue, then the final step would be getting his brothers on board. Ben considered their possible reactions. Jason didn't seem happy here. Besides, no gay boy could resist Gotham. He would be a yes vote. Cade wouldn't be thrilled with the idea, but he'd be fine as long as everyone stayed together. That left Quentin. He had a girlfriend and was a sophomore in high school. He would certainly be the most resistant. And, knowing Quentin, he would have no problem voicing his objection.

"ARE you crazy?!"

They sat at the kitchen table, eating breakfast. Which, since Travis had disappeared, consisted of bowls of cold cereal. Ben tried to ease his way into the conversation, working in some of Colin's arguments as to why they should consider this a good thing. From the tone of Quentin's reaction, he had clearly failed.

"I am not moving to New York. I hate that place. It smells like rotting garbage."

"You've only been to visit once."

"And that's all I needed! This is the worst possible solution. On top of losing our mom and dad, now you want to take away our home too. We've lived in this house our whole lives!"

"Calm down, little brother." Ben put a decidedly condescending tone in his voice.

"Don't talk to me like I'm a child."

"Then stop acting like one." Ben doubted he should be having this conversation in front of Jason and Cade, but that train had already left the station. "You know damn well this isn't the worst possible solution. Don't throw a fit pretending there wasn't a *much* worse option on the table last week. You are not the only person in this family, Quentin."

"So now what? You have absolute power?"

Ben didn't have a chance to answer him because Cade started crying.

"Shit," said Ben. "Cade, I'm...."

"Put a lid on it," barked Quentin.

"No, you put a lid on it." Ben got up and walked around the table next to Cade. He squatted down and the boy fell into his arms. "I'm sorry, buddy. You know how we talk to each other sometimes. Hey, look at me." He pulled back so that he could see Cade's face. "This conversation is not about anybody splitting up. The four of us will be together no matter what. You have my word on that. Tell him, Q. Even if we move to New York, you'll be there with him."

Quentin didn't speak. Ben felt his resentment from across the table and could practically see the steam shooting out of his ears. Ben had played a dirty trick, and they both knew it. *Dirty*, he thought, *but effective*.

"It's all good," Quentin said, reaching over to pat his brother on the head. "No way we're splitting up. Even if he drags us to Alaska."

Cade laughed and wiped his nose on the sleeve of his sweatshirt.

"See?" Ben said. "So enough with the crying. It's time to man up."

"Jesus, Ben. He's only twelve."

"Twelve, not eight. Next year thirteen. If we were Jewish, he'd be a man soon. I'm just saying. Your idyllic childhood is over."

"Fine," said Cade. "But you two stop fighting. You got that?"

Ben looked at him, impressed. "We got it," he answered. Ben went back to his chair and his bowl of Froot Loops.

"Can I say something?" Jason asked.

Ben nodded. "Please. You don't see your brother asking permission, do you?"

Jason took a deep breath and rolled his head back and forth.

"We can't leave this two-bit cattle town fast enough for me!"

Then he gave out a yelp of joy.

"Wait," said Quentin. "Can there be a little accommodation here?"

"How so?" asked Ben.

"Can we at least finish out the school year? It's only five months. If this place where you work loves you so much that they're gonna pay for all this, then surely they can give you five months. Not even half a year."

Ben looked at Jason, whose face betrayed his obvious disappointment.

"Cade?" Ben asked, gesturing with his spoon.

The youngest Walsh brother digested the information. "I agree with both of you. We should go to New York but not until after school's over."

Ben finished his cereal and drank the remaining milk straight from the bowl. "Then I will take that deal back to my client. You know, this just might work out. I don't care what people say about you," he joked. "You boys are alright."

They all laughed. Even Quentin.

TRAVIS stayed away that day. The brothers didn't question it since they figured he was with Trisha. Ben kept them in the dark about what happened the night before, and since Ben had mastered the art of takeout long ago, they didn't go hungry. Their neighborhood even had some decent restaurants. As usual, they passed the day and night watching more movies. On Friday morning, the Walsh boys sat in the living room eating cereal and watching *Donnie Darko* (one of their favorites). Shortly before noon, they heard a knock at the door.

"Probably Travis," said Quentin. "Poor fool can't stay away for more than a day."

Ben got up and headed toward the door. Poor fool. But when he opened it, there was no Travis.

Instead, Colin stood on the front porch, his arms outstretched, grinning wildly.

"Yeehaw, Walsh! Look at me. I'm in Texas."

That's when someone stepped out from behind him.

"Hey, stud."

It was David.

EIGHT

"WHAT are you doing here?"

"Surprise, Walsh. I knew if I asked, you would say no. And since I hate to travel alone, I thought it would be a nice gesture if I brought your boyfriend along. It doesn't hurt that he can walk onto a plane anytime he wants."

"I hope it's okay," said David, his voice deep and comforting. Ben's spirits lifted when he saw him. David looked like the kind of guy that can only be found in glossy magazines and high-class porn. Ben knew he could hold his own in that department, but when they went out in New York, everyone looked at David with lust and Ben with envy. He hadn't thought about sex since the phone call, except for a few stray mental images of a shirtless Travis, but his cock woke up when David looked at him sheepishly and ran his fingers through his wavy brown hair.

"Of course it's okay," said Ben. "Come on in."

As they grabbed their bags and filed past him, Ben leaned forward and gave David a kiss.

"Hey, sexy. It's good to see you."

"Likewise," said David, kissing him back.

Ben led them into the living room, where his brothers were sitting up with varying looks of surprise on their faces.

"Boys, you remember Colin, from New York. And this is our friend David. This is Quentin, Jason, and Cade," he said, pointing each of them out as he went.

"Wow," said David. "They're like Xeroxes of you."

The Walsh boys had heard similar comments for years and their reaction had always been the same—smile politely and nod. Colin and David sat down and gave a brief summary of their trip. Ben noticed his brothers didn't have much to say at first, and he wondered if this was a good idea. Not like Colin had given him a choice. Then he saw Jason eying the two visitors with awe, as if they were some kind of exotic creatures at the zoo. Ben kept on stealing glances at David. He thought about crawling into bed with him, naked, feeling his skin next to his own. He considered how to maneuver him to the bedroom. His parents' room? Still creepy, but he'd get over it. He decided to hold off, though. His brothers didn't need to confront his sex life just yet.

As the afternoon wore on and they hung out and talked, the brothers warmed considerably to both of his friends. Colin possessed a natural charisma that almost everyone found infectious. He had also met Ben's brothers when they visited him the one time in New York. Jason started asking questions about the city, and Colin looked at Ben with a knowing smile. As he answered the questions, Colin went to his bag to pull out brochures of three New York prep schools. *He's campaigning already*, Ben thought.

"This one is my alma mater, so of course I'm partial. But the other two are top-shelf. What are your grades like?"

"He got a B once," Quentin answered for Jason. "A few years ago."

"Private school?"

Jason looked at Ben.

"No," Ben answered for him. "They go to public school. It was a thing with my dad."

"I admire that. But if you're moving to New York City, public schools are not an option for him." He turned to Jason. "You are clearly a young genius like your brother."

"Public school is just fine with me," insisted Quentin.

Colin grinned knowingly. Ben laughed when he saw that. Mostly because he knew that Colin always had a plan and was probably two steps ahead of Quentin. He reached into his bag.

"Which is why I brought you these," he said, passing two brochures to Quentin and stunning him into silence. "The first is for LaGuardia Arts, the *public* school for visual arts." Quentin looked up at him, puzzled. That's when Colin took a book from his bag and pulled out a paper napkin from between the pages. He handed it to Quentin. "Look familiar?"

"Where did you get this?" An elaborate pen drawing of a New York City street scene, viewed from inside a restaurant, covered the napkin. Cade and Jason both looked over his shoulder.

"Hey," said Cade, "that's one of yours!"

"That's right," Colin confirmed. "I picked it up off the table when I had dinner with your family. During your visit to New York. You have a great eye."

Quentin scoffed at the suggestion. "You kept this?"

"Of course. It's one of the coolest things I've ever seen. Am I right, David?"

"It is pretty cool," David agreed.

"Let me see." Ben held out his hand and Quentin passed him the drawing. Quentin had been scribbling on napkins in restaurants since he was three, and they had all stopped paying attention years ago. Clearly that was a mistake, since Ben could see Quentin's talents had developed considerably. "This is awesome, little brother. The detail is amazing."

"In case you haven't noticed, Walsh, your brother is an artist."

"I'm not an artist," Quentin protested.

"My friend Stephanie, who owns a gallery down in Soho, begs to differ. I showed it to her. She said if you did napkin drawings of scenes all over New York City, she could make a show out of them."

"No way," said Quentin.

"This is Colin, Q. He makes things happen."

"The other brochure," Colin continued, "is for a private visual arts school." Then he reached into his bag and casually added, "That's if you can't get into LaGuardia."

"Please," Quentin scowled. "I could totally get into that place."

Nothing like throwing down a challenge to a Walsh, Ben thought. *Well played, Colin*. Colin pulled out one more brochure and handed it to Cade.

"This is Bolton Academy. It's an all-boys school that emphasizes athletics as well as academics."

"You mean like *Dead Poets Society*?" Cade asked.

"Yes," Colin answered. "But without Robin Williams. Or the unfortunate suicide."

Ben sat back, amazed. Colin had absorbed all that about his brothers from one dinner two years ago. "I don't suppose there's anything in that bag for me?"

"Of course there is, Dorothy." Colin reached into the bag and pulled out a small white box.

"Are those…?"

"Peanut butter-chocolate brownies from your favorite bakery on Forty-Eighth Street."

"I love you, man," Ben wept, taking the box and smelling it. He opened it up and bit into one of the sweets. "You've got to try these," he said, passing the box to Quentin, who took one and then passed it to Cade.

"Do you work at the same place as Ben?" Jason asked Colin.

"No," Colin answered, chuckling. "I could never work for my family."

"Colin has loftier ambitions," Ben explained. "He works for the ACLU."

"Cool!" Jason cooed.

"You a lawyer too, David?" Quentin asked.

David grinned and shook his head.

"No. I'm a pilot with JetBlue."

"No way!" exclaimed Cade. "You fly planes?"

"Yes, I fly planes."

"Where'd you learn how to do that?"

"In the Air Force."

That led to a barrage of questions from Quentin and Cade. They wanted to know everything about flying planes. Colin and Jason sat next to each other, looking over the brochures and whispering conspiratorially. Ben knew that Colin had taken him under his wing, and remembered once again that he needed all the help he could get.

When they left for dinner, Ben noticed that Travis's truck was in the driveway. They hadn't seen each other since Wednesday night. Two days. It seemed odd, but he brushed the feeling away. When they got home, the truck was gone.

That night, Ben was horny and wanted David to himself. So he looked for the shortest two movies he could find, which turned out to be *Clerks* and *Office Space*. Almost three hours later, the boys went off to bed and Colin politely retired to the guest room with a wink.

"We'll see what Grindr has to offer."

"Behave yourself," Ben chided. "There are children in the house."

"Yes, Dad."

After he left, Ben grinned at David. They were sitting on opposite sides of the room.

"Your brothers don't know we're dating."

Ben got up and moved to the other sofa. He reached his hand out and put it on David's knee.

"No. But I'll tell them if you think I should. In the scheme of things, it hasn't been important."

"Gee, thanks."

"You know what I mean."

David looked down.

"You haven't called me since the airport."

"I know. But when I saw you on the porch today... I'm glad you're here. I mean that."

"I'm not going to make a big stink about it. You pretty much get a pass when both your parents die. I just need to know that you want me here. That it wasn't a mistake, me coming."

Ben stood up and extended his hand.

"You know I'm not good with words. Can I show you instead?"

David took his hand and allowed himself to be pulled up off the sofa. Ben put his arms around David's waist and lowered his hands until they were cupping the cheeks of his ass. He squeezed and kissed him. The stubble from David's chin brushed up against Ben's lips. He found the bottom of David's shirt and lifted it over his head. David had a powerful torso and chest covered by a sexy coat of dark, coarse hair. Ben lowered his head and ran his tongue over David's left nipple, at which he jumped and gave out a small cry.

That's when they both heard a knock on the door.

"Shit," Ben muttered.

"Who would be stopping by at this time of night?"

"I'll take care of it. Wait here."

Ben went to the front door and opened it, knowing exactly who would be there. Travis started talking immediately.

"Ben, I'm so sorry about Wednesday night."

"Travis...."

"No, please. Let me say this. I had one shot of tequila, which is no excuse, I know that. But I've been beating myself up for what I said to you. Honestly. I ain't thought about nothing else for two days. Ben, I need to tell you something. I...."

"Who is it?"

David had stepped up behind Ben, still shirtless. Travis looked confused.

"Travis, this is David. From New York."

Travis didn't move. He tried to look away, but he couldn't stop staring at David, who wrapped his arms around Ben as he offered his hand.

"Nice to meet you, Travis."

Travis reached out and shook it. "I'm sorry. I didn't know you had company."

"Neither did I until he and Colin showed up today."

"Unexpected," Travis said, looking down. "I didn't mean to interrupt. I'll... talk to you later. I'm sorry. Nice to meet you, David."

"You too."

Travis spun around and headed down the steps toward the street. Ben closed the door and turned back to David.

"Who's that?"

"Just some guy my dad took in. He's nobody, really. Now, where were we before he knocked?" Ben lowered his head and ran his tongue over David's other nipple. A low bass moan rose out of David's chest. "That's where we were. I think it's time we took this to the bedroom."

"Good idea."

Ben reached down and took David's hand, intertwining their fingers. He led him into the master bedroom, where his parents had slept. He pushed the ghosts to the corners of his mind and sat David down on the bed, then turned around to close the door.

"Take off your pants," Ben ordered.

David stood up and kicked off his shoes, knowing better than to remove his socks. He unzipped his fly, pushed his jeans to the floor, stepped out of them, and tossed them into the corner of the room with his foot.

"Get on your knees."

David obeyed, eying Ben's crotch as he stepped in front of him. Ben reached out and grabbed the back of David's head, forcing his mouth onto Ben's denim-covered dick. David gnawed at it while Ben moaned. After a moment, Ben pulled away and stepped back.

"Look at me."

David tilted his head up and their eyes met. He looked hungry, ready for a fix. Ben peeled off his shirt.

"Shoes."

David bent over and undid the laces of Ben's running shoes, then pulled them off. He almost reached for the socks but thought better of it and pulled back.

Ben paused for effect.

"Socks."

He lifted each foot as David peeled off the socks.

"Look at me."

David looked up again. Ben undid his zipper and opened his pants. He pulled out his cock and held it at the base. There were bigger dicks in the world, Ben knew that, but he'd never seen anything as perfect as his own cut eight inches. His cock was a work of art, straight as an arrow and beautifully proportioned. David sat back on his heels and looked at it, waiting for permission to take it into his mouth. With his jeans still on, Ben stepped forward and slapped him on the face with it. He teased David by rubbing the head along his lips, knowing full well that he wouldn't try to suck it until Ben gave him permission.

"What do you think?"

"Please let me suck it."

"I don't know," said Ben doubtfully as he continued to rub his cock on David's face. "You gonna do a good job?"

"It will be the best blow job you've ever had."

"You going to take it all the way down your throat?"

"Yes, sir."

"Even if you choke?"

"Yes, sir."

"And what if you beg me to stop?"

"Don't listen to me, sir. Just keep fucking my throat."

Ben stepped back again and shucked his jeans.

"Good answer."

David looked at him, and Ben made sure to put a cocky grin on his face.

"Have at it, airman."

David reached out and pulled Ben toward him while he took the stiff dick into his mouth. He didn't stop until Ben's cock rammed down the back of his throat. He went perfectly still, breathing through his nose, concentrating on the suppression of his gag reflex. Ben knew he would stay that way until tears started streaming down his face. Finally, they did. David choked and pulled off. That's when Ben grabbed the back of his head and pushed him back down on his wet prick.

"Oh, no you don't."

Ben started to fuck the back of his throat, which made David go wild, moaning and crying at the same time. It was so hot Ben thought he might come, so he grabbed David by the hair and tilted his head back, then bent over and kissed him. He could feel David trembling. He pulled away and said, "Facedown on the bed."

David sprang up off the floor and lay down on his stomach. Ben reached over and peeled off his briefs. On the long list of things that Ben appreciated about David, his ass came in at number one. Most people called it a bubble butt, but Ben heard someone call it an onion ass once, because that was an ass that made you cry. Ben liked that better.

"Get your cheeks in the air."

David complied.

Ben knelt down between David's legs and spread his ass cheeks, revealing the entry point. He bent forward and ran his tongue lightly over the crack. David jumped.

"Sir, please eat my ass."

"You can do better than that."

"Sir, I'm begging you to fuck me with your tongue. Please, sir."

So Ben thrust his tongue deep into David's asshole. They were both in heaven. Ben could eat ass all day and night, and he pushed David further and further, until he was biting down on one of the pillows and clenching the bedsheets with his fists.

"Sir, I don't know how much more of this I can take. If you don't fuck me...."

David had brought his bag into the room earlier that evening and set it next to the bed. He reached down while Ben continued to rim his ass and undid one of the zippers. He pulled out condoms and lube and threw them back onto the bed next to Ben. Without stopping his tongue assault, Ben ripped open one of the packages and rolled the condom onto his cock, and then rubbed it with a small dab of lube. He lay down on top of David, rubbing his dick against his ass crack. Without using his hands, Ben guided the head of his cock into position against David's puckered asshole. Their bodies stopped as Ben entered him and inched forward.

Ben reached down and ran his fingers through David's thick hair, then ran his chin across the back of David's neck. David bucked up and got about four inches of cock at once, which caused him to squirm and pull away.

"Get on your back," Ben said.

David flipped over underneath him. He lifted his legs and guided Ben's dick back into his ass. They looked at each other and smiled. David's eyes flashed as if he had a card to play. He lifted his legs higher, until his socked feet were rubbing all over Ben's face.

"You fucker," Ben growled.

"Come on, stud. Get those socks off."

Ben peeled off the socks and buried his face in the soles of David's feet. Ben became instantly enthralled and David knew it.

"You like those big slabs of airman feet, don't you?"

"You know I love 'em, fucker."

"Show me, sir."

Ben licked the soles and then took each toe into his mouth. After he had showered David's feet with attention, Ben leaned in to kiss him and they started to fuck in earnest. They discarded their characters and held onto each other as Ben pounded away. David didn't touch himself while they screwed. Ben hated when he did that and wasn't shy about telling him so. As he threw his thrusts into fifth gear, Ben felt the heat of orgasm rising in his balls. David urged him on.

"Come on, Ben. Fuck me harder. Slam your cock into me. Give me your fucking dick. You know how I feel. You know what I want."

"Say it."

"Fuck me harder."

"Say it, goddamnit!"

"I'm only happy when your cock is in my ass."

Ben fucked in a frenzy until he was arching his back and coming into David's butt. He could feel the spurts before his orgasm began, wave after wave of pleasure coursing through his body, depositing itself into David's now battered asshole. Finally, Ben collapsed on top of him, reaching down to grab the condom as he pulled his dick out. He tossed it on the floor next to the bed and knelt down between David's legs. It took Ben less than a minute to get him off. He loved sucking dick and went down on David's with gusto, working him with his hand and mouth until Ben felt the familiar taste of come at the back of his throat. Afterward, Ben wanted to lie there in the stink of sex, but David hopped off the bed and went into the bathroom to clean up.

As they fell asleep, Ben thought about the unexpected day. He liked having a friend who knew him well enough to show up like that. But then he thought about Travis. What was that look on his face when he'd seen David? Was he jealous? And what did Travis need to tell him? Ben just didn't buy that their argument was all a misunderstanding. Travis knew he was pushing up against his knee at dinner. They both did. And that comment at midnight, about nobody to kiss but each other? Please. Ben had no room in his life for games. Much better to be with someone who knew what he wanted. He wrapped his arms around David, rubbing his stubble against the back of David's neck, reminding him of fucking and making him hard again. He reached over to the nightstand and got another condom. He put it on and gently maneuvered his cock into David's ass. After a few minutes they fell asleep like that, legs intertwined, one inside the other, breathing softly.

NINE

BEN squeezed Travis from behind, his arms around him, holding him close. He ran a finger down his neck, up the slope of his shoulder, and then across his arm. His alabaster skin felt cool to the touch. Travis looked like he had been carved from marble, his form smoothed to perfection by the incessant sanding of an overenthusiastic sculptor. His red hair, flecked with blond and gold, caught the morning sunlight in crazy ways as it streamed through the east window. He only pretended to be asleep. He pushed his butt up against Ben. Maybe he could rub his knee under the table and call it an accident, but he wanted to see Travis talk his way out of this one. Ben kissed him on the earlobe.

Travis responded by reaching back and pulling him in closer.

"I want you to fuck me, Ben."

"It's about time."

"Ben? Stop. Are you asleep? Wake up, Ben."

BEN sat up as David turned around in bed.

"Shit," Ben said. "Sorry, I was still asleep. Did I hurt you?"

"No, of course not. It's just that you aren't wearing a condom."

"Oh." He had been dreaming of Travis but about to fuck David. "Sorry about that."

"Don't apologize. Put one on and keep going."

Ben thrust his head back onto the pillow and pulled away. Everything felt wrong in the light of day.

"I think we should probably skip the morning round. Cade will be up soon."

"Got it," said David, obviously disappointed.

They dressed and went into the kitchen, where the others soon joined them. Ben kept his distance from David for the rest of the day. The more he thought about the dream, the more uncomfortable he felt being around David. He wanted to talk to Travis and hear what he had to say, but Colin and David weren't flying back to New York until Sunday. Colin rented a car *and* a driver to take Jason shopping. David took Cade and Quentin to a Longhorns basketball game, which Cade loved and Quentin tolerated because he thought David was kind of cool. They were giving Ben some alone time, which he appreciated. He just wished that Travis would come home.

That evening everyone gathered in the kitchen as David prepared a gourmet spread. His style stood in stark contrast to Travis's, even though they shared the same intent. They both liked to take care of people with food. Ben didn't even notice that Quentin had left until he heard the front door open, followed by the sound of Travis's voice. A few seconds later, the two of them came into the kitchen.

Ben had never been happier to see anyone in his life.

"Travis!" yelled Cade, running over to give him a punch and a hug.

"We hadn't seen him in a few days," explained Quentin. "So I had to make sure he was still alive. He was eating a bowl of cereal for dinner."

"I'm sorry, Ben. I tried to tell him no, but…."

"It's true. I dragged him out of the house against his will."

Travis looked disheveled, like he hadn't showered or slept in a couple of days.

"What's wrong with you, Travis?" Cade asked. "You look kind of sick."

"I'm fine, little man. Been working a lot, that's all."

"Come on in," Ben insisted. "It's fine, really. I'm glad you came over. Meet my friends. This is Colin. We went to law school together."

Colin eyed Ben suspiciously and then stepped forward to shake Travis's hand.

"Ben told me you've been helping out with his brothers."

"I'm trying to do what I can."

"That's very decent of you. It's a pleasure to meet you."

"And," continued Ben, "you met David last night. We didn't go to law school together."

"Hi, Travis," David said, stepping around the kitchen island to shake his hand. "I hope you're hungry?"

"I'm starving, actually."

"Great. Then let's sit down to eat."

THEY had to squeeze an extra chair in to make room for seven people. Everyone gave their compliments to the chef, who had produced a wide assortment of appetizers from around the world.

"When did y'all get in?" asked Travis as he munched on some Korean spring rolls. Ben looked at him and wondered if his tousled appearance had anything to do with their argument on New Year's Eve and David's subsequent arrival.

"You know," Colin said, "I hear that all the time in movies but I never believed people actually talk that way. This is a genuine Texas moment I'm having."

Travis looked confused.

"Colin," Ben said. "Stop being a douche."

"I apologize, Travis. I have never heard anyone use the contraction *y'all* before. I mean, not in an actual conversation. It's not a comment about you. Clearly I need to get out of Manhattan more." He turned to Jason and whispered, "I embarrass your brother sometimes," which made Jason giggle. There had been some major bonding during their shopping expedition. "Anyway, to answer your question, we came in yesterday. Uninvited, I might add. Walsh has a problem asking for help."

"Men have a problem asking for help," said Travis.

"Amen," agreed Colin.

"Well, I'm sure you're gonna miss having him around New York."

"Not if I have anything to say about it."

That's when Jason blurted out, "We're moving to New York City!"

Travis looked at Ben, startled.

"Not right away," Ben explained, hesitating. "They… want to finish out the school year and then… yes, it's likely that we'll all be heading back to New York."

Travis picked up his glass of water and took a large gulp.

"Boy, a lot's changed since I've been gone."

"I'm going to go to an all-boys school," Cade told him.

"Really, Cade? That's great."

"Too bad you had to work today. You could have come to the basketball game with us."

"Yeah, that's too bad." Travis said.

There was a long silence at the table.

"So," Colin said, changing the subject, "what are you studying, Travis?"

Ben froze.

Shit.

He had forgotten all about the lie he told to Colin. He never dreamed the two of them would actually meet. He scrambled to think of an explanation, but he had boxed himself into a corner. He could feel Travis looking at him.

"Did Ben tell you I was a student?"

"Yes, he did," Colin answered. "It's nothing to be ashamed of. Most PhDs are six or seven years, and a law degree is only three. We'd still be in school too if we weren't lawyers."

David and Colin, of course, noticed nothing at first. Quentin, Jason, and Cade knew that Travis fixed cars for a living and didn't understand why Ben would have told Colin otherwise. Ben's heart broke when he saw the ashen look on Travis's face and knew that he had made a terrible mistake.

"Why would you tell him that?" Travis pleaded.

"I'm sorry, Travis. I didn't think…."

"Are you ashamed of me?"

"What's going on here?" David asked Quentin.

"Travis is not a student. He's an auto mechanic. It seems Ben lied and told Colin otherwise, though I haven't figured out why that was necessary."

"What?" exclaimed Colin. "Why would you tell me he was a grad student if he wasn't?"

"Because," Ben answered. "You were asking me twenty questions and I didn't want to hear some 'grease monkey' comment when I told you what he did for a living. It was a stupid thing to do. If I had known…."

David interrupted him. "Why were you asking him twenty questions?"

"You really screwed the pooch this time," Quentin said.

Travis got up from the table.

"Don't leave," Colin protested. "So he told a little white lie. Since he can demonstrate absence of malice, why don't we all settle the case and move on?"

"Do you always cover his ass like that?" asked Travis.

"Excuse me?"

Travis looked like he might be sick to his stomach.

"I gotta git," he said, flying out the front door without bothering to close it behind him.

No one said anything for several moments. Ben gazed down at his plate but could feel everyone staring at him, especially Quentin and Cade. Finally, he looked up at David, who wore his own brand of renewed disappointment.

"That," Colin whispered to Jason, "is how they do it *Jersey Shore* style."

"Shut up!" David barked. "Ben, can I talk to you? In private?"

"Do we have to do this now?"

"I can leave now if you want, or we can talk and then I can leave. It's up to you."

"David," Colin interrupted. "You're overreacting. Everyone's overreacting."

David ignored him. "Ben?"

"Okay. Let's step outside. The rest of you stay where you are."

Ben followed David to the front door and then stepped out onto the porch. He looked across the street.

No more lights.

"Do you have feelings for him?" David asked once Ben had closed the door behind him.

"What are you talking about? I met the guy two weeks ago."

"And you met me two months ago. You would only be embarrassed about what he did for a living if you had feelings for him. That's why you lied to Colin. You were ashamed to tell your best friend you're into somebody who fixes cars for a living."

"You're insane."

"No, something's going on. You told me he was nobody, but that's not true. I saw it on his face when he stopped by last night. He's somebody. He needed to talk to you. And this morning, when you were still asleep, you were dreaming about someone else. I'm sure of it. It was him, wasn't it?"

"No."

"Don't lie to me too."

"Okay," Ben said in surrender. "Yes. It was him. Are you happy now? I'm as lost as any human being on the planet. I don't know which end is up or what direction I'm going in. I know you want us to move forward, but I can't be responsible for you right now. I just became a dad to three teenage boys! I'm ten years younger than you, David. I don't have space in my head for this."

"Then why did you fuck me last night?" David asked, accusing him, his eyes glassy with tears.

"I don't know. I was lonely and horny and I ended up thinking with my dick. But I was happy to see you. You're an amazing guy. It's just…."

"Not going to work out."

Ben paused. Then he said,

"No, it's not. Not the way you want it to." He reached out his hand but David moved away.

"This was a mistake after all. Coming here. I should never have listened to Colin."

"David, it's better this way. You can go back to New York and get on with your life. Instead of waiting for me."

"I would have, you know. Waited for you."

Silence.

"I'll sleep on the couch tonight."

Ben nodded. "I'm sorry."

David turned around and walked back into the house. Ben stayed on the porch and thought about what he would say to his brothers, not to mention Travis. A moment later, Colin opened the door and stuck his head out.

"Is it safe to approach?" he asked.

"Yes, come on," replied Ben, waving him onto the porch. "I'm sorry you got involved in all this."

"Please," said Colin as he stepped out and closed the door behind him, "don't apologize to me. Well, maybe at least tell me it was a momentary lapse in judgment. Do you honestly think it matters to me if you date a mechanic?"

"I'm not dating a mechanic."

"Not yet. But there's clearly something going on."

"I know, but what? The whole thing makes my head hurt."

"It doesn't matter. You know I don't really like the term, but in this case it's appropriate. You were a douche, Ben. You owe Travis an apology, prospective boyfriend or not. And I'd do it tonight, if I were you. Honestly, do not go back in there and face your brothers until you patch things up with him. Now, across the street with you. Git, as he would say."

"Okay, I'm going. Tell them where I am?"

"Of course. As it was so eloquently pointed out to me this evening, I always cover your ass, Walsh."

"I know. Thanks for that."

BEN headed across the street and knocked on Mrs. Wright's side door. He knew that Travis would be able to hear him. He could see light coming from underneath the closed door of the back bedroom. As soon as he knocked, he saw a shadow dart randomly along the thin strip of light at the bottom of the door.

Mrs. Wright called from the living room. "Travis! Someone's knocking."

A few moments later, Travis opened his door and saw Ben's face, visible through the glass panes. Travis looked panicked and uncertain, but finally grabbed his jacket and passed through the living room to the kitchen.

"Who's at the door, Travis?"

"It's just Ben, Mrs. Wright. From across the street."

"Oh, those poor boys. Tell him we'll be praying for his family tomorrow at church."

"I will."

Travis opened the door and Ben stepped off the stairs onto the driveway. Travis locked the door behind him and then turned to face Ben.

"Your eyes are red."

"We should take a walk," Travis said, ignoring Ben's comment. "Mrs. Wright says she'll be praying for you tomorrow."

"Yeah, I heard. God knows I need it."

"You ain't gonna hear no arguments from me."

Ben turned and started to move down the driveway, lagging enough until Travis caught up with him. The street where they lived was a cul-de-sac, though in Texas they didn't bother with the French and just called it a dead end. They walked in the middle of the dark street, making their way onto one of the main thoroughfares and then past St. Paul's Lutheran church, which had a bell tower that played seasonal hymns every day at noon and six. Ben considered it one of the perks of living in its shadow, infusing the neighborhood with an air of grace. Eventually, Travis stopped and took a seat on a bus-stop bench.

Ben pulled out his phone and looked at the time.

Eight thirty-eight.

He sat down next to Travis on the bench. They gazed out at the street, watching the cars race by.

"Why are we here?" asked Travis.

"Catching the bus?" Ben's attempt to lighten the mood fell flat. "Sorry. I want to apologize."

"So apologize."

"I need to know something first."

"What do you need to know?"

"Who I'm apologizing to."

Travis glanced over at Ben and frowned.

"What does that mean?"

Ben turned his head and looked at Travis.

"Who am I apologizing to? Because it makes a difference. Are you the guy across the street who's helping out in a pinch, maybe even a good friend? Or are you something more than that?"

"Like what?"

"You tell me. You look like shit, Atwood."

"Geez, thanks a lot."

"Does that have anything to do with what happened a few days ago? People don't usually lose sleep over something like that unless…." Ben stopped short of saying it himself.

"Unless what?"

"Unless they feel something more than friendship."

"I'm not gay, remember?"

"Yes, I remember. Then why all the Sturm und Drang?"

"I don't even know what that means."

"It means that one minute you're calling me a faggot and the next minute you're showing up on my…."

"Okay, okay." Travis paused. "You were right about the knees under the table thing."

Ben exhaled. "Finally. So, you acknowledge something's going on here?"

"Maybe. I don't know. I thought we were friends, Ben. At least that. But then something changed and… damn if I ain't baffled by it. I don't think of nothing else. I can't eat or sleep. And I sure as hell don't know where to go from here."

Ben turned toward Travis.

"I think I do."

Without any warning, Ben leaned over and kissed him. Travis's lips trembled from the shock, his eyes wide open. But he didn't pull away. Ben backed off for a second and then kissed him again. And again. Six, then seven. And eight. On the eighth kiss, Travis kissed him back.

Ben had his answer.

He pulled away and stared into Travis's eyes. A number 10 bus drove up. Ben turned and waved it on, then settled himself back on the bench.

"David and I broke up. I don't want you to think I'm kissing you while I have a boyfriend. Now, the apology. I'm a defense attorney, and if I were my own client, I would suggest going with temporary insanity." He looked down, talking to his hands. "I'm not always a strong person. Like you said, I'm Lonely Boy. I don't really fit into Colin's world, but I can certainly act like a dick trying. It was a moment of weakness and I apologize."

"Well, I'm sorry I used the F word."

"We'll chalk that up to a moment of weakness too."

Travis yanked his coat collar up to stay warm. "Maybe I'm the wrong person for you, Ben. Are you ashamed of being… *whatever* with someone like me?"

"No. Absolutely not. I promise you right here that nothing like this will ever happen again. I'm a work in progress, Travis. God knows I know that. But this is not going to be an issue and I was a fool to lie to Colin. I am truly sorry."

"Why did you kiss me?"

"Why did you kiss me back? Because you did—on number eight. You definitely kissed me back."

Travis turned away and stared out at the traffic.

"I don't understand what's going on."

"I know you've never fooled around with a guy. But you avoided my question last week. Did you ever want to?"

Travis paused and bit down on the corner of his mouth.

"The thought has crossed my mind. Recently."

"Recently, as in since you met me?"

"Yes."

"But not before that?"

Travis shook his head.

Ben huffed and rolled his eyes. "See, I just don't buy that. I know there are supposed to be these straight guys out there who go gay for that one special dude. But it's a fantasy. It doesn't really happen, except maybe in romance novels and gay porn."

"I can't explain it."

Ben decided to drop the subject. He had more important things on his mind. "Say you forgive me, Travis."

"Of course I forgive you. As long as you forgive me for using that word."

"Deal."

Ben thrust out his hand and Travis shook it. Firm and sturdy. Travis looked at Ben and then pulled his hand away, turning his gaze back to the street.

The two men sat in silence for several moments.

"So," Travis said. "Here we are."

"Here we are," Ben repeated.

"You're not gonna ask me to decide anything tonight, are you?"

"Of course not."

Ben looked over at Travis. He had a worried look on his face. That's when Ben realized.

"You're not okay with this. Are you?"

"With what?"

"Liking a guy. Kissing a guy. The possibility of being with a guy."

Travis paused. "I…."

For a moment it looked like he might lay it all out on the proverbial table, but then he stopped himself.

"I don't know."

Ben nodded thoughtfully.

"Okay, then. Muddy waters."

"What's that?"

"Something my dad used to say. When everything is confusing and murky, he told us to treat it like muddy water. Stop. Sit still. Let the dirt settle and eventually the water will clear up."

"Does that mean you don't want me coming around no more?"

Ben laughed. "No, that is not what I mean. I'm just saying that we need to step back. Take it easy. See how things go. Before we decide if we want to take our bromance to the next level."

Travis laughed and rubbed his eyes. "Our bromance? You crack me up."

"I know. It's one of the things I like about you. Now, let's go. I'm sure everyone is wondering what's going on."

They got up off the bench and walked back to their block. When they reached Mrs. Wright's house, they stopped under the streetlamp. Travis looked down at his feet but clearly wanted to say something.

"What is it?" Ben asked.

Travis kicked a pavement stone with his boot.

"There's something you should know about me. That is, mostly I'm a sorry-ass coward. But since I met you, well, it's made me not want to be a coward so much. It's made me want to take chances, which is what I'm trying to do here. We both know that nothing in life is for certain. So if we decide not to"—he grinned meekly and looked up—"you know, take our bromance to the next level, could you do it one more time?"

Ben looked confused at first, but then he understood.

"You mean kiss you?"

Travis nodded. "Yeah. Just so I'll remember what it feels like, in case things… don't work out."

Ben looked at him and swallowed. He didn't need any arm-twisting. He leaned down slowly until their lips were about an inch apart. Then he stopped. They looked into each other's eyes.

"What will the neighbors think?" Ben asked softly.

"We need a good scandal on the block."

Ben arched forward and brushed Travis's lips. A little at first, and then, after a moment, more intense. Travis wrapped his arms around Ben's neck as Ben invaded his mouth with his tongue. Ben pulled Travis close to him, wrapping his arms around his waist, unleashing all his pent-up frustration from the past two weeks. He pushed, grabbed, and practically strangled Travis, allowing him to open up the unexpected floodgates of his grief. Soon Ben could taste his salty tears as they melted into their kisses. He stopped and rested their foreheads together.

"I feel it," Ben said. "It's here. They're not coming back, are they?"

Travis held him as he broke down weeping.

"No, Ben. This is it. They're not coming back."

TEN

AFTER Ben regained his composure, he and Travis sat on the curb and talked for another hour. Ben explained how the New York solution came about and it gave them another reason to put the brakes on their budding relationship. After they finally said good night, Ben went inside and convinced his brothers that he had patched everything up with Travis. The next day, after Colin and David left, Travis knocked on the door. He had a new recipe and wanted to know if he could try it out.

"Jesus," Quentin muttered under his breath to Ben as Jason and Cade helped Travis carry groceries to the kitchen. "He comes up with some moronic excuses to hang out with you."

Ben looked surprised. "What are you talking about? He was hanging out here for months before I showed up."

"But he never came up with something like trying out a new recipe. I don't know, big brother. I think he might be gay for you."

After the kiss, Ben was pretty sure Quentin was right, but he was also sure that full disclosure to his brothers wasn't a good idea yet, so he played dumb.

"You don't go gay for one person," Ben said, rolling his eyes.

"According to Kinsey...."

"That dude was a quack. There was no control to his studies, and they were anecdotal at best. The latest research from 2005 suggests sexual orientation in men is fixed. Google it."

"Mark this day on the calendar," Quentin announced. "I know something you don't."

"Not possible."

"Afraid so. Because I *did* Google it, loser. A Northwestern study last year used new criteria to select people for their study. Their conclusion was that bisexuality is totally real and comes in all different system configurations. Which is so obvious. You're using an outdated argument to cover up what you know is true."

"I'm a lawyer, Quentin."

"Travis has been acting different since you got here."

"Differently," Ben corrected him.

"That's just my natural aversion to adverbs. And then last night, when he found out you threw him under the bus like that, did you see his face?"

"I didn't throw him under the bus."

"Heartbroken. That's how I'd describe it. Wouldn't you?"

"He was not heartbroken. I told you, we patched things up."

"And I'm impressed. Really. What is it about you that everyone finds so damned charming?"

"When you figure it out, please let me know."

"Shit," Quentin said. "I bet you a hundred bucks he's into you."

Ben considered it. As he saw it, either way he won.

"You're on."

That night, neither Travis nor Ben mentioned the kiss. The next day would be the boys' first back to school since the death of their parents, and Travis didn't stick around long after dinner. A couple of nights later, though, he came back. The two of them got along great as long as they didn't discuss the elephant in the room. So they didn't, and after a few days, they found it easier to pretend that the kiss never happened, even though Ben thought about it every time Travis said good night.

Muddy waters, he reminded himself.

In the meantime, Ben occupied himself with figuring out how to run a house—or at least who he had to hire. If he could pay someone to do a task, any task, he would. Laundry, house cleaning, even many of the meals—Ben outsourced them all. His father left behind plenty of life insurance, not to mention Ben's salary from Wilson & Mead, so the Walsh boys had no problem with money.

His brothers adapted because life really didn't give them a choice. They didn't want to move on. In fact, their grief deepened as winter unfolded. With a fire in the fireplace and the cold banished to the outside, they often spent evenings and weekends on the couches watching movies, even though Travis constantly suggested dinner out or a basketball game for Cade.

Travis became an integral part of their lives. He helped out with the meals and getting the boys here and there. Ben needed a caretaker as much as his brothers, and Travis did that too. He would listen to Ben ramble on for hours. He had been in his shoes; he knew what it was like to have no parents left in the world. When Quentin, Jason, and Cade looked at Travis, they saw a constant, a through line, but when Ben looked at Travis, he saw a goddamned hero.

Ben spent the rest of his time planning the Walsh transition to Manhattan. His boss had agreed to the five-month sabbatical, something else Ben chalked up to Colin's intervention. As for his first brushes with parenting, well, no one would have said it came naturally to Ben.

Cade got into a fight at school because someone called his brother a fag. Ben didn't ask which brother. Cade had little to say about the incident, except that he would do it again, and at the end of the day, Ben chose not to discipline him. Cade knew what the word "fag" meant and that Ben was one of them. Ben understood the expectations of the moment—he was supposed to tell Cade about other ways to deal with conflict. Peaceful ways. But he didn't do that and dropped the whole thing instead.

Jason hated his school, but when Ben asked him if he was being bullied, he said no. He withdrew even more than usual, staying in the living room when the rest of them watched a movie but reading a book instead. Somehow Ben managed to avoid the topic of Jason's make-out session. The time never seemed right and the topic made Ben uncomfortable for some reason. Colin steadfastly refused to disclose anything he and Jason discussed, standing in stern defense of Jason's right to privacy.

Quentin managed to keep Ben on his toes. "Look," he told Ben one evening, "I understand the pressure you're under. Really, I do. And I'll do my best to respect that. But I'm sixteen years old. We both know this will probably mess me up a little. I promise you, I'm gonna make mistakes. Big ones. Well, not the pregnancy one, but something stupid, I'm sure. Still, I promise to do my best because I know you're gonna do the same." He paused for a moment, then said, "And, speaking of my age, I need to take my driving test."

"You haven't done that already?"

"I flunked the first time."

"Really? Did you choke or what?"

"Kind of."

Ben wanted to support Quentin, not make fun of him.

"It's not a big deal, Q. Colin doesn't even know how to drive. We'll go down there next week and get you squared away." Quentin passed his test the second time. Ben gave him a long leash, even though secretly he decided to use technology to his advantage, sneaking a GPS tracking app onto Quentin's phone so he could at least see where he went.

By the end of January, Ben noticed that, one day at a time, despite their funk, he and his brothers had survived the initial shock of an unspeakable loss. Ben could see the outlines of a plan starting to form. Maybe life wouldn't suck after all.

Finally, Ben tried to wrap his brain around the situation with Travis, a straight guy who turned out to be not so straight. Gay for Ben, maybe? It was confusing. And certainly the move back to New York made any step toward a relationship... insane? Irresponsible? Unnecessary? But then there was the kiss. It was a game changer. They couldn't deny that, either. During January, every lingering hug good night, every casual touch in the kitchen, every whisper in his ear reminded Ben of that kiss. He knew all the reasons why they had backed off, but Ben thought that if he brought them out into the open, maybe they could figure out a way to move forward together.

SO ON a Saturday night at the beginning of February, as Ben and Travis sat in the living room of the Walsh house, Ben decided to make his move. They had finished a movie and Travis was off work until Monday. The brothers had already gone to sleep. As Travis put on his boots, Ben stood up and went to his father's rolltop desk and took out two pads of paper. He grabbed some pens and tossed them onto the sofa next to Travis.

"What's this for?"

"We're going to play a little game," Ben answered.

"What kind of game?" Travis asked.

Ben sat down and took one of the pads and a pen.

"We are each going to make a list. The top five things we're afraid of... "

"What is this? Have you been watching Oprah's final season?"

"... with each other," Ben finished.

Travis paused. Without saying anything, he picked up the other pad.

"The top five things, eh?"

"The top five reasons that, one month later, we sit here having never repeated that kiss. There, I brought it up. Remember? A month ago we made out and then went back to being friends. But I think the bromance portion of this little adventure is over."

Travis considered the proposal. He picked up a pen and wrote "My List" at the top.

"Let's gitty on up, then," he said.

Ben looked down at the blank pad of paper in his hand. He didn't want to go too fast and rush Travis. After all, this was Ben's idea, and he had already thought his list through. Out of the corner of his eye, he watched as Travis thought, then wrote, then thought some more. When it looked as if Travis was nearly finished, Ben wrote,

Ben's List
1.   I'm afraid you're not gay.
2.   I don't want to screw up your relationship
               with my brothers.
3.   It's a lot of pressure being your one and only guy.
4.   I don't see a future for us.
5.   We're moving to New York in four months.

They put their pens down at the same time.

"How do we do this?" Travis asked.

Ben didn't answer. He tore the top sheet off his pad and handed it to Travis. The two men exchanged lists. Ben looked down and began to read.

My List
1.   Not sure I'm gay
2.   What if I'm not a bottom ☹
3.   Quentin/Jason/Cade
4.   Don't trust you (bastard)
5.   Y'all are moving to NYC in 4 months

They sat in silence for several moments. Ben took his time mulling over every word choice. He felt a bit stung, but at least he could see they were on the same page, more or less.

"You don't trust me?" asked Ben.

"Not a hundred percent."

"Why did you call me a bastard?"

"It was a joke. Well, kind of. Actions have consequences, Ben. No matter what you say, you were ashamed to tell Colin that I'm a mechanic. I wish to God that'd never happened. Things can change with time, but right now that's how I feel."

Ben decided to cut to the chase.

"Do you think about sex? With me?"

Travis blushed, but he didn't look embarrassed.

"Of course I do. All the time. If you want to play a game, let's play top five reasons we should."

"Okay," Ben nodded. "Let's play."

"Number one. Who cares if I'm gay or not? I spent the last month thinking about nothing but you, so right now I'm feeling pretty gay. And I reckon I'm doing just fine."

"My number two and your number three are the same. My brothers."

"We can't do nothing to upset 'em."

"So, then, let's agree to that. No matter what we do, nothing changes with them."

"I'm good with that."

"There's only one way to find out if you're a bottom."

"And you're gonna have to get over being my one and only man. I think you can handle the pressure, Obi-Wan."

"You don't trust me."

"Not yet. But then you don't see a future for us."

"Not yet."

They stopped and read the lists again, each considering reason number five. Travis took a deep breath and spoke.

"It's difficult reading those last ones considering the past six weeks. Like I said before, we of all people know that nothing in life is certain. Should we really make decisions based on what might happen four months from now?"

"You're saying we could both be dead."

"That's what I'm saying."

Ben paused.

"I had a dream about you."

Travis grinned. "When?"

"The night David was here. In the morning. I had a dream that it was you. In bed with me. I run that kiss in the street over and over again in my head. Travis, I want to have sex with you. I know there are five really good reasons why we shouldn't, but right now, all I can think about is the one amazing reason why we should."

Travis looked at Ben directly. "I get the picture. And I'm in."

"I don't want you to be confused."

"I'm a big boy, Ben. I know what I'm doing. Maybe I was confused a month ago, but I ain't no more."

They looked at each other.

"If we do this, it will be your first time with a guy."

Travis kept smiling. Ben saw something new in his eyes.

"I'm more excited 'cause it'll be my first time with you."

"Are you ready?"

Travis sat up.

"Yep. I'm ready."

Ben got up off the sofa and waited. Travis stood in front of him.

"No more guest room," he said.

Ben laughed and took his hand. They went into Ben's room and closed the door. They sat down on the bed, side by side.

"Those boys know better than to barge in here, don't they?"

"What do you think?" Ben replied.

Travis kicked his boots off and grinned.

"I think I been on my feet all day. I could sure use a foot rub."

"You turkey," Ben joked.

Travis jumped onto the bed behind Ben. He scooted forward until his chest rested against Ben's spine. Travis wrapped his legs around his waist and put his white-socked feet in Ben's lap. Ben reached down and peeled the socks off, revealing little slices of heaven. He touched and rubbed Travis's feet, feeling their perfection between his fingers. He pushed Travis back and flipped over as they came face to face with each other, Travis's legs still wrapped around Ben's waist. Ben leaned down and kissed him, allowing the length of their bodies to press together. Travis wrapped his arms around Ben's neck.

"You're a good kisser," Travis said.

"Thanks, so are you."

"I like the way your stubble feels. But we got too many clothes on."

Travis began pulling at Ben's shirt. They stood up and everything flew off at once until, seconds later, they faced each other in the open room, naked.

"Good golly," said Travis, staring at Ben's hardening cock. "It sure is big."

Ben reached out and took hold of Travis's dick. It looked like a solid seven inches. Ben could see the blue veins running underneath the pale skin. Travis moaned as Ben ran his thumb through the soft red pubic hair and then cupped the smooth balls with his hand. He watched as Travis stared down at Ben's now protruding erection.

"Go ahead," Ben said. "Touch it. I want you to."

Travis hesitated at first, but then reached out, determined. He wrapped his hand around the base of Ben's now rock-hard cock. He slowly moved his hand back and forth, sometimes squeezing, sometimes running his fingers lightly along the underside of Ben's shaft.

"What do you think?" asked Ben.

Travis smiled and laughed.

"It's hot."

Ben dropped to his knees and looked up at Travis, then down at the throbbing prick in front of him. Ben put his mouth on Travis's cock, all the way to the base. Ben could easily deep throat him and enjoyed engaging those skills now. He grabbed Travis's hands and moved them to the back of his head, encouraging him to be a little rough. When Travis resisted, Ben pulled off his dick and looked up at him.

"I won't break. Sex with guys can be a little more...."

"It's not that. It's just that if you keep sucking me, I'm gonna blow a load right off and I want to take my time with this."

"Oh," Ben said, standing up. He reached out and took Travis into his arms, and the two men embraced. "Lay down," he said.

"On my stomach?"

"However you feel comfortable. On your stomach, on your back, whatever you want."

Travis lay down on his stomach.

"I know what you want to see," he smirked, wiggling his butt. "Ain't that right?"

Ben looked down and the sight of Travis's ass practically knocked the breath out of him. It looked just like it had in his dream—as if sculpted from marble. He reached down and caressed it, spreading the cheeks and revealing the virgin puckered hole waiting for him in between. Ben dove in with his tongue and showed no restraint. He lapped at the asshole with hunger. Travis reacted as if he knew exactly what he wanted. He didn't yelp or pull away, but instead pushed back against Ben's assault, reaching around and forcing his tongue in deeper. Ben lifted his hand and brought it down on Travis's white ass cheek with a loud *whack,* but that only made Travis push back harder.

They continued like that for several minutes, until Travis pulled away and flipped onto his back. He lifted his legs into the air and dangled his feet in front of Ben's face. Ben grabbed them and tasted each toe.

The footplay drove Ben so wild that he pulled some condoms and lube from the nightstand drawer and threw them onto the bed. Travis looked at them and Ben saw anxiety flash across his face.

"So," Travis said. "Here we are."

"Here we are. Unless you want to back out."

"No, we're gonna do this. I got to know what all the fuss is about. No more being a coward."

"You're sure?"

Travis threw his head back and laughed. "Fuck, yes, I'm sure!"

Ben wrapped his cock and thought about how to begin. Bottom on top could work, but he had to take the lead on this. He wanted them to look at each other and kiss. So he nestled in between Travis's legs and lifted one of his knees. He kept shifting his position until the tip of his dick rubbed up against Travis's waiting hole.

"I'm the first guy to fuck you?" Ben asked. "Ever?"

"Ever."

"That is so hot."

Ben pushed a little. At first he felt only resistance, so he pulled back. He started to kiss Travis, brushing and licking his lips while he gently rubbed the tip of his cock against the tight hole. Finally, the tip slipped in and Travis gasped.

"Don't pull away," Ben insisted.

Travis held steady but tightened his grip around Ben's neck.

"It hurts."

"Count to eight."

"Why eight?"

"I don't know, but it always works."

Travis began to count.

"… five, six, seven, eight."

"Now kiss me," Ben said.

Travis kissed him full on the mouth, holding on for dear life. His whole body relaxed, and Ben moved his cock forward in painstakingly slow motion.

"Does it still hurt?"

"Nu-uh."

"See, I told you."

"Eight seconds," Travis mumbled.

"What's that?"

"Eight seconds. It's how long a rider has to stay on the bull. At the rodeo."

Travis rubbed the back of Ben's neck and ran his fingers through his hair. Ben could feel him opening up as their lips met again.

"Travis?"

"Yeah?"

"I'm in. All the way."

Travis took a deep breath. Ben pulled him up so that they sat Indian style, facing each other, Ben's dick piercing upward into Travis's ass.

"Put your arms around my neck," Ben told him.

"I ain't too heavy?"

Ben laughed.

"No. I got you. Trust me."

Travis put his arms around Ben's neck and kissed him again. They stayed that way in a kind of facing-lotus position, kissing softly and humming with pleasure. Travis would occasionally grind his butt onto Ben's dick, lifting up and down as he surveyed its length and girth. Ben pulled back, and they looked at each other. That's when he saw it. Travis's eyes rolled back into his head.

"Good fit?" he asked.

"Good golly," Travis moaned. "I had no idea. Perfect fit."

Ben pulled his legs under him and rolled Travis onto his back. While he kissed him, he pulled his cock all the way out and then slowly thrust it back in, making Travis arch his back and lift his legs so that he could accommodate the entire length. Ben repeated the motion again, and then a third time, until he was long-dicking Travis's ass at a steady pace. After that, Ben short-fucked him, using only the first inch of his dick with an increasingly quickened rhythm.

"What are you doing?" Travis moaned.

"I'm loosening up your hole."

"You're teasing me is what it feels like."

"Is it working?"

"Hell, yeah, it's working. Give me more, Hotshot."

So Ben went in deep, full up to the hilt, and then started to really fuck, rocking back and forth on the bed, increasing his stride with each thrust. Travis tightened his arms around his neck again and increased the pace of his breathing.

"Ben? I think...."

"What's wrong?"

"Nothing. Don't stop. Keep fucking me. But I feel like I'm gonna shoot."

Ben didn't respond but slammed into Travis with an extra hard pound. He started to fuck faster as a growl escaped from Travis's mouth. Ben moved his lips across Travis's cheek and kissed him furiously. He could feel Travis's body tense up and knew what he needed to do. He slowed his pace but increased the power of his thrusts, providing Travis with the long and muscular strokes he needed. Travis threw his head back and muffled his cries.

"Fuck. Fuck. Fuck me."

Come started to spray from Travis's cock. He shot long streams of semen into the space between their bodies, which sent Ben over the edge. He reared up and dumped his seed deep into Travis's butt, wave after wave of juice spurting out of his body. Ben looked down and locked onto Travis's eyes.

Travis pulled him close and whispered into his ear, "My ass is yours."

Ben thought he might start crying but instead collapsed on top of Travis, allowing the tension in his body to ooze out of every pore. He'd just had the best sex of his life. The revelation of their orgasm, combined with everything he already felt for Travis, produced an entirely foreign emotion. Was this what he'd been missing all along?

After a moment, Ben rolled over onto his back and lay next to Travis.

"How is that even possible?" Travis asked.

"How is what possible?"

"Coming without touching myself. I couldn't even control it. It ain't always like that, is it?"

Ben laughed. "I don't know. I've seen it before, but it's rare. Who knows? Maybe it's always like that for you."

"Damn, I'm in trouble, then."

"Why?"

Travis stopped himself.

"Nope. I need to shut my pie hole." He rolled over until he was on top of Ben. "Any regrets?"

"Are you kidding? You?"

"Nu-uh. But now I just want you to turn into a pizza."

"Typical guy," Ben said. "You need to clean up?"

"Nope. I like the way it smells."

"Good answer. Let's head to the kitchen so you can make us something to eat."

But they started making out again and didn't get far. They both grinned wildly and laughed when they came up for air and looked at each other.

"What?" Ben asked playfully.

"Am I spending the night?"

"I would like you to."

"You got more condoms?"

"Listen to you," Ben said as he got up and rummaged around the floor for their underwear. He tossed a pair of briefs to Travis, who lifted up his legs and slipped them on. "I got a whole box. Be careful what you ask for, though."

"Why's that?"

Ben put on his boxers and opened the bedroom door.

"Ancient Chinese proverb," he said, heading toward the kitchen. "He who butt-fucks all night wakes up with sore asshole."

Travis laughed and followed him.

"Well, as my mama used to say, if you ain't sore then you're not doing it right."

ELEVEN

WHEN Ben woke up the next morning, he thought he might be dreaming again. After all, there was Travis in his arms, the curve of his shoulder and arm exactly as he had imagined it. He felt Travis push against Ben's morning wood. Ben reached over to the bed stand and grabbed another condom. He slid his cock into Travis's asshole and the two of them moaned together.

"That's more like it," Travis said.

This was no dream.

"Good morning," Ben whispered.

"What time is it?"

Ben looked over at the alarm clock.

"Two minutes after seven."

"When do the brothers wake up?"

"Cade gets up first. We have about an hour."

"They don't go to church no more?"

"No. But that was their decision."

Ben continued to fuck Travis gently as they talked.

"Are we gonna tell 'em anything?"

Ben hadn't really thought about it. He'd been mesmerized by Travis's ass all night.

"What do you want to tell them?"

Travis huffed and reached around, grabbing Ben's ass and pulling him in deeper.

"You're exasperating sometimes, do you know that? Do you even realize you answer questions with questions?"

"I picked that up in law school."

"Well, it's damn annoying."

Ben started to pull away.

"Oh, no you don't," ordered Travis, pulling him back in. "Don't you dare stop what you're doing. I ain't mad. Don't mean I want to change you or nothing. Just that sometimes I want to box your ears."

Ben smiled and kissed the back of his neck.

"Now," Travis continued, "what should we tell 'em?"

Ben didn't have to think about it long. "We'll tell them the truth."

"So what's the truth? Are you ready to DTR?"

"What's DTR?"

"Define The Relationship."

Ben chuckled and slammed his cock in deeper. "No, I'm not ready for that. How do you feel about sneaking around for a while?"

Travis didn't speak for a moment; then he said, "I'm okay with that. For a while."

SO FOR two weeks, Ben and Travis fucked on the down low. Since they could hardly keep their hands off each other, that meant taking advantage of every opportunity. Travis stopped by the house almost every day at lunch. Every night, they waited until the brothers went to bed and then did it again. In the morning, before Travis slipped out of the house, Ben often woke up with a condom on his cock and Travis waiting to mount him. Every chance they got, they fucked. They never sucked each other off or bothered with any kind of foreplay. When Travis wanted to have sex, and he pretty much wanted to have sex all the time, it meant Ben's cock in his ass. Once he got it inside him, they explored a lot of variety in pace and position. But if Ben tried to pull out, Travis would whimper and protest. Ben had to admit, it turned him on, especially since Travis could fuck for hours at a time. Often they would have entire conversations while they screwed, Ben slowly moving his cock in and out of Travis's ass. Other times they fucked like dogs, literally, as Travis discovered the specific joys of being on all fours with his butt in the air. When Ben wanted to make him come, all he had to do was pound away at a certain angle and soon Travis would be spewing jizz.

Finally, on a Friday morning that also happened to be Valentine's Day, Travis woke up and didn't want to leave. He curled up in Ben's arms and nuzzled into the crook of his neck.

"I need to 'fess up. I ain't okay with sneaking out before your brothers wake up. Not anymore. It's Valentine's Day. Wouldn't it be nice if we could have breakfast together? We need to tell them what's going on."

Ben agreed. "Let's do it. Stay for breakfast and we'll tell them. Better yet, make breakfast and we'll tell them. Everything goes down better with your pancakes."

The conversation went as well as could be expected. Ben didn't beat around the sex bush. He explained that Travis would be spending the night in his bedroom for the foreseeable future. He looked sideways at Travis, not wanting to assume. From the smile on his face, it didn't look like he had a problem with that.

Quentin, of course, displayed no surprise when he heard the news. Ben laid five twenty-dollar bills on the table and pushed them his way.

"Thank you," Quentin said, gathering up the bills and then stuffing them into his pocket. "Glad it worked out for you two lovebirds. Welcome to the family, Travis. Again."

"What was that all about?" Travis asked.

"I'll tell you later," said Ben.

Cade didn't understand how Travis could like girls all his life and then all of a sudden like boys. Ben said he wondered the same thing, but Travis explained that life is full of surprises.

"Some things you just know are true. Even though you can't explain 'em."

"I don't know," Cade said. "This house is getting super gay. But if you're happy then I'm okay with it. I guess."

Jason didn't have much to say, and Ben knew he needed to sit down with him. But that would have to wait. Again. Ben had a little plan for Valentine's Day, which would be his first official date with Travis, and it required some rehearsal. So after he dropped the brothers off at school and Travis went to work, Ben sat down at his mom's piano in the living room and brushed up on his skills. The arts council in Austin had placed upright pianos all over downtown. One of these pianos sat on the Lamar Street pedestrian bridge. Ben did some musical theater in high school and could bang out a few chords. He looked through his mom's sheet music, which she kept under the cover of the piano bench. He found the Rodgers and Hart classic "My Funny Valentine." Perfect. He practiced it a few times, simplifying the chords to suit his skill level.

Since everyone and his brother had a dinner reservation on Valentine's Day, Ben got barbeque takeout for the two of them instead. He knew by now that nothing made Travis happier than a plate of brisket and some Elgin sausage. When Travis showed up after work, Ben ushered him into the backyard, where he had set up dinner on the small table between the two lawn chairs.

"What have you gone and done, Obi-Wan?"

"I thought we could have a romantic dinner out here. To celebrate our coming out. To the brothers."

"Good golly. This is real, ain't it?"

"This is what you said you wanted," answered Ben, smiling. "No more sneaking around. So, here we are."

Travis threw his arms around Ben and kissed him. "Here we are," he repeated. "Did you get brisket *and* sausage?"

"It's Valentine's Day, Travis. Of course I got both."

The two men sat down to eat. Dinner included a bottle of Shiner Bock for each of them, which they used to toast their evening. Travis devoured everything on his plate, including the spicy beans, mayonnaise potato salad (which, in Texas, was quite different from mustard potato salad), pickles, onions, and several slices of soft white bread.

"You should drop by the shop," Travis suggested in between bites.

"Are you sure you're ready for that?"

"Well, maybe give me a week or two. I just got to figure out how to tell 'em."

"Maybe we should go downtown this evening and take a walk around Town Lake. It's a nice night."

"Look at you, taking it to the next level."

"Why not? If I'm on a date with you, I definitely want to show you off."

Travis blushed. "Seriously, Ben. You're too much of a good thing sometimes."

After dinner, Ben drove them downtown in his father's pickup truck, parking near Seventh and West Streets. "We should walk toward the river," he suggested, "but first let's stop by Whole Foods for some chocolate-covered strawberries. We have to indulge in at least one cliché tonight."

After they finished their dessert, Ben steered them toward the Lamar Street bridge.

"Can I hold your hand?" Ben asked.

Travis laughed. "Are we okay down here?"

"Yes. You live in a very gay-friendly city. Just so you know."

"I kind of figured. I seen plenty of boys holding hands in this town." He took a deep breath. "So, yes, you can hold my hand."

Ben grinned from ear to ear as he reached down and meshed Travis's fingers with his own. He knew that people were staring at them, which was all part of the plan. When they reached the bridge, Ben looked down the span and spotted the piano. He heaved a sigh of relief when he saw that it was empty.

"Do you see that?" Ben asked, pointing toward the piano as they stepped onto the bridge.

"Are we gonna see the bats?" Travis replied.

"Sorry, Atwood. The bats only fly in the summer. No, I mean the upright piano down there. You see it?"

"Yeah, I see it."

"I wonder what that's for?"

Ben stopped and spoke to a young woman who was standing near the railing with her boyfriend. "Excuse me. Do you know why there's a piano on the bridge?"

"They put them all around downtown," the boyfriend answered. "People just sit and play something. It's cool."

"Thanks, man," Ben said, walking away and pulling Travis with him. "Do you play the piano?"

Travis laughed. "Nu-uh. My mama would have never spent her hard-earned cash on music lessons. Why, do you?"

Ben shrugged. "Let's find out, shall we?"

He sat down at the piano bench and checked the keys for tuning. Then he launched into the opening chords of "My Funny Valentine."

"What in God's creation are you doing, Obi-Wan?"

People had already begun to stop and linger in anticipation of a show.

"Ladies and gentlemen," Ben announced at full voice, speaking to the gathering crowd while he continued to play the song's introduction. "My name is Ben and this is my date, Travis."

Random people in the crowd said hello to them by name.

"This is the first time Travis has ever been on a date with a man. Which means that, today, I won the lottery."

"Welcome to the club, Travis," a young man yelled from the edge of the crowd.

"Thanks," Travis replied, turning several shades of scarlet.

"My funny valentine...," Ben began to sing. Travis stood and listened, completely awestruck and beaming with pride and happiness. "But don't change a hair for me...," Ben continued to croon as people pulled out their phones, took pictures, and started tweeting about the event. Ben hammed it up through the middle section but then brought it down to a quiet note at the end. As the last chord faded out on the piano, Ben asked, "Travis, would you be my Valentine?"

Travis looked around at the crowd. "Well, I couldn't exactly embarrass you in front of all these people, so I reckon the answer is yes."

Everyone cheered and Ben stood up to plant a big kiss on Travis.

ON SUNDAY night, Ben decided it was time for him and Jason to finally get some face time. So they left Quentin and Cade behind with Travis and went to dinner at Hyde Park Bar & Grill.

"How are you doing?" Ben asked once they were seated.

A busboy sat two glasses of water onto their table and then walked away. Jason shrugged.

"I'm okay, I guess."

"Quentin told me. About the boy in your room. I'm sorry it took me so long to bring it up."

Jason didn't speak at first. Then he said, "Am I in trouble?"

"No, of course you're not in trouble."

A young man approached the table. He told them his name was Joe. "Anything else to drink, boys?" he asked.

"I'll have a Dr Pepper," answered Ben.

"Me too," said Jason. "And can I have some HP fries to start, please? With extra sauce?"

"You got it. Coming right up."

Joe walked away and Jason took a sip of his water.

"It wasn't me, you know."

"What do you mean?"

"I didn't start it. He kissed me first."

"Does it matter?"

Jason shrugged again.

"Who was this boy?"

"Jake McAlister. He's a freshman."

"How did you meet him? You're still in junior high."

"Out Youth potluck."

"You went to an Out Youth potluck? By yourself?"

"Sure, why not? I can't exactly get into Oilcan Harry's."

"Have you seen him since then?"

"No, not really. Mom kind of freaked out, which freaked him out because his mom is cool with… whatever. He texted me a couple of times, and I saw him at the holiday potluck, but he didn't have anything to say. Just hey, how's it going? Lame stuff."

"Is he cute?"

Jason blushed.

"A-list adorable. A total Justin."

"Justin?"

"That's what the girls at school call a cute guy."

"As in Timberlake?"

"As in Bieber."

Ben shook his head and laughed. Joe returned with their drinks and Jason's fries. Hyde Park fries were a local legend, battered before they were deep fried and then served with a kind of modified tartar sauce. Joe set them down in the middle of the table. Ben ate one. He had forgotten how delicious they were.

"So, you and Colin seemed to hit it off."

Jason's eyes lit up as he munched on the fries.

"OMG, finally an uncle I actually like. He told me to call him Uncle Colin. Is that okay? Did you know his family has a yacht?"

"I've been on that yacht. And you will too someday."

"Really?"

"Sure. Once we move to New York, I bet you'll get an invitation first thing."

Ben grabbed another fry.

"What about Travis?"

"What about him?" Ben asked.

Jason looked puzzled.

"Aren't you and him boyfriends now?"

"I… I don't know what we are. But not boyfriends. Yet."

"He told me what you did down on the bridge. You're totally crush-worthy, Ben. But if you think he's not your boyfriend, well… let's just say you'd better DTR."

"We're not ready to DTR, thank you."

"Are we moving to New York without him?"

Ben looked down at the menu. "What's good here these days?"

Jason munched down on another fry. He got the hint and dropped it.

"Did you think about calling me?" Ben asked.

"When?"

"When Mom and Dad found out. Why didn't you pick up your phone?"

Jason looked down at his menu.

"I did."

"What do you mean, you did?"

"I called you. You said you were in the middle of a deposition or something and you'd call me back."

Ben sat there, stunned. He remembered the call now.

"And I never did."

Jason shook his head.

"I'm sorry."

Jason nodded. "It's okay."

"No, it's not. I'm not really happy with the way I've behaved these past few years. I should have been there for you."

"You're here now. Let's go during spring break."

"To New York?"

"Yeah. Travis too. Maybe he'll want to move there when he sees it."

Ben thought it over.

"That is not a bad idea. Colin was right about you. You are a young genius."

WHEN they got home, Ben told Travis he needed to call Colin and debrief. He went into his room and closed the door.

"We're doing it," Ben announced when Colin answered the phone.

"What?"

"Me and Travis. We're fucking like Mormons."

"Since when?"

"Since about two weeks ago."

"Good Lord. What's come over you, Walsh? I thought the straight ones were off limits."

"I break my own rules all the time. Besides, he doesn't seem so straight when my dick is in his ass. I got it bad, Colin. I can't keep my hands off him."

"Well, I can't say I'm surprised. I could see it coming a mile away."

"We had our first real date on Valentine's Day. What would you think about me bringing him to New York? With my brothers? Show them around during spring break."

"Good God man, you do have it bad. You want to move him here?"

"I didn't say that."

"You didn't have to. I think you're not thinking straight, pardon the expression. But you know I'll support you regardless."

"You don't like him?"

"I like him just fine. But why do you have to take a perfectly good *Bridges of Madison County* romance and turn it into an LTR? Relocation never works. He'll only end up resenting you in the long run."

"I'm not twisting his arm. I haven't even brought it up to him yet. I was going to bring him along and let the city charm him. He can decide what he wants to do. What's wrong with me giving him an option?"

"There is nothing wrong with it. But what if he doesn't do what you want him to do?"

"I'll cross that bridge when I come to it."

"I hate that expression. It negates the very concept of planning. By the way, I got a text from Jason while you two were at dinner. He said you were having *the talk*. It's about time."

"This Jake McAlister sounds dreamy."

"He sounds like a little prick to me. Hardly talked to him after your mom caught them making out."

"The kid's fifteen. And if you'd ever seen my mom freak out, you wouldn't blame him. Besides, I thought you weren't supposed to tell me anything."

"Oops. Let's shuffle back to you and Travis. How is he in bed?"

Ben couldn't hide his excitement.

"A-list amazing."

LATER that night, after a round of fucking, Travis curled up into Ben's arms.

"Do you want me to sing you a song?" he joked, tickling Ben under the ribs.

"Can you sing?"

Travis cleared his throat, and in a clear but slightly off-key tenor voice, crooned the opening line of Michael Jackson's song "Ben."

"You do know that song is about a rat, don't you?" Ben asked.

"Are you shittin' me?"

"I am not shittin' you. Hey, Jason threw out an idea at dinner tonight."

"Oh, yeah? What idea?"

"That we all go visit New York during their spring break. What do you think? I'd love to show you around."

Travis didn't answer.

"What's wrong?"

"Nothing. Everything. Is this a try-out or something? It's crazy to be even thinking about it, but are you floating the idea that I might move to New York with y'all?"

"I'm inviting you to come with us for a visit. No obligation. But come on, Travis. Isn't it obvious? This is not just about sex. For me, at least. And if we are still like this in May and the furniture is on the truck, I'm going to be pretty fucking bummed if I'm leaving you behind."

"Well, I'm gonna be pretty bummed too."

"So at least consider the possibility, then. This could be our way forward. A future."

"Okay, okay. I'll ask for the week off from work. I pay my own way, though. I can afford a plane ticket and motels and stuff. I got a nest egg."

"Keep your nest egg. We'll stay with Colin's family."

"I don't think that's such a good idea."

"Stop it. You'll charm the pants off them."

"Just 'cause you see me that way don't mean New York high society will."

"Nonsense," Ben said, kissing him full on the mouth. "You'll be my own little Molly Brown."

"Who the hell is Molly Brown?"

"Kathy Bates in *Titanic*."

Travis looked confused.

"That was a real person?"

THE next morning, Ben woke up with a sore throat, throbbing head, full body aches, and a high temperature. He had the flu and it knocked him out flat. He had been too busy to get a flu shot last fall, unlike the rest of the people in the house. They all felt fine. Ben slept for five days. He knew Travis woke him up at regular intervals to feed him soup. He got up to go to the bathroom but often didn't make it back to bed on his own. At a certain point, he didn't know how long he'd been down. He started to have fever dreams in which he rewrote law briefs over and over again in his head. He wondered if they would take him to the hospital at some point.

Then one night he woke up and looked at the alarm clock:

3:14.

Ben looked out the window into the dark night.

The bedsheets felt wet and his head was clear. His fever had broken. He looked around but didn't see Travis. He went into the bathroom and took off his T-shirt, then dried himself with a towel. He went back into the bedroom and put on a fresh shirt. He heard sounds coming from the kitchen. Who else but Travis would be up at this hour of the night? *He's probably worried sick*, Ben thought. He headed toward the kitchen to give Travis an update.

"Hey, Trav," he said, opening the door, expecting to see him making pancakes or something. "I'm feeling…." He stopped.

"Ben, did I wake you up? I sure didn't mean to do that, but since you're here, what the hell, have a seat. I'm fixing migas and I know how much you love 'em."

Ben didn't believe his eyes. This couldn't be happening.

Because standing in front of him, dicing a fresh tomato and scrambling some eggs, was his father.

TWELVE

"WHAT'S going on?" Ben asked.

"Sit down, let's have some breakfast."

"It's the middle of the night."

"That never stopped you before. Remember when you were a boy and couldn't sleep? We'd come in here and fix something to eat. Afterward you were always right as rain."

"What are you doing here, Dad? You're dead."

"Life is full of surprises," he answered, throwing up his hands in a gesture of resignation. "Sit down."

Ben took a seat at the kitchen table. His father finished scrambling the eggs and vegetables, throwing in the tortilla strips at the last minute. He split the contents of the skillet onto two plates, sprinkled them with grated cheddar cheese, and brought them over to the table. His father went to the fridge and retrieved a jar of salsa. Finally, he sat down and inhaled the aroma of the food in front of him.

"Ah, smells great, doesn't it?"

He put a couple of spoonfuls of salsa onto the Tex-Mex egg dish and then shoveled a forkful into his mouth.

"Dig in, Ben."

Ben picked up his fork and tried the migas. They tasted perfect. He added some salsa and watched his father while he ate.

"What are you doing here?" Ben asked.

"Checking in, mostly. The world whacked you upside the head pretty dandy, didn't it, son?"

"Pretty dandy, Dad. I wish I could say I've been this superhero who swooped in and rescued everyone, but so far I suck at this. I wasn't too happy when I thought I was going to be moving back here, either. I was really pissed off."

"Yes, I know that. Get it off your chest. You've always had a selfish streak, even when you were a child. You never wanted to share your toys with other kids. I suppose you don't remember throwing a fit in the middle of Aunt Julie's living room? With your cousin Billy? Over a Tonka truck, no less. But, son, it doesn't matter what mood you're in on the road to doing the right thing. You're allowed to bitch and moan all the way. You still got there, that's my point. And you don't *suck* at this. As long as everyone's alive, you're doing just fine, and the last I checked, they were all still breathing. You don't need to be a superhero."

"You set the bar too low."

"I wouldn't be upset if you turned out to be a better man than I was."

"It hasn't been all bitching and moaning. I like my brothers. I never appreciated them before this happened. I had no idea they were so interesting, really. I mean, Quentin is a handful but I love him to death. Jason I just want to shelter. And Cade... well, you had to see it. He reminds me so much of you. Every day it becomes more and more apparent. Quentin sees it too. I catch him watching Cade with this sad look on his face. He's going to miss you most of all, Dad."

"Which one? Cade or Quentin?"

"Cade."

"Well, that's where Travis comes in."

Ben smiled. "Travis is a part of the family now?"

"Son, life is pretty much a process of problem-solving. Sure, I've studied as much philosophy as the next English professor, but at the end of the day, the most successful people are the ones who recognize how to match solutions to their problems. Cade has interests that none of you share. That's a problem. If you don't recognize Travis as a solution—as a part of your future—then you're simply not paying attention. I'm going to tell you a 100 percent true story. On the day I first met him by the curb, I came into this very kitchen and said to your mother, 'Grace,' I said, 'that boy has Ben written all over him.' Well, she thought I was crazier than a shithouse rat. And now look at you two. 'Lovebirds', isn't that what Quentin called you?"

"You were never okay with the gay thing, were you?"

His father scoffed at the suggestion.

"Horseshit. I was fine with the gay thing. We're all fine with the gay thing."

"Then why did you tell Travis everything about me except that?"

"Because *that* was something he needed to hear from you. Your problem is that you play up the gay thing because you don't think you're interesting enough without it."

"That's not—"

"Be careful."

"—true. Mom's family is not okay with it."

"Maybe, maybe not. Here's what you don't know. You and Travis would be what you are even if you weren't gay. You two are not an accident and you have more history than you'll ever realize. But you're also not pony rides and sunshine. This is going to be a hard road for both of you. One of these days you're going to ask yourself, is it worth the...." His father paused. "Never mind. It's not fair for me to say anything more. Just remember, match your solutions to your problems. And if you lose your way, listen to Quentin."

"Quentin?"

"He's an old soul."

Ben looked at his father and blinked.

"I don't really know what I'm doing."

"That's okay. I didn't really know what I was doing either."

"You were an awesome dad."

"We both know that wasn't always the case. I never even managed to get Christmas lights on the damn house."

"Well, you're not going to hear any complaints from me. According to Travis, I turned out alright." Ben paused. "I feel like I'm waiting for that moment, though. When things will make sense to me again. When I won't be so angry. I know that you're gone, even though I'm sitting here talking to you. I've acknowledged that. But our lives have no... forward momentum. Does that make sense?"

"Let me tell you a story. It all began back when I was a boy and my folks took me and your Uncle Tommy on vacation to the lake house. Every summer. This was in the 1970s. I was maybe thirteen or fourteen. My father drove a Chevy Impala. I mean, this was a boat of a car. The backseat was so big that me and Tommy could both sleep lying down. My dad built this bench that went in the space between the back and front seats. My mom took the towels and bedding we brought for the rental cottage and made a mattress. So we had this bed in the back because we drove for ten hours, straight through. Tommy slept the whole way there. Me, most of the time, I would sit with my arms on the front seat, my head propped up between Mom and Dad. I liked to watch my father drive.

"He always drove with his right hand at twelve o'clock and his left hand on his left thigh. Every so often, he would open up his right hand, rotate it to the right, like he was airing it out or something, and then close it back down on the wheel. He did this maybe every ten minutes or so. Open, Close. Wax on, wax off. And I watched this from the backseat, summer after summer."

"Did you ever ask him about it?"

"Never. I just watched. It was a secret that I shared with him. I knew that something was going on, even if I didn't know what it was. I knew it was a part of him and that made it a part of me too. It was a mystery that lasted my entire childhood.

"So, when I turned sixteen, I started driving. We still had that old Impala as a second car, and my dad said that if I was going to wreck something, I could wreck that. So I wasn't allowed to drive the new car. One day Mom and I were going to Dallas for some back-to-school shopping, and I wanted to drive, but of course that meant we had to take the old Impala. She wasn't crazy about the idea but gave in eventually. So we're heading up I-35, and this is probably the longest

I've ever driven on the freeway. I'm talking to my mom and trying to pay attention and making sure I signal and this and that. And without even noticing it, I end up with my right hand at twelve o'clock and my left hand on my left thigh."

"Just like your dad."

His father winked.

"I look down at the dashboard. Now, this was an old-style dashboard, where the speedometer spans about ten inches across. It's not a tiny little dial like you see today. It was this big sprawling thing that goes from zero on the far left to 120 on the far right. And in the middle was 55, which was the speed limit at the time. This was back when we were trying to conserve gasoline. Now, I'm driving along with my mom and I want to make sure I'm not speeding. So I look down. At the dashboard. I can't see the needle on the speedometer because my right hand is at twelve o'clock, blocking the middle section, where 55 was. So without even thinking about it, without any understanding of what I was about to do, I open up my hand and rotate it to the right, so that I can see the needle and check my speed, and...."

Ben's jaw dropped. "Wax on, wax off."

"Yes. In that instant, I understood my father. All those years I sat in the backseat, watching him drive. All those years I wondered why he lifted his palm up every ten minutes. The answer was simple. It was to see the speedometer. But I couldn't see that from the backseat. I couldn't know that from my point of view."

"Did you ever say anything to him?"

"Sure I did. He confirmed it. That's what he'd been doing all along, which he said he would have told me if I had bothered to ask. That was the day my father lost all his mystery to me. Utterly. It was an Oedipal strike against him. I stepped into his point of view."

"And now I'm stepping into yours."

"Well, you're not quite there yet, but when it happens, you'll know it. And that's when you'll feel this forward momentum you're talking about."

"Hmm," Ben murmured. "I see."

His father added some more salsa to his migas. "You're moving the boys to New York?"

"That's the plan. What do you think?"

"Who's paying for all this?"

"Colin's family."

"And you're okay with that?"

"I have a job there, Dad. My life is there. Colin's family is a resource for me, and I need all of those I can get right now. I'm matching a solution to a problem."

"Fair enough. But do you believe this solution comes with no strings attached?"

"What do you mean?"

"If they pay for all this, you're bound to them, correct? What if you want to go to another firm in ten years? Or better yet, what if you want to start your own firm? Do you think they'll let you go?"

"I hadn't thought about it."

His dad paused while he finished up the last of the migas on his plate. "Maybe you should. You land on one space and think that's the only option. Then you land on another space and think that's the only option. Have you thought about keeping your options open? If they pay for this, then you're selling your soul to somebody. I'm not exactly sure who that is at this point, but whoever it is, you'd better believe they'll be around to collect someday."

"It's not like that."

"Do me a favor. Humor me."

"How?"

"Register for the Texas Bar Exam. It's only given twice a year, in February and August. If you end up moving, you don't have to take it. But at least register—as a favor to your old man. Will you do that for me?"

"Sure, Dad."

"Good. Thank you."

They were quiet for a moment.

"How long can you stay?" Ben asked.

"Not long. Your mother will get worried if I'm not back soon," he said, snorting a chuckle at his own dead joke. "Seriously, Ben. You're doing a good job with your brothers. I'm proud of you. Just try to be patient with Travis. It's going to take him awhile to...."

"I'm falling in love with him, Dad."

His father nodded. "I know."

"I'm falling in love with him and I don't know what to do about it. He doesn't feel permanent. Do you remember when I did *Brigadoon* in high school?"

"That's the one where the Scottish village only appears for one day every hundred years?"

"Right. I played Tommy, who falls in love with Fiona on that one day, and after that, she's gone. That's how it feels with Travis. Like he's only here for one day, and when it's over, he's going to disappear for another hundred years. And I'll be left wandering the highlands of Scotland looking for him. I'm trapped in a Broadway musical. That's how surreal my life has become."

"Muddy waters, Ben."

"Yes, I know that. But for how long?"

His father got up from the table and cleared the plates away to the sink, rinsing them off as he always did before placing them immediately into the dishwasher.

"You should go back to bed. That fever took a lot out of you. Get some sleep and you'll feel better tomorrow."

Ben didn't move. "For how long?"

"For as long as it takes," his father answered. "It won't be this way forever, Ben. For a while, yes. But not forever."

He looked at his father one last time.

"Thanks, Dad."

"I love you, son."

Ben got up from the table.

"One more thing," his father said. "Do you remember how that musical ends?"

Ben stopped at the door to the kitchen but didn't look back. "Yes. He loves her so much that the village reappears and he's able to get back to her."

"Something to keep in mind."

BEN left the kitchen. He looked for Travis in the living room, but he wasn't there. When he got back to the bedroom he found it empty too. Maybe Travis had crossed the street to his room in Mrs. Wright's house. Or maybe Travis was only a figment of his imagination, like his father—an imaginary character that Ben created to cope with the death of his parents. Or maybe he was still delirious from the fever.

Ben crawled under the covers and let his heavy eyelids close. He would figure it out tomorrow, he thought, as exhaustion overcame him. He slowly drifted away into the space between consciousness and slumber. And that's when he saw it, a vision dancing across his mind. He was sitting with Travis, holding his hand. The horizon had vanished. All he could see were clouds and sky, no earth, and no line where the two should meet. The present disappeared and only this future horizon remained. As the last minutes of night slipped away and Ben surrendered himself to sleep, the corners of his mouth curled into a smile and he mumbled a question under his breath.

"Will you put lights on the house this year?"

THIRTEEN

"BEN? Wake up."

Ben opened his eyes and squinted to block the morning light.

"What time is it?" he asked.

"It's after nine."

"What day is it?"

Travis laughed.

"Saturday. Your fever broke last night."

"Where did you go? I got up and couldn't find you."

"You must have been dreaming. I didn't go nowhere."

Quentin stuck his head in the door.

"You gonna live, big brother?"

Ben rubbed his head.

"I think so. I talked to Dad last night."

"Oh, really?" replied Quentin, looking at Travis and then rolling his eyes. "Did you have your very own *Lost* flashback?"

"Something like that."

"I'm fixin' to head to the shop," Travis interrupted, "now that you're out of the woods. I'll be back when I get off at six." He leaned down and kissed Ben on the lips.

"Aw, shucks," Quentin said. "Look at you two."

Travis glared at him as he headed out the door.

"Take care of your brother while I'm gone."

"Bye," Ben said to the back of his head. "What's wrong with him?" he asked once Travis had left.

"Who do you think's been taking care of everything all week? He's Nurse Jackie and Phil Dunphy rolled into one."

"Is he okay?"

Quentin waved off the question. "He's fine. Just a little frazzled. He missed a lot of work and his boss wasn't exactly thrilled. You were pretty out of it for a while there. We even discussed putting you down at one point."

"Very funny," Ben said.

"So are you gonna get out of bed or what? I need help with a history project if you can walk."

"I can walk," Ben insisted, throwing back the covers. "What's the project?"

"We're supposed to trace the civil-rights struggles of African-Americans, Latinos, or gay people in Austin. I was going to do the gay one since... well, since I have two gay brothers. But there's not much online."

"I can help you out," Ben replied, sitting up on the edge of the bed. "I knew someone at UT that did his master's thesis on the gay rights movement in Austin. There's a hard copy in the graduate library." Ben got up and went into the bathroom. "Hey," he called, "did Travis mention spring break?"

"Yes," Quentin yelled back. "It's not going to work, you know? Taking him there."

"You don't know that. He's never even been to New York. Anything is possible." He grabbed a bottle of mouthwash and took a swig.

"That chick Stephanie called me."

Ben poked his head out of the bathroom door, talking as he gargled. "The one that Colin showed your napkin to?"

Quentin laughed. "Yeah. She's serious about the drawings."

Ben stuck his head back in and spit the mouthwash out.

"She told me she can really sell the teenage-artist angle," Quentin continued. "The art crowd eats that shit up. And she says the fact that I'm so good-looking doesn't hurt either."

"It's a curse we all share," Ben said, crossing through the room. Quentin followed him into the kitchen, talking to the back of his head as he went.

"Art is 90 percent marketing these days. Seriously, she asked if I could speak with a Texas accent."

"So are you going to do it?"

Quentin shrugged as Ben opened the fridge and took out a carton of orange juice.

"I ain't gonna pretend that I talk like Travis," Quentin said, imitating his Texas drawl.

Ben pulled a glass from the cupboard and filled it with juice.

"No. I mean, are you going to do the drawings?"

"I don't know. I guess so. She said if I wanted to get into LaGuardia that a Soho gallery exhibit would seal the deal. I could become an art world celebutard at sixteen."

Ben took a swig of the juice. He grimaced before turning around and spitting it into the sink. "Gross. Mouthwash and OJ don't mix. Anyway, thanks, Q. For giving this a chance. The city will make you think big, I promise. You're really talented."

"Whatever. Get dressed so we can go to this place you mentioned. What'd you call it again? A library?"

"That's right, kid. Before Wikipedia there were these things called books."

BY MONDAY, Ben felt normal again. Travis had been quiet for two days, and they hadn't had sex in over a week. When the brothers came home from school that afternoon, Ben explained to them that he needed some alone time with Travis.

"I gotcha covered, big brother. Since I have my license now, I can drive us up to the Highland 10 to catch a flick. Jason's been wanting to see *The King's Speech*."

"Yes!" Jason confirmed with glee.

"That should give you until nine or so."

"Thanks, Q."

"You're paying for the movie, though."

"And the popcorn," Cade said.

They headed out to the movie around six thirty, and Travis showed up shortly after that. Ben noticed that he didn't knock anymore. He just walked right in. He must have made that transition while Ben lay dying.

"What's that smell?" Travis asked, hanging up his coat on one of the pegs near the front door.

"Pot roast," Ben answered as he sat up on one of the sofas in the living room. "Come here." Travis walked over to him. "Sit down," Ben said, letting slide an evil grin. "Put your feet up."

"Pot roast, eh? You're cooking?"

"I have a few tricks up my sleeve."

"Did you put some balsamic vinegar in with the beef broth?"

"Sit."

"But it really makes a…."

"*Sit*," Ben insisted.

"Okay, okay." Travis sat down and plopped his feet onto Ben's lap. Ben unlaced and removed his work boots and thick white socks. Travis lay back and closed his eyes while Ben began to massage his feet.

"That does feel mighty nice. What'd I do to deserve the royal treatment?"

"You took care of me when I was sick. Thank you for that."

"I was in a sorry spot last week, Obi-Wan. I was missing a heap of work and wondering if I should take you to the hospital or call a doctor or something." Travis opened his eyes and sat up on his elbows. "But Quentin said no, it's the flu, don't overreact. He was right—the sixteen-year-old was right. But with you in a coma, I was the only adult within spitting distance. Me! I took 'em to school, made sure they ate an' all. I was the back-up plan and it scared the bejeezus out of me."

"Wow, someone's been holding their stuff in."

"Sorry about that."

"Don't even. This is the first I'm hearing about it, that's all. Trust me, I can relate to your panic. I *share* your panic."

"Yeah, I know." Travis closed his eyes and lay back again, obviously enjoying the attention Ben lavished on his feet. "I missed you."

Ben grinned. "I missed you too."

"I'm glad you're back in charge. I like being the right-hand man but I don't like being you. Does that sound strange?"

"Not at all. I don't like being me either. But oh well—here we are."

"Yep. Here we are."

"Whatever it is we're doing, it involves those three boys. So we suck at it sometimes and it scares the shit out of us. The bottom line is, they don't feel alone. Score a point for us."

"So just what is it we're doing?"

Ben paused.

"You want to DTR?"

"You know I do," Travis answered, sitting up again.

"Well, then, I'm ready. But I want you to go first. What do you want out of this? I know you're going to visit New York, and a big part of me is excited about that, but do you really see yourself with a man? I mean, long term?"

Travis took a deep breath. "Where are the brothers?"

"They went to see *The King's Speech.*"

"Damn, I wanted to see that."

"Relax, Atwood. We'll go see the late show if you want. Now talk."

Ben continued to rub Travis's feet.

"Okay. Obviously, this whole business has been crazier than tits on a fish. I never expected nothing like this to happen to me. Ever. But like I already said, I ain't confused no more. I can't explain it, mind you, why I would one day wake up in bed with another man. But that's a whole other thing than being confused. I want to be with you, Ben."

"Exclusively?"

"Yep—110 percent."

"What if you don't like New York and we end up moving anyway?"

"I'll skin that cat when the time comes."

"But otherwise, you're ready to be gay?"

"Well, I ain't thought about marching in no parade or nothing. Do I got to buy a T-shirt to get into the club?"

Ben shook his head and laughed. "No, the T-shirt is free. In theory, everyone gets to define themselves however they want. Or not. But we don't live in a theoretical world. If we're holding hands in public and someone calls you a fag, they're not going to apologize just because you tell them you're only gay for me. Not to mention that marriage isn't even an option for us. Once you experience some of that and realize being with me means you're now a second-class citizen— regardless of what you call yourself—well, you might rethink that whole 'marching in a parade' thing."

"Then call me gay. I'm fine with that. I told the boys at work that I'm dating a dude."

"You did?"

"Of course. I told you I was gonna. When I missed all that work last week, it was the perfect opportunity."

"How did they take it?"

"They were kinda quiet for a day or two. I think they thought you were gonna croak or something. But now they're giving me all kinds of grief, which means they're just fine with it."

"So can I come by some day and bring you lunch?"

Travis laughed. "You can come on by anytime you want."

Ben smiled.

"So it's your turn," Travis said.

Ben took a moment. "I feel vulnerable. Which I know makes me sound like a total pussy, but there you have it. I'm crazy about you. I want this to continue and that's the problem. We're probably moving in three months and I don't know if you're coming with us. I wish I shared your 'skin the cat' attitude, but I don't. How can we define the relationship until you make that decision? You have to see New York. I get that. But if you choose to stay in Austin, I don't know what other options are available to us. My job is important to me and it's back there. I haven't signed my soul away yet, but this deal is in motion, and we both know that the deadline is approaching. Fast."

Travis grinned. "Sounds like we could both end up getting hurt real bad. Guess that means there's only one question left to ask."

"What's that?"

"Is the possibility of eight seconds of glory worth the risk of getting thrown off the bull?"

Ben thought it over.

"Yes. It's worth the risk. I love that metaphor, by the way. And if things don't work out, we'll pick up the pieces and move on. Travis, I've never felt this way about anyone. I've never wanted to be with someone so much." Ben broke out laughing. "I want to fuck you all the time. My stomach hurts when you go to work and I check my messages to see if maybe you said howdy or forgot something. But as much as all that's true, I have got to get back to New York."

"I understand." Travis nodded. "I'm not opposed, really. It's worth the risk to me too. But frankly, I'm scared to death and more than a little bit cautious."

"As we both should be. Cautious, I mean, not scared to death. I don't want you to be scared to death. But how do you feel about waiting to use the B word?"

"What's that?"

"Boyfriend."

"I ain't never used that word."

"I know. It's just that Jason asked me the other night if we were boyfriends now. And I didn't have an answer for him. I still don't."

"So you want to wait until I decide? Before I get the title?"

"Something like that."

Travis sighed and rolled his eyes, clearly unhappy with the proposition. Ben, however, silently stood his ground.

"Fine," Travis conceded. "But I would like to know that you're not sleeping with no one else. Can you at least give me that?"

"Travis, don't be ridiculous. You know I'm not sleeping with anyone else."

Travis tried to pull his feet away but Ben grabbed them and pounced on top of him to lighten the mood.

"I ain't ridiculous!" Travis protested as Ben began tickling him.

"Ridiculously hot, maybe."

"Stop it," Travis said through his laughter.

"Maybe I should fuck you instead."

"It's about time, Hotshot. No way I'm calling someone my *boyfriend* who leaves me for a week with no sex."

"Ouch."

"I'm just saying," he said, imitating one of Ben's favorite expressions. "You can't get me addicted to cock and then close the barn door."

"Well, why don't we open it back up, then?"

"What about the pot roast?"

"It's not going anywhere. We'll have a late dinner with the boys."

Travis wiggled out from underneath Ben and jumped to his feet. He peeled off his T-shirt as he walked toward the bedroom.

"You coming, Obi-Wan?" he said over his shoulder. "My ass ain't gonna fuck itself."

Ben followed him into the bedroom, undressing as he went. In less than a minute, they became intertwined. Travis slipped a condom onto Ben's stiff cock and lightly coated it with lube. He lifted his legs into the air and pulled Ben down on top of him. He reached under and guided Ben in so that the tip of his dick sat ready to split Travis wide open.

"Look at me," Travis demanded.

No one told Ben what to do in bed. Nonetheless, he followed orders and locked his gaze on Travis.

"No other man has ever fucked my ass and no other man ever will."

"I promise you, Travis, I will be worthy and faithful and true."

And as corny as that sounded, Ben meant it.

He made love to Travis, even though Ben didn't dare use that word yet. But he wanted to. After a week without sex, Travis didn't last long and shot them both in the face with his load. Ben licked the come off Travis's chin and then fed it to him. He reached down and grabbed the condom.

"Don't stop just 'cause I came," Travis said.

"I thought we might try something else. Something new."

Travis lifted up and allowed Ben to withdraw his dick.

"Like what?"

Ben grinned as he removed the condom.

"What's your favorite number?"

Travis understood immediately.

"You want to sixty-nine?"

"Look, I can't believe I'm even saying this. I'm the guy that used to think a blow job was a brief stop on the way to the main event, which was always fucking. But now I miss it. You've never sucked my dick. Ever. Dan Savage says any model that doesn't come equipped with oral should be returned to the factory."

"Who the hell is Dan Savage?"

"That's not important."

"So you're gonna return me to the factory if I don't give you a blow job?"

"I'm just saying."

"You're just saying, eh? Well, let's give this a try, then."

Travis slid down until he was staring right at Ben's hard prick. He took it in his hand and stroked it. He moved his head a little closer and looked up at Ben.

"So you want me to lick it? Like this?"

Travis ran his tongue along the underside of Ben's shaft, starting at the base and working his way, ever so slowly, up to the tip. He flicked his tongue all around the head, making Ben thrust involuntarily toward Travis's lips. When he did that, though, Travis pulled back.

"Where did you learn to do that?" asked Ben, panting.

"I watched some gay porn. While you were sick. You like it?"

"Uh, yeah."

"You want some more?"

"Please."

Travis teased Ben again with his tongue, running his lips back and forth over Ben's now throbbing cock, pulling away each time Ben thrust upward. When Ben grabbed the back of Travis's head and tried to force him down, Travis quickly reacted by catching Ben's wrists and pinning his arms to his sides. At the point where Travis knew Ben would overpower him, he took the whole of Ben's cock into his mouth and wrapped his lips around the base. Travis went at it with full-force gusto, unable to completely deep-throat Ben's eight inches, but the giver of a championship blow job nonetheless. Ben thrust his hips off the bed, keeping rhythm with Travis's sucking. He reached down to feel Travis's cock and discovered that it was hard again. Without any prompting, Travis swung around until he straddled Ben in the sixty-nine position, never once taking Ben's dick out of his mouth. Ben looked up and saw Travis's cock jutting out above him. He pulled it down and wrapped his lips around it, running his tongue over the head and relishing the taste of precome before taking the whole of it into his mouth.

After a minute, Travis came up momentarily for air. "Jesus, Mary, and Joseph. So that's what a blow job's supposed to feel like?"

And then he went back down on Ben's prick. They rolled over onto their sides, and Ben took Travis all the way down to the base. Ben encouraged Travis to fuck the back of his throat, something that caused Travis to buck wildly. Ben could feel his own orgasm rising when Travis started to work him with both his hand and mouth. Without a sound or warning, Ben felt his mouth begin to fill with the bittersweet taste of Travis's come, sending him over the orgasm cliff. As he started to sense Ben's release, Travis pushed down as far as he could onto his cock so Ben literally shot down Travis's throat. Finally, Travis pulled off so that the last spurts landed across his lips and cheek.

"Good golly," he panted. "That was the hottest thing I've ever done."

Ben slowly let Travis's cock slide out of his mouth.

"Seriously?"

"Seriously," Travis answered, still catching his breath. "Fucking hits a deep spot, don't get me wrong. But that was hotter than a billy goat with a blowtorch. I love your come. I love tasting it. I love feeling it splatter on my face. You don't get that with a woman."

"You're really getting into this whole gay-sex thing, aren't you?"

"Damn if I ain't. I love that you have a dick. I never been into guys, but it's one of my favorite things about you. I never want to go back."

Ben flipped around and kissed him. Abandoning all logic, his heart took over and nothing could stop it.

"Then don't. Say you'll move with me to New York."

"You know I have to visit first," Travis insisted.

"No. Say it now. Tell me you'll come with me now, before you see it. Have faith in me, Travis. Have faith in us."

"That ain't fair."

"I know!" Ben said, giddy with laughter. "Life's not fair. I'm asking you to take a leap of faith with me. Tell me that you're permanent. Please. Tell me that you're not going to disappear for a hundred years. Now, before we go."

"Whoa there, Trigger, slow down. First, a hundred years? What's that all about? And second, where's this coming from? You're the one who said we should be cautious. Wait to use the B word, remember?"

"I know. But everything amazing in my life has been the result of *not* being cautious. What I really wanted you to say is that you're a part of my life no matter what."

Travis shook his head stubbornly. "Nu-uh. I ain't gonna say *nothing* 'til you say something else first."

"I love you," Ben blurted out. "I have been in love with you since Valentine's Day, probably even before that. I believe you are my present and my future—and for some reason that I can't explain, even my past. I know I can do great things if you're with me, Travis. I want to call you my boyfriend. I'm ready to make you the happiest man in the state of Texas, if you'll just let me. So please tell me. Now. Before we go."

Travis looked overwhelmed, but he lifted up his head and kissed Ben softly. "Okay. Yes. I'll move to New York with you."

THE next morning, Ben registered for the Texas Bar Exam.

FOURTEEN

DURING the three weeks running up to spring break, the Austin weather warmed up and the Walsh brothers, plus Travis, began to spend their weekend afternoons at Barton Springs. A naturally fed pool, the Springs had a consistent temperature of sixty-eight degrees year-round. Too cold for March, but a dip in the summer could keep a person cool in the Texas heat for almost an hour. Barton Springs also served as a kind of town square, a gathering place of grassy slopes where people could meet and catch up. Quentin generally went off with his buddies or his girlfriend, Dakota, a waifish lass with blond hair and the severe cheekbones of a supermodel.

"It's pretty cool what you guys are doing," she said one day, talking to Ben and Travis. "Taking care of everybody, I mean."

"Thanks, Dakota," Ben replied, deciding right there and then that he would take the direct approach when it came to this parenting thing. "Did Quentin tell you about our no pregnancies policy?"

"Jesus," Quentin complained.

Dakota laughed. "You don't have anything to worry about, Mr. Walsh. Your moving away kind of put the brakes on things."

"Oh," Ben replied. "Sorry about that."

Travis leaned over to kiss his boyfriend. "Mr. Walsh."

"You like this whole PDA thing, don't you?"

"I'm getting used to it."

"I'm going to hurl," Quentin said.

Travis spent a lot of his time tossing a football or playing catch with Cade. Ben and Jason, on the other hand, preferred to lie out and soak up the springtime sun or sit under one of the large oak trees and read. Afterward, they often headed to Huts for burgers and onion rings.

"One of these things is not like the others."

Their waitress, a colorful woman with bright orange hair and pancake makeup, surveyed the Atwood-Walsh clan, trying to figure out how Travis fit in. She looked at him and whispered, "The milkman didn't have red hair, did he?"

"I'm the boyfriend," Travis explained.

"Well," she replied, winking at Ben. "Aren't you the lucky one, then."

One day, Ben walked over to Travis's shop and surprised him with some doughnuts, which he'd made himself from scratch. Travis's boss and the three other mechanics stopped their work to come over and meet him. Travis beamed as he introduced them. Darrell Cook, the boss, who couldn't have weighed more than 140 pounds wet, shook Ben's hand. With his square jaw, buzz cut, and USMC tattoo, Ben could tell that no one gave Darrell any crap. The mechanics—Ed, Topher, and Royce—each shook Ben's hand as well and tried the doughnuts.

"Damn," Royce said. "That's better than Krispy Kreme."

"I'm not really that domestic," Ben explained. "I just have a lot of free time on my hands." He looked around at the cars and trucks hoisted into the air. *Every night,* he thought, *Travis comes home from this place, the setting of erotic fantasies and classic guy-on-guy porn, his muscles sore and butt aching to be fucked.* He did a man's work. Ben thanked himself for wearing baggy pants that easily hid the thickening of his cock.

"So you're the one taking Red away to New York," Darrell said. "He's my best monkey. You couldn't have taken one of these bozos?" He motioned to the three other mechanics, all of whom were eminently bangable.

"Thanks a lot," Topher said with his mouth full.

Ben laughed and looked at Travis, who continued to grin. *I make him happy*, he thought. "I would if I could, Mr. Cook. But Travis came with a strict no-return policy, so I'm afraid I'm stuck with him wherever I go."

"Well," said Darrell as he popped a doughnut into his mouth, "it was worth a shot. But really, I wish you both the best of luck. God knows no one deserves it more than Red."

Ben could have stayed in that idyllic zone for longer, but soon they only had days until their trip. The more they talked about it at dinner, the more excited everyone got, even Quentin, who'd set up a schedule with Stephanie to go around the city and do napkin drawings from inside famous restaurants. Travis bought tickets to a Knicks game at Madison Square Garden for himself and Cade, and Colin had lined up tours of several prep schools for Jason, who continued to express his boundless enthusiasm for New York and its many possibilities.

WHEN the Saturday of their flight arrived, things seemed to start off smoothly. They got to the airport without incident, but when they arrived in Newark, they hit their first snag. All the checked bags came through except Jason's. They waited for two hours only to be told that it would not be coming in until after midnight. The airline rep apologized and assured them that it would be delivered as soon as it arrived. They made their way into the city and over to the Upper East Side. Colin's parents lived in a four-story brownstone on Sixty-Eighth Street. They had more than enough bedrooms for everyone. Colin's seventeen-year-old sister, Catherine, came home from boarding school for her spring break and took an instant liking to Quentin.

At dinner that evening, the brothers had less to say than usual. The opulent and tastefully decorated Mead house, with its art on every wall, dwarfed their home in Austin. Two years ago, it was given a featured spread in *Architectural Digest*. Ben, of course, had visited many times, but he remembered how the place had intimidated him the first time too. Mr. Mead, a boisterous man who skipped the law in favor of a fortune in real estate, doted on the Walsh boys like grandchildren. He took a special shine to Cade and asked him about college football and if he thought the Longhorns would be ready to take another national championship next season. Colin arrived late and sat next to Jason for dessert, talking with him in hushed tones.

"The stupid airline lost my luggage," Jason complained.

"Don't worry," Colin assured him. "If it doesn't come by tomorrow, I'll take you shopping and replace everything."

"You can do that, Uncle Colin?"

"Jason," he answered, "you can do anything with a black American Express card."

"Uncle Colin?" Catherine said, raising her perfectly shaped eyebrows. "I don't recall having children yet."

"Cathy, you know that Ben is like a brother to me."

"Don't you dare call me that."

Ben knew the quickest way to Catherine's bad side was to call her Cathy. She asked Quentin about his napkin drawings, which he downplayed as no big deal.

"Did you see our Manet on the second floor?" she inquired.

"No," replied Quentin. "You have an original?"

"Yes. Granddaddy bought it at auction a few years ago but couldn't find anywhere to hang it. Can you imagine? Buying a Manet and not having a place to put it. Absurd, really. So he gave it to Mommy and Daddy for their twenty-fifth."

Ben felt Travis tug on his pant leg under the table. He put his arm on the back of Travis's chair and discreetly leaned in so that Travis could whisper into his ear.

"Who's Manet?"

"A painter," Ben whispered back. "French impressionist."

"He a big deal?"

"Very."

"Travis," said Norma Mead, a quiet and gracious woman, "you've hardly said one word since you arrived. Ben tells me this is your first trip to New York."

"Yes, ma'am."

She smiled a sad smile. "I can still remember my first trip. What do you think so far?"

"Well, ma'am, I ain't seen much yet, but it's as big as all hell and half of Texas—pardon my French."

Mrs. Mead laughed with delight. "And how long have you known our Ben?"

Travis paused to run the calculation in his head.

"Three months."

"My," she said, returning to her sad smile. "Such a big decision for such a short time."

The next day, an airline rep delivered Jason's bag and Mother Nature delivered a torrential downpour of rain that lasted all week. Manhattan, a wonderful place to visit when the weather was temperate and inviting, turned depressing and difficult when it rained. They all attempted some sightseeing together, but the wet and cold made it impossible to enjoy anything. On Monday, Ben headed into the Wilson & Mead offices to talk to his boss, and Travis planned to take Cade down to Ground Zero, which Travis insisted he could do on his own. Ben gave him a map of the subway system and detailed directions about how to get there, but an hour later Travis called in a cold sweat. He had taken the uptown train instead of the downtown train and ended up in Spanish Harlem. Ben told him exactly what to do, but when they got back to the Mead residence, they were both soaking wet and visibly shaken.

The next morning, Cade woke up with a vicious cold that kept him in bed for the rest of the week. Ben volunteered to go to the basketball game with Travis that evening, but he had spent the entire day at the office and couldn't work up any enthusiasm for the sport. They ended up leaving at halftime, much to Travis's dismay. On Wednesday, with Cade still in bed, the Mead's real estate agent, a perky woman named Gail D'Angelo, whisked the rest of them through a tour of Manhattan apartments. She showed them at least ten different places, none of which could satisfy everyone. Travis openly expressed his shock at the lack of space. Quentin and Jason balked at the suggestion that one of them might have to share a room with Cade. Ben became increasingly frustrated by the whole experience and was seething with resentment by the end of the day. Travis had no idea how to deal with him when he got that way and steered clear altogether. When they crawled into bed that night, they barely spoke or touched.

Quentin's plan to spend most of the week doing napkin drawings fell apart from the beginning. The rain made everything gray and murky, but Quentin had his own issues. When the drawings turned into work instead of something he dashed off during a meal, they became arid and uninspired. When he showed them to Stephanie on Thursday, she tactfully expressed her criticism and told Quentin that perhaps she had spoken prematurely about a gallery show. Quentin brushed it off as no big deal, but Ben knew otherwise. He could read Quentin's moods at this point because it turned out they weren't that different from his own. They both hated failing at anything, and although Quentin tried to downplay it, Ben knew the rejection stung.

On Friday night, Colin invited Ben and Travis to a dinner party at his apartment in Chelsea, and Catherine invited Quentin to a birthday party for one of her friends. When Jason got wind of that, he begged to tag along until the two acquiesced. Cade, finally out of bed and feeling better, had spent the afternoon with Mr. Mead in the study, learning how to play chess.

"He's a shark," Mr. Mead told Ben as he and Travis stood in the foyer, getting ready to go out for the evening.

"Thank you so much for taking care of him this week."

"It was our pleasure," said Mrs. Mead. "It breaks my heart that he will grow up without a mother."

"You two have a wonderful evening and tell my son we expect him for dinner on Sunday."

"I'll remember to tell him."

They walked over to Lexington Avenue and Ben hailed a cab. He and Travis said little during the ride downtown to Colin's apartment on Twenty-Third Street. An exhausted Ben allowed himself to think that maybe he had made a huge mistake about everything.

When they arrived, Ben saw David in the living room. Colin had failed to mention that he would be there. David gave Ben a hug that lasted a little too long, and Travis looked at them both, confused. Ben ignored the look. He said hello to Martin and Johnny, two people who always had the ability to cheer his heart. Colin and Ben had met Johnny in law school, and he and Martin had proven to be good friends over the years. They greeted him enthusiastically and made a point of sharing their condolences in person. Martin introduced himself to Travis and immediately tried to make him feel at ease, though from the look on Travis's face, he had his work cut out for him. Blaine Webster, a friend of Colin's from prep school, and Blaine's boyfriend Stewart, rounded out the party. Once Colin completed the introductions, he excused himself and disappeared into the kitchen. Since Martin still had Travis engaged in a conversation, Ben decided to follow Colin.

"What is David doing here?" Ben asked once they were safely out of earshot of the others.

"That sounds like an accusation, Walsh."

"Why would you invite my ex-boyfriend and my current boyfriend to the same dinner party?"

"Because I needed an even number. And the last time I checked, this was still my apartment and my guest list. Not everything is about you, my friend."

"But...."

Colin held up his hand and Ben stopped. "You're acting like a child. David is a great guy and you are the one who brought him into our lives. We are not in high school. Just because you broke up with him does not mean the rest of us have to."

Ben stared at him, the wheels of his brain spinning.

"Do you like him?"

Colin laughed off the suggestion. "You've been gone for three months, Ben. Life goes on. You'd better get back in there and save your boyfriend. You don't want Blaine digging his claws into him."

Ben decided to drop the deposition. "Your father asked me to remind you about dinner Sunday night."

"I got it. Now leave me alone so I can finish in here."

"Why didn't you have this catered?"

"Because I don't need someone to do everything for me anymore. Now, please, git."

Ben returned to the living room, where Travis was now sitting next to Martin. He looked up when Ben came back and tried to smile. Ben knew Travis needed some reassurance, but instead, he sat down in the only available seat, which was next to David, who asked about his brothers. Ben gave him a brief rundown of their trip so far.

"Sounds like you've had a rough week."

"That's an understatement. Murphy's Law was in full effect." Ben looked across the room and lowered his voice. "I'm sorry if this is awkward. With Travis, I mean."

"We're good," David replied. "That was three months ago. I've moved on."

Blaine stepped into their conversation.

"So sorry to hear about your parents, Ben."

"Thanks, Blaine."

"Tragic," Stewart added.

"Let's change the subject," Ben insisted. "What have you been up to these days, Blaine? Still working on that PhD?"

"I'm afraid so."

"What are you studying?" asked Travis.

"I'm doing a post-structuralist reading of Joyce's *A Portrait of the Artist as a Young Man*. Are you familiar with it?"

"Nu-uh," Travis answered. "I never heard of her."

Stewart suppressed a giggle and everyone else looked down, embarrassed for him.

"What did I say?"

"Nothing," Ben insisted. "It's a man. James Joyce."

"Oh. Sorry, I...."

"Martin," Ben interrupted, "are you going to DC to catch the new revival of *Follies*?"

"Of course," Martin answered. "We're going in May. It's sure to be epic. Whenever Bernadette does Sondheim, it's historically epic."

"We have a line-item in the budget now," Johnny added. "For *Follies* tickets after it transfers to Broadway."

Martin dismissed him with a wave of his hand. Ben looked at Travis, who was staring down and trying to remove the ever-present grease from underneath his fingernails. Ben felt bad for him but still did nothing.

"I cannot wait to see what Bernadette does with the big numbers," Martin continued. "I'm not so concerned about 'In Buddy's Eyes', but 'Losing My Mind'? I mean, the Dorothy Collins original is iconic. Still, it's the single greatest song about heartache in the musical theater canon, so… how can she go wrong?"

Everyone fell silent for a moment.

"Travis," David said. "What do you think of New York?"

Ben appreciated David's question, an attempt to steer the conversation away from modernist literature and Sondheim musicals. Travis, however, didn't see it that way.

"I don't much like it."

"Excuse me?" Blaine replied.

"People have been asking me that since we first got here, and I been trying my best to be polite and all. But the fact of the matter is, this place is as worthless as chicken crap on the pump handle. It's cold and wet—I mean, really, is that turd-floater out there ever gonna end? I almost got mugged on the second day we were here. Everything's crowded and cramped. The apartments we looked at were the size of my closet at home. Ben's fit to be tied half the time. Quentin got his heart broken yesterday when that Stephanie woman told him his drawings weren't good enough. Frankly, I can't imagine why anyone would want to live here."

His words stunned the room into silence.

"Well," Stewart said after a few moments, "aren't we a Negative Nancy?"

"We've had a difficult week," Ben said, trying to contextualize Travis's comments.

Colin returned from the kitchen. "Dinner is served," he announced. He looked around the room at the blank stares. "What did I miss?"

"Nothing at all," said David. "They were just discussing Joyce and Sondheim."

"Ugh, what a bore. Everyone into the dining room."

Travis didn't say another word all evening and barely touched the food on his plate, pushing it around with his fork instead. The others ignored him and engaged in a spirited political discussion about the next presidential election. Ben tried to participate, with limited success. He couldn't help but wonder if Travis had just broken up with him in front of his friends. Had he changed his mind? Was the move off, at least for him? Ben lost his appetite and excused himself.

"I need to use the john."

"Charming, Walsh. In the middle of dinner?"

Ben didn't answer. He got up and went down the hallway to the bathroom. He took a piss and then threw some cold water onto his face, looking at his reflection in the mirror as he dried himself with a hand towel.

Is this worth it?

Ben froze at the thought. He remembered the conversation with his dad in the kitchen. He returned the towel to the rack beside the sink. He opened the door and practically knocked David over.

"Sorry," David said. "I needed to piss too."

Ben stepped out into the hallway.

"It's my fault. I should watch where I'm going. Jesus, this has been the worst... well, second worst week of my life. I can't believe he just went off like that."

"Cut him some slack. It can't be easy."

"I'm done caring."

"Don't say that."

"I want to crawl into bed and bury myself under the covers."

"Do you love him?"

"I thought I did. But right now all I feel is broken down."

David reached out and touched Ben's arm, gently caressing it in a gesture of comfort. Ben heard some shuffling and looked down the hallway, where Travis stood with tears rimming his eyes, looking crestfallen and alone. David immediately jerked his hand away.

"Travis," David blurted out. "It's not what you think."

"It don't matter what I think no more." He grabbed his jacket off the coat tree next to the door. "I'll get a cab back on my own."

"Shit," Ben said as he watched Travis open the door and flee. "Tell Colin we had to go. I'll call him later."

He grabbed his coat and ran after Travis, down two flights of stairs and onto the street. He looked both ways and saw him heading toward Eighth Avenue. Ben called his name but he didn't stop. He ran until he caught up with him, then he grabbed Travis by the elbow and turned him around.

"Would you wait for me, please?"

"What's the point?"

Ben stood silently on the sidewalk. He didn't have an answer.

"What, you ain't got nothing to say now?" Travis asked in a loud voice. "We both know I don't belong here. How could you do that?"

"So now it's my fault you don't know who James Joyce is?"

"Fuck you. You could have helped me out in there."

"How?"

"Would it have killed you to sit next to me? Maybe—oh, I don't know—treat me like I'm your goddamned boyfriend?"

"You're an adult, Travis. I wasn't aware I needed to hold your hand during a dinner party. Shit, I'm in charge of three boys. I don't need a fourth."

"You are a cold person, Ben Walsh." He turned to walk away but then turned back. "And by the way, thanks for throwing David in my face. That was a real treat."

"Fine. You're right. So let's just have it out."

Travis reeled back and punched Ben in the jaw.

"What the...."

"You made me promise!" Travis's eyes were ablaze with fury. "You made me say I'd come with you before I even knew what I was getting myself into. You and your fucking leap of faith. I was doing just fine before you came along. And now look at me. I don't even recognize myself no more!"

"I never put a gun to your head."

"I fell in love with you, Ben. I was walking in tall cotton. I finally had a real family. Someone was gonna love me and take care of me and let me love them back. If being gay was gonna bring me all that, then damn if it wasn't the best thing that ever happened to me."

"We've had a bad week."

"I heard you in there. I was standing right there when David asked if you love me. I heard your answer."

"I'm exhausted, Travis. Don't pay attention to that."

"You thought you loved me? What, so now you've changed your mind?"

"Travis...."

"No. You've ruined my life. If you're done caring then so am I."

Ben didn't know what to say. A couple of women walked past them, averting their eyes so as not to intrude on their painfully private moment.

Ben noticed that the rain had stopped. "So that's it?" he asked. He had stood here before, at the edge of the relationship cliff. He recognized it. A few well-chosen words would send them crashing onto the rocks below. Usually Ben would exhale a sigh of relief at this point. Usually *he* took his boyfriends to this place, but he didn't like being brought here against his will. He wanted to pull them back from the edge.

Ben's phone rang and he took it out of his pocket.

Quentin.

He slid his thumb across the screen and put the phone to his ear.

"Ben, you need to come get us. Something's happened to Jason."

"What do you mean, something's happened to Jason? Where are you?"

No answer. He heard Quentin talking to somebody. Travis looked at him, and Ben was sure he could see the panic on his face.

"What's the matter?" Travis asked.

"I don't know yet," Ben whispered over the mouthpiece.

Quentin's voice returned.

"Broadway and Tenth Street."

"Okay, hang tight and keep your phone handy. We're about ten minutes away. I'll call you when we get there."

"I'm sorry, Ben."

Quentin hung up.

"Shit," Ben said. "Let's go."

"What's wrong?"

"I have no idea."

They ran to the corner and furiously waved down a taxi. Ben gave the driver the intersection and told him it was an emergency. His knee twitched up and down while the taxi maneuvered downtown toward the Village and then east toward Broadway.

"Is there any way to go faster?" Ben asked the driver, who pretended not to hear him.

"Everything's gonna be okay," Travis assured him.

"Bullshit." Ben looked out the window. "Nothing is going to be okay."

They finally pulled up to the intersection in front of Grace Church. Ben threw several bills at the driver and jumped out of the cab. He saw Quentin and Catherine standing across the street, next to an NYU dorm. Jason sat on the sidewalk. Ben and Travis ran over to them, and Ben immediately squatted down to check on Jason.

"What happened?" he barked.

Catherine answered. "It's my fault, Ben. I wasn't paying attention."

"I wasn't talking to you, Catherine. What happened, Q?"

"It was like a scene out of *Twelve*," Quentin explained. "They had 'Happy Birthday' spelled out on the coffee table. In lines of coke."

Ben looked up at him. "You let your brother do coke?"

"Jesus, of course not. Catherine introduced him to some of her gay friends, and I thought he would be okay."

"He was having a good time," Catherine added. "Then Nathan came and told me that he'd taken a tab of Ecstasy and was falling out."

"Jason," Ben said to his brother. "Can you talk to me?"

"I love you, Ben," he answered, clearly disoriented but remarkably lucid. "You're the best brother in the whole world."

Ben looked up at Catherine. "Do you know how much he took?"

"Nathan said just the one capsule. It's pure MDMA."

"Are you sure it wasn't cut with anything?"

"I'm sure. Nathan only buys pharmaceutical grade."

"Has he thrown up yet?"

"Yeah," Quentin said. "Just after I called you. What happened to your lip? Did you two get into a fight?"

Ben didn't answer. He needed to think the situation through. He couldn't take Jason back to the Mead house until he came down. He considered what his father would do. He'd take him to the hospital immediately. But Ben thought he had a better idea. And that's when he felt it.

Forward momentum.

Ben was in the driver's seat now and needed to follow his gut. His point of view was the one that mattered, not his father's. A hospital would only freak Jason out. As unorthodox as it sounded, he needed to turn this experience around for his brother.

"Jason," he said. "Can you stand up and lean on me?"

Jason put his arms around Ben's neck and allowed himself to be pulled to his feet. He kept his arm around Ben's shoulder and leaned against his older brother.

"Catherine, can you get Quentin and Travis back to your house for me?"

"What are you going to do?" Quentin asked.

"Not now, Quentin. I'll deal with you later. Catherine?"

"Of course. Anything. We can catch a cab right now."

"Don't say anything to your parents, please. If they ask, tell them Jason wanted to see the Village at night. Make something up, I don't care."

"I understand."

Catherine grabbed Quentin by the sleeve of his coat and pulled him toward Broadway.

"Ben...."

"Please, Travis. Go with them. I got this, I promise. Leave me alone with him."

Travis hesitated for a moment and then followed Quentin and Catherine as they crossed Broadway and hailed a taxi. Ben pointed himself and Jason in the opposite direction, toward University Place. After a few steps, Jason got his sea legs and could walk with only limited assistance from Ben. He looked up at the sky.

"It stopped raining."

"That's right, buddy. How are you feeling?"

"Like nothing in the world can hurt me ever again. Because I see how it's all meant to be."

"I know, Jason. Do you want to talk about it?"

"Talk about what?"

"Anything. Life. The universe. Mom and Dad, maybe."

"Do you think we'll ever see them again?"

"I hope so."

Jason paused. "Me too. Ben, can I tell you something?"

"You can tell me anything, Jason."

"You saved my life. You saved us all. Quentin told me they were going to split us up. I don't know what I would have done if you had sent me to live with Uncle Nick. Or Uncle Sam. They hate me."

"They don't hate you."

"They do. And they hate you too. Didn't you know that?"

"No one's splitting us up. Nothing bad is going to happen to you again. Ever."

"Oh, Ben. Don't you know you can't say things like that and make them come true? I read, you know. A lot. You have no idea how many books are about the loss of innocence. I'm fourteen years old and I'm not supposed to understand that yet, but I do. You know you can't protect us forever, right?"

"I can certainly try."

Jason laughed. "Ben, do you think I'm too young to fall in love?"

"You might be. No need to rush into anything. Besides, you have lots of people who love you."

"That's not what I mean. I mean like you and Travis. Do you think anyone will ever love me like that?"

Ben's mind flashed back to the dinner party and the argument on the street.

"You're going to have all the boys lined up, young man. And the one who loves you is going to be the luckiest guy in the world."

"Really, Ben, I'm not interested in boys lining up. If we're being totally honest, I really liked Jake. A lot."

They crossed University Place and continued down Tenth Street toward Fifth Avenue.

"Do you think you can walk on your own?" Ben asked.

They stopped and Jason removed his arm from around Ben's shoulder. He stood still.

"Where are we?"

"The West Village."

"Why are the streetlights so bright? And why is my skin tingling?"

"Do you remember taking something at the party?"

Jason smiled and began walking. "Nathan. He asked me if I'd ever done E before. I didn't want to sound like a hick so I said sure. Am I in trouble?"

"No," Ben assured him as they walked together. "You're not in trouble. If anything, I'm in trouble. So tell me more about Jake."

"He kissed me, Ben. He made my toes curl. Does Travis make your toes curl?"

"Yes, he does."

"I thought so. But now he won't talk to me. I mean, he'll talk to me, but he doesn't want to hang out anymore. Mom really flipped when she found us and he never recovered from that."

"Can you blame him?"

Jason laughed again, louder.

"She really was the best mom ever, wasn't she? But he said it was too much drama for him. Of course, I haven't seen him since Mom and Dad died."

Jason stopped.

"I think that's the first time I've said that out loud. They're really gone, aren't they?"

"Yes, Jason. They're really gone. But I'm here."

Ben put his arm around his brother and continued walking.

"Hey," Jason said, "maybe we can go to an Out Youth potluck sometime. You and me."

"Of course we can do that. But first, let's stop at this deli and get you something to drink. Only thing is, we're going to be quiet while we're in there. We don't want the guy listening to our conversation, okay?"

"A secret. I understand."

Ben steered them into the deli and quickly snatched an orange juice and a bottle of water from the refrigerated section. He added a pack of sugarless gum and paid for the items, after which he got them back out the door.

"Here, drink this," he said, opening the orange juice and handing it to Jason. He took a large gulp and then handed it back to Ben, who opened the bottle of water. "Now this," he repeated, handing the second bottle over. Jason took a swig and tried to hand that back as well. "No, you keep that. And chew this," Ben instructed, opening up the pack of gum and then unwrapping a stick for Jason, who took it and popped it into his mouth.

"Yum. Grape. What happened to your face, by the way?"

"Travis hit me."

Jason started laughing. "Really? What did you do?"

"I asked him to make a promise he couldn't keep."

"Ben, for being so smart, you're not too bright sometimes."

"Yeah, I know. Now let's keep walking. Try to go easy on the gum chewing, but without it, you'll start grinding your teeth. And I want you to drink that water or else you'll get dehydrated."

"Okay," Jason agreed, now heading toward Sixth Avenue. He looked around at the buildings, the trees on the street, the lights in the windows, and the people passing by. "I missed you so much when you were gone, but now I can see why you had to be here. It's like another world. Are we really going to move?"

"I don't know," Ben replied. He now seriously doubted that they could live together in this place. "Do you want to move here?"

"I don't know either. I lied when you asked if I was being bullied at school. Some of the boys call me a faggot and tell me I need to use the girl's restroom. How do they know? I haven't told anyone at school and no one at the potluck would have said anything."

"Nobody said anything, Jason. They just know. I'll be talking to someone when we get home. I promise. And we'll get you into a private school next year. No matter where we are."

"Really? You would do that for me?"

"I'd do anything for you boys."

"Dad said that public schools were the backbone of our educational system and look what they did for him."

"Yes, I know that. But maybe he didn't understand the specifics of the case, and if he did, I think he would rule in my favor."

"I disappointed him. Do you think he forgives us for being gay?"

Ben looked over at his brother.

"There's nothing to forgive. We didn't do anything wrong."

"You know what I mean."

"Yes, he forgives us."

"How do you know for sure?"

"Because I talked to him about a month ago. He made me migas."

Jason slapped Ben on the arm. "What's wrong with you? Dead people can't make migas."

"I know that. But he told me he was fine with the gay thing. So you can put those worries to rest, okay?"

"Okay. Can we walk around some more? There's got to be some cool stuff in this neighborhood."

"Sure, Jason. Let's keep walking, and I'll show you some of the cool stuff. You remember Thomas Wolfe? The guy who wrote *Look Homeward, Angel*?"

"One of Dad's favorite books! I just finished it," Jason said, quoting, "We can believe in the nothingness of life, we can believe in the nothingness of death and of life after death—but who can believe in the nothingness of Ben?"

"That's right. I like that part. He used to live right up here. So did E. E. Cummings. And Edgar Allan Poe."

"They all lived here?"

"Yep. Let's keep walking and I'll show you."

They walked around Greenwich Village for another hour or so. Ben pointed out the homes of all the famous authors he knew. Then they went down to Christopher Street, and Ben showed him the Stonewall Inn and explained how the gay rights movement started there back in 1969. Finally, Jason stopped walking and looked around as if he had been suddenly dropped onto the street.

"What happened?" Jason asked.

Ben turned toward him and looked into Jason's eyes, which were beginning to dilate normally again. The ride had ended.

"You feel like you just dropped out of warp?"

Jason nodded.

"Okay. So, I want you to listen to me very carefully. You were at a party and you took a drug that someone gave you. Ecstasy. Do you know what that is?"

He nodded again.

"You're not in trouble. But if you do this again, you will be. Do you understand?"

"Yeah."

"Now, here's what's going to happen. You're not going to get much sleep tonight and you're going to feel like shit warmed over tomorrow. But we're going back to the Mead house and we're not going to say anything about this to anybody. Do you hear me?"

"I hear you."

"And when we get home, you and Quentin and I are going to have a long talk. And you're never going to do anything like this again.

Because if you do, I will lock you in your room until you're eighteen. Understood?"

"Understood."

"Good. Now let's catch a cab and get back before Mrs. Mead calls the cops."

THEY flew back to Texas the next morning. The Meads asked no questions regarding the events of the previous night, even when faced with Ben's swollen lip. As expected, Jason felt like he had been hit by a freight train. Quentin didn't speak and Cade watched a movie on his phone, oblivious to the sour moods of his brothers. When he heard that Travis had clocked Ben on the jaw, Cade's reaction had been entirely sympathetic.

"I've wanted to do that a few times myself."

Once airborne, Ben knew that he and Travis needed to finish their conversation from the night before.

"We need to talk," he began.

"Yep, I know."

"I'm sorry that I pushed you into something before you had all the facts. It wasn't fair to you at all."

"Apology accepted. I'm sorry I hit you."

"I probably deserved it."

The flight attendant pulled a cart up to their seats and asked if they wanted anything to drink. They each requested a Coke and some shortbread cookies.

"So now what?" Travis asked.

"Maybe if the whole thing with Jason hadn't happened last night... things might be different. But it did. And the fact is, I've been distracted. By my grief. By my single-minded need to get back to New York." He paused. "By my relationship with you. I haven't been paying attention. I'd like to blame Quentin for what happened last night, but I didn't even ask where this party was. Or who was throwing it. Or if there would be any supervision. Any of the things that any parent would ask. I just trusted Catherine, even though I'm the one who's responsible. So it turns out Julie was right: I'm not prepared for this at all. I had no idea what it means to be a parent. But if anything happened to one of those boys, I would never forgive myself. The list of my regrets is already too long."

"I get it."

"Do you?"

"Ben, I was scared to death last night. If that was me, I wouldn't have known what to do. What *did* you do?"

"I turned a bad trip into a good trip. When they told me he had thrown up, I knew the drug was already in his system. And I know that pure MDMA is not a deadly drug. So, he was going to go on a ride and there was nothing anyone could do to stop it. He needed his brother, not a hospital."

"How do you know all this?"

"Come on, Travis. I'm a twenty-seven-year-old gay man living in Manhattan. I've been to the Black Party. Do you think I've never done Ecstasy before?"

"So what did you do with Jason?"

"We walked around the West Village and talked. And boy did he have a lot to say. That's Ecstasy for you. Everything poured out of him. I found out he *is* being bullied at school. I don't know what my uncles have said to him, but for some reason, he thinks they hate him. He's got the biggest crush on a boy named Jake. As we were talking... I don't know. He came first, before everything else in my life. My brothers need to be my number-one priority. Before my job. Before myself...."

"And before me."

"I'm sorry."

Travis turned his head away and looked out the window. Ben fought back tears and saw Travis doing the same as he turned back and wiped his eyes dry.

"Are you still fixin' to move in May?"

Ben didn't have an answer for him.

"I don't know. I need to talk to them about it. It was a disaster, but it was only one week. I need to figure out if there's a real problem there. And if I mean what I say about putting them first, then ultimately it's their decision. They have absolute power."

"Quentin and Jason ain't never gonna say no to you. Not after last night. I sat up with Q for two hours waiting for you. He was beating himself up, talking about your daddy and how disappointed he would be in him. But he was singing your praises."

Ben tried to smile. "Maybe it was necessary. The whole trip. We were living in a bubble for three months. It was bound to burst at some point."

Travis looked back out the window, and the two men didn't say anything for several moments.

"So, where do we go from here?" Travis asked, still staring at the clouds floating by.

"I wish I had answers for you. Honestly, I do. If we end up moving, I certainly don't expect you to come with us. I know you don't belong there. But if we stay in Austin… well, I still need to get my priorities straight. Maybe I'm the wrong person for you, Travis, at least right now. I want you to be a part of their lives. I want you to be a part of my life. But I don't know how to be a boyfriend and a parent at the same time."

"I'll wait until you figure it out," Travis said, turning back to Ben.

"No. I can't ask you to do that."

"You didn't."

They fell silent.

"Okay," Ben finally said. "But I need a time-out."

"For how long?"

Ben shook his head. "I don't know."

Travis took a gulp of his Coke. "Okay. Then at least let me tell you I didn't mean half the things I said last night. Some things I did, but I can't remember when I've been so riled up. I don't know what came over me. It was wrong of me to say that you've ruined my life. The fact of the matter is, I feel just the opposite. You woke me up, Ben, and I ain't talking about the gay part. I know someday I'm gonna look back on this and realize meeting you was a turning point in my life. No matter what happens." He choked up and had to turn away again. After a moment, he wiped his eyes and continued. "I don't know if I'll ever feel this way about nobody else, but at least now I know I can. Feel this way, I mean. I know it's in me, and that's a whole hell of a lot more than I knew before. I love you, Ben, and I've never said that to no one and meant it more."

"I love you too, Travis. I would never have gotten through these past three months without you."

"That ain't true, but it's nice to hear."

They didn't say much after that.

When they got home, Travis crossed the street to Mrs. Wright's house. The brothers plopped down in the living room and turned on the television, glad to be home and to see their New York ordeal come to an end.

TRAVIS didn't come around after that. Cade asked about him, but Ben explained that he wouldn't be hanging out for a while and Cade didn't press the issue. Ben sat down with Quentin and Jason that week and the three of them had a long talk. He told them about what happened with Travis and they both said they were sorry if they'd played a role in it. They talked about the party and the drugs. Ben couldn't preach to them as if he were their father, but he nonetheless reconsidered his hands-off approach and laid down a few rules. When they demonstrated good judgment then *maybe* he would loosen the reins.

A week later, Ben received a contract from Wilson & Mead in the mail. Fifteen pages long, it detailed the terms of the firm's financial assistance to the Walsh brothers. It took him about an hour to read through the whole thing, until he stopped at page fourteen. He read it over several times as his father's words rang in his ears. The contract contained a 'do not compete' clause. By signing it and accepting the money, Ben effectively agreed that if he ever left Wilson & Mead for any reason, he could not practice law in the state of New York for twenty-five years.

After their trip, Ben had already begun to seriously question moving his brothers to New York. This clause in the contract only finalized that decision. He would never agree to it and he knew Colin couldn't fix it. Besides, Ben felt the need to grow up and stop relying on Colin so much. He thought back to that day in New York when he'd gotten the phone call from Father Davenport, when his biggest problem had been what kind of gift to get David for Christmas. It seemed like a lifetime ago now, and he realized how childish he had behaved immediately after his parents' death.

At dinner that night, he'd told his brothers they would be staying in Austin. He would take the Texas Bar Exam in August and have a job by Labor Day. All three boys expressed their relief, even Jason, whose brush with fast-lane Manhattan teenagers had left even him gun-shy and reluctant.

One afternoon in early April, Ben noticed that he hadn't seen Travis's truck parked across the street for several days. Ben missed him and had begun to regret their conversation on the plane ride back from New York. He decided to cross the street and investigate. Ben knocked on the front door and waited. He heard Mrs. Wright shuffle around and yell, "Who is it?" from inside.

"It's Ben Walsh. From across the street."

A few seconds later, she opened the door and smiled.

"Oh, I've been expecting you, Ben."

"You have?"

"Yes," she answered. "But first I need to ask you a question."

"What's that, Mrs. Wright?"

"Are you moving to New York City or staying here in Austin?"

"Well, turns out we'll be staying. Why?"

"Travis told me I was only supposed to give you this if you and the boys are staying." She turned around and picked up a manila envelope from the lamp table next to her sofa, handing it to Ben. "Here you go."

He looked down at the envelope. Travis had scrawled his name on the front in black magic marker.

BEN

"Where did he go?"

"He didn't say. Just packed up a few days ago and moved out. Said you would understand when you got this."

Ben felt the blood drain from his face. His mouth went dry and he cleared his throat. "Thanks, Mrs. Wright."

"How are your brothers doing?"

"They're doing fine, thanks for asking. I need to get back, though. I have to pick them up from school soon."

"Well, we always include you in our prayer circle at church. Lord knows, it can't hurt."

"Thanks for that. I expect you're right." He turned to go and then stopped short. "If he calls or anything, could you let me know?"

"Of course, dear."

He left her house and crossed the street, his heart racing. He rushed through the back door and sat down at the kitchen table. He stared at the envelope for several minutes, terrified that it was a letter telling him good-bye. He picked up the envelope and felt it with his hands. It wasn't a letter. Finally, he tore it open and emptied the contents onto the table in front of him.

It was the map of Alaska Ben had given to Travis for Christmas. On the front were three words, scribbled in the same black magic marker.

I'M COMING BACK

FIFTEEN

"WHAT'S this?" Quentin asked, holding up the map of Alaska. Ben had picked them up from school, after which they gathered in the kitchen to discuss dinner plans. "What does 'I'm coming back' mean?"

"Travis left that for me. I went over to Mrs. Wright's place this afternoon to ask about him, because I hadn't seen his truck in a few days. She said he packed his things and left. Didn't tell her where he was going, though."

Cade walked around the table and took the map from Quentin.

"Duh. He went to Alaska."

"But that doesn't make any sense," Ben countered. "If he went to Alaska, then he would have taken the map. That's why I gave it to him."

"You don't think like Travis," Cade insisted. "He likes puzzle movies. If he left you a map, that's him telling you where he went. He's always wanted to see a place where the sun never sets. Have you looked inside?"

"No," answered Ben. "Why?"

"One of Travis's favorite movies is *Indiana Jones and the Last Crusade*. X marks the spot. Remember? In the library?"

Cade opened the map and laid it out on the table.

"See?" he said, pointing toward the northern part of the state.

In the same black magic marker, Travis had put an **X** on the city of Barrow.

"It's on the north coast of Alaska," Jason said, "inside the Arctic Circle. The sun won't go down for half of May and the entire months of June and July."

"How do you know that?" asked Ben.

"He told us all about it," Quentin answered. "He'd been researching it for a while. I think he even had a job lined up. Two and a half months of wall-to-wall daylight. He was pretty stoked."

Ben stood silently in amazement. He had called a time-out in their relationship and that was exactly what Travis had given him. *I'm coming back.* He hadn't said when, but Ben figured it would be sometime after Labor Day. No guarantees, though, just a note scribbled on a map. Still, it might turn out to be a good thing. Ben *did* need to focus on his family and get his act together. He would probably spend most of the summer studying for the bar exam anyway. Maybe he would reconnect with some friends in town and start socializing again. As for dating, Ben could have put Travis behind him and moved on, but he kept hearing his father's words in his ears.

Muddy waters.

So he decided to wait.

SHORTLY after Travis's disappearance, Ben made an appointment with the principal of Jason's school and told her about the bullying. She promised to address the issue, but Ben suspected there was little she would (or could) actually do. He had to get Jason out of there next year. When he asked around about private schools, everyone he spoke to mentioned the same two names: St. Stephen's and St. Andrew's, both Episcopal. So Ben made appointments at each of them and discussed Jason's situation. After looking at his grades, both schools expressed a keen interest. Ben figured the dead parents and the gay angle probably didn't hurt, either, the Episcopal church being about as gay-friendly as Christianity got. He knew these kind of schools loved diversity and both had strict no-bullying policies. After visiting each himself, Jason finally decided on St. Stephen's. He made a calendar for the fridge that counted down his final days in the public school system. "Next year," he said, "it gets better."

IN MAY, Ben went with Jason to the monthly Out Youth potluck.

"So," Ben said as they entered the room with their dish of grilled steak and vegetable kabobs, "I want you to point out this Jack McAlister to me."

"It's Jake," Jason corrected him, scanning the room. "He's over there at the table with the two lesbians. The ones with the matching fauxhawks. That's his mom sitting at the table next to him. The one wearing Chanel and talking on the phone."

"How progressive of her. Where does he go to school?"

"Westlake."

Ben nodded. "You know how to pick 'em, don't you? You were definitely right about the Justin part."

"Gross."

"What? I can't tell you I think your boyfriend's a hottie?"

"No. Please refrain. And you know he's not my boyfriend, so I would appreciate it if you wouldn't embarrass me in front of him."

"Trust me, Jason. I'm not Dad. What are some of his interests?"

"He wants to work in the film industry. He knows a lot about movies."

"Hmm. Like a modern-day Dawson Leery."

"Who's that?"

"What does he like to do for fun?"

"He loves the water. His father has a speedboat but he told me he really wants to learn how to sail."

"What does his father do?"

"He's a lawyer."

Ben laughed.

"This is going to be too easy. Okay, I'll take care of the heavy lifting, but when I do this" —he flicked his index finger across the tip of his nose, à la Paul Newman and Robert Redford in *The Sting*—"you step in with the invitation."

"What invitation?"

"You'll figure it out. Just pay attention."

After dropping their dish at the hot food table, Ben and Jason walked over to where Jake McAlister sat with his dyke friends, his mother next to him but at an adjacent table.

"Hi, Jake," Jason said. The lesbian couple looked up from their place across from Jake, who turned around.

"Hey, Jas, what's up? Is this your brother?"

Jake stood up while his mother glanced over her phone at Ben.

"Yeah, this is Ben. Ben, Jake."

Ben extended his hand and Jake shook it, smiling.

"Nice to meet you, Jake."

"You too. This is my mom."

Jake's mother turned sideways and put her phone to her shoulder, extending her right hand.

"Sarah McAlister. Nice to meet you."

"Ben Walsh," he said, shaking her hand. "Do y'all mind if we join you? This is my first time, and it would be nice to sit at the cool table."

Everyone laughed.

"Please," she said, "have a seat."

Ben went around and sat across from Sarah McAlister. Jason sat down next to Jake and across from Brenda and Debbie, the two fauxhawks.

"I've got to go," Sarah McAlister said into her phone. "I'll call you later. Yes, I agree with you. We'll talk about it when I get home. I promise. Good-bye." She turned off her phone and shut it away in her clutch. "Excuse me, I didn't mean to be rude. Ben, I'm so sorry about your parents. Can I call you Ben?"

"Please do. Sarah?"

"Of course." Ben sized her up. She had money, but wasn't filthy rich by any means. She wasn't getting her roots done as often as she should. Under thirty-five. Probably a teenage mother. "Thanks, it was a rough winter for all of us but now spring is here so we're getting on with it. That outfit looks great on you, by the way. Is it Chanel?"

"Yes, it is," she answered, blushing. "Thank you."

Jake rolled his eyes. "Jason told me you lived in New York. Did you have to move back here? After... you know...."

"Yeah, I did."

"That sucks."

"Jake, please," his mother scolded.

"Well, it does." he insisted. "How would you like it if you had to come back here from New York and start all over?"

Ben liked this boy already.

"Did you find a job yet?" Jake continued.

"No, not yet."

"What kind of work do you do?" Sarah inquired.

"I'm a trial lawyer."

"Really? My husband's a lawyer. Maybe he can help you. Look over your resume or something."

"That would be great. Does he work for Harrison & Pope, by any chance?" Ben watched as Sarah McAlister's smile turned upside down. "They want me to sign on now, but I think I should wait until fall to make a final decision. My father always told me to keep my options open."

"Isn't that one of the firms Dad wanted to work for?" Jake asked his mother.

Perfect, Ben thought.

"You have an offer from Harrison & Pope?" she asked, ignoring her son.

"Yeah, but like I said, I don't want to make a decision until September. I plan on spending the summer with my brothers, maybe take them back to Southampton and do some sailing."

Jake sat up.

"You sail?"

"I sure do. One of my buddies from Columbia Law took me out a few years back and I was hooked. Last summer we sailed from New York to Miami. And back again."

"No way!" Jake exclaimed.

"Columbia Law?" Sarah murmured.

"Jason?" Ben continued. "Am I telling the truth?"

"He's telling the truth."

"First I need to teach Jason and his brothers how to sail, though. I was thinking of renting a boat for Memorial Day weekend. Go out on Lake Travis and show them the ropes. Maybe camp at night."

"That sounds...." Jake stopped. "I wish my dad would do something like that. All he cares about is his stupid speedboat."

Ben flicked his index finger across the tip of his nose.

Jason's eyes widened. "Do you want to go with us?" he asked.

"Seriously?" Jake responded, his jaw slack.

"Is that okay, Ben?"

"Sure," Ben confirmed, turning to Sarah. "I run a very tight ship, and my buddy Colin will be with me. He's been sailing since he was a boy. And Jake will share a tent with one of Jason's brothers."

"Please, Mom, can I go?" Jake pleaded.

"Well, I'll need to talk to your father first, but I'm sure he'll be more than fine with the idea."

"Oh my God," Jake said, turning to Jason. "We're gonna have a blast!"

Jason looked like he might jump out of his skin.

"I know!" he cheered.

"Let's go get some food," Jake suggested as he stood up and pulled Jason's chair out for him.

Ben leaned over and whispered to Brenda and Debbie, "You should try the steak and veggie kabobs. I made them myself." They smiled and assured him they would, but ended up changing tables when a group of their friends showed up a few minutes later. That left Jake and Jason to talk amongst themselves while Ben tossed a long series of questions at Sarah about parenting teenagers. When it was time to go, they exchanged numbers and Ben told her he would be in touch the following week about the sailing trip.

"You should come out to the house for dinner before then," she suggested. "Dan would love to meet you, I'm sure. He'll feel better about the trip that way too."

"We would love that. What do you say, Jason?"

"Yeah, that sounds great. Thank you, Mrs. McAlister."

On their way home, Jason could hardly contain his excitement. "I've never seen anything like that! I'm going to spend Memorial Day weekend sailing with Jake McAlister? Someone pinch me! Please."

"Calm down, there," Ben cautioned. "This will be a good opportunity to really get to know him. Start with a friendship before you decide if he's worth kissing again, and if he is, tell him I'm not going to kick him out of the house. You're going to be fifteen in two months. Nothing wrong with kissing boys at your age. Lord knows I was."

"Don't worry. Uncle Colin already had the sex talk with me."

"So I heard. Speaking of Uncle Colin, you'd better text him. Tell him to book a plane to Austin for Memorial Day and that he's going to be giving sailing lessons to you and your potential new boyfriend. No way will he be able to say no to that."

"It's also Cade's birthday that weekend."

"This'll be perfect, then. He'll love learning how to sail. We have to come up with a major present, though."

"He wants—"

"Wait," Ben interrupted. "I've been trying to do better and pay attention, so I should know this. He's... wait—he's complained a lot about his bicycle, hasn't he? Of course, this is an easy one—he wants a new bike."

"Bingo."

"Jason," Ben said, grinning, "we are going to find our little brother the baddest ride on two wheels."

BEN enjoyed dinner at the McAlisters' immensely. Dan McAlister's tone of voice betrayed that mixture of admiration and envy Ben had come to accept in other lawyers. Since Jake had no brothers or sisters, dinner consisted of the five of them, and the conversation inevitably turned to Ben's once and future career.

"Columbia Law?" Dan asked. "What was that like?"

"The best three years of my life."

"No kidding? I can't say the same."

"Where did you go to law school?"

"Here, at UT. Like half the lawyers in Austin." He quickly changed the subject. "So you're going sailing, I hear. I'm more a speedboat man myself."

"Yes," Ben confirmed. "My buddy, Colin Mead, is coming down from New York to show everyone the ropes. He's been sailing since he was a boy."

"Mead? He related to Joseph Mead?"

"He's his grandson. I was a litigator at Wilson & Mead. Colin and I went to law school together. I learned to sail on one of Joseph Mead's boats. And honestly, I'm only saying all that to connect the dots, not to...."

"Good Lord," Dan exclaimed. "You're the guy! I heard a couple of people talking at the courthouse the other day, something about Joseph Mead's protégé moving to town. No wonder you already have an offer from Harrison & Pope. Firms must be lining up for you."

"I have offers from several firms," Ben admitted. "But my plan is to stall a bit and hope the offers get better."

"Smart man, because they absolutely will. By the way, Sarah and I wanted to thank you for inviting Jake along on this trip. I know he's going to have a great time with your family. And he will absolutely behave himself, won't you, JJ?"

"Yes, Dad."

Ben continued, "You and I should have lunch sometime, Dan. I would really like to hear your lay of the land."

Dan sat up a little straighter in his chair.

"Absolutely," he said. "No one's lining up offers for me, but I've been around awhile and know who the players are, that's for sure."

"Would you mind?"

"It would be my pleasure."

"Thanks. I'd really appreciate it."

"So, Jason," Sarah said, ready to move past the shop talk, "Jake tells me you're going to St. Stephen's next year."

"Yes, ma'am. Only nine more days in the public school system."

"Hey," Jake protested. "I go to a public school."

"Oh, please," Jason rebutted. "Westlake High School is an elite private institution masquerading as a public school. To be a student there you have to live here first, which is impossible unless you're wealthy. It's the reinforcement of privilege via economics and zoning."

Jake laughed. "You gonna get on your class-warfare soapbox now, Walsh?"

"I just might," Jason replied. "No offense, Mr. and Mrs. McAlister."

"None taken, son," Dan assured him, smiling.

"Our father encouraged us to… argue at the dinner table," Ben explained.

"He liked a good fight," Jason openly admitted.

Ben laughed. "I hope we don't go too far."

"Don't you worry," Sarah assured him. "Whatever your father did, it turned out an Ivy League lawyer. So if a heated political discussion over the pasta gets my son into Columbia, I'm all for it."

MEMORIAL DAY weekend looked like something out of *White Squall*—two men and four boys on the open water. Lake Travis could not exactly compare to the Atlantic Ocean, but they still had some serious fun. Jake fit in with little effort and hung on Colin's every word as he taught the boys how to sail. Ben couldn't remember when he'd seen Colin so happy.

"You're loving this, aren't you?"

The sun had set long ago, and the boys had already crawled into their sleeping bags for the first night. Ben and Colin sat next to the campfire watching the last embers fade.

"I do enjoy me some male bonding," Colin admitted. "And this camping thing is so very *Brokeback Mountain*." He bent in close to Ben so that he could whisper and still be heard. "What do you think of Jake?"

"He's a good kid," Ben whispered back. "They seem to be having a great time."

"He's a natural. He can really feel the boat."

They stopped whispering and changed the subject.

"So," said Colin. "How the hell are you doing?"

"I'm okay. I'll be studying for the bar this summer. Can you believe it? Again? I thought I was past all that."

"Don't sweat it, Walsh. You could probably ace it without all the studying."

"Thanks for the vote of confidence, but I'm not going to take that chance. How are things going with you?"

"Not bad. I should probably tell you that David and I are seeing each other."

Ben shook his head and smiled. "I knew it."

"Are you okay with that? I'm not very good with the bro code or whatever it's called."

"Colin, I'm okay with it." And he meant it. "You guys are perfect for each other, actually."

"Have you heard from Travis?"

Ben shook his head. "No. I don't expect I will until he gets back. If he gets back."

"Alaska, eh? I kind of like him now. Not that I didn't before, I was just very Switzerland about the whole thing. Look, we all have our Scudder fantasy but—"

"Colin, please. Travis is nothing like Alec Scudder. I never once met him at the boathouse without fail."

"Would you let me finish? First, Scudder was hot. Second, I was wrong to limit Travis with my narrow view of the world. There's something there. You called a time-out and he called your bluff. Good for him, because frankly, it was a stupid idea to begin with. It's a relationship, not a football game. And third, I'm sorry for inviting David to dinner that night."

"It's all water under the bridge. I've said it before and I'll say it again—other than my brothers, you are the only person I love unconditionally. You know I'm always going to depend on you, no matter what...."

"Yes, I know."

"And someday... I haven't forgotten."

"And neither have I."

"So enjoy yourself with David. He's an awesome guy and deserves someone like you."

The second night of the sailing weekend, Colin and Jason surprised everyone with a cake for Cade's thirteenth birthday (his new bike had already been unveiled at home).

AS JUNE stretched into July, Dakota and Jake became semipermanent fixtures at the Walsh house. One night in midsummer, Ben got a call from Dakota's mother, Ingrid Hayes. She invited him and Quentin to dinner. Ben politely accepted, and they combed their hair and shinned their shoes in an attempt to make a good impression.

"Just don't be a dork," Quentin reminded him.

Ben found dinner at the Hayes's house pleasant enough, though not as warm as the McAlisters'. Dakota's parents were a tad too uptight for his taste. After dessert, Gregg Hayes politely asked his daughter and Quentin to leave the room.

Uh-oh, Ben thought.

Quentin and Dakota went into the living room, leaving Ben alone with Gregg and Ingrid Hayes.

He waited.

"We just wanted to get your impression," Gregg began, "of the relationship Quentin is having with Dakota."

Ben measured his words carefully. "My brother is an awesome kid and I know you're not saying that he isn't. But that's part of my impression." Ben decided that, once again, the direct approach was best. "I think what you're really asking, though, is do I think they're having sex?"

Ingrid nodded.

Ben took a deep breath and continued. "No, they're not—at least not yet. But they're both seventeen. In the state of Texas, they can now legally consent to a sexual relationship with each other." Ben laughed. "Not like that would have stopped them before. They just haven't been ready. Why didn't you talk to her about this?"

Gregg and Ingrid looked at each other.

"We did," Gregg said. "She told us they weren't."

"And you didn't believe her?"

Their silence spoke volumes.

"Look, I am not Quentin's father, but I am his guardian, and I think part of what that means is knowing when to let go. That's where we are. This is their decision to make, and I have a feeling it's right around the corner. I think what we can do for them is provide information and be supportive if their hearts get broken. Which, inevitably, they will. I'll be honest with you—I've already talked to both of them about this on more than one occasion. I hope you don't think I've crossed a line or something."

"No!" Ingrid assured him. "I'm... terrified of what she might go through. But I can't protect her from it."

"And you wouldn't want to," Ben added. "This is a part of growing up. Trust me, I've explained to Quentin that pregnancy is not an option. I think that condoms in combination with another form of birth control would be a good idea. Whatever you think is best, Mrs. Hayes. But I think the condoms are important for Quentin. They can be his responsibility—to remind him of the consequences and make him a participant in all this."

Gregg nodded. "We're on the same page. I hope you understand why we brought it up."

"Of course, I understand. I have no idea what I'm doing half the time. Really, I'm learning most of this as I go along. Do you have any other kids, though?"

"Yes," Gregg answered.

"Another girl and a boy," Ingrid continued. "We sent them to their grandparents for the evening."

"Well, Quentin and Dakota have known each other for a year and a half. Why didn't you have this conversation with my parents when they first started dating?"

"I'm afraid we had our heads in the sand," said Gregg.

"I'm just saying that you have other children. And now you don't have your heads in the sand."

"You're right," Ingrid said. "It's not like we know what we're doing, either, Ben. Dakota is our first teenager. We're all learning as we go along."

Austin parents, to Ben's surprise, were at least cool about their denial. On the way home, Ben noticed Quentin had little to say.

"What's wrong?" Ben asked.

"Nothing."

"Doesn't sound like nothing."

Quentin paused.

"Okay, I'm scared. I mean, what if I'm no good at it?"

"Are we talking about sex?"

"That's what all that was about, wasn't it? Sending us into the living room?"

"Yes. Her parents are concerned. I told them what you told me."

"And that's the truth. You're my brother, Ben. I'm not going to lie to you about *not* sleeping with my girlfriend. We talk about it a lot but… what if I'm no good at it?"

Ben smiled in the dark truck. "Quentin, let me just say that no one's good at it right out of the gate. But you have an honest heart and a sense of humor. Now all you need is practice. You'll be great at it. I promise. It's not rocket science."

"How old were you?"

"When I lost my virginity?"

"Yeah."

"Sixteen to a girl. Fifteen to a boy."

"Fifteen? Jesus."

"He was really cute. Look, if you want my advice, then don't wait too long. Don't turn this into… something else. I know you care about her. It's a good thing to express it. Besides," Ben said as he punched Quentin on the arm, "it will also make you less angry, which for you could be a good thing."

"Eff you. Chicks like brooding. It's a known fact."

"At first, maybe. But… you're lucky, that's all. You have someone you really dig. That's what it's all about."

IN LATE July, Ben quietly celebrated his twenty-eighth birthday with his brothers. He remembered it was Travis's birthday too. He wondered if someone threw a party for him up there in Alaska. That night, Ben finally tried calling the cell number he had for him, but Travis, who favored cheap, pay-as-you-go phones, didn't answer. He had no doubt picked up a new phone with a local number. As Ben was putting the phone back into his pocket, it started to ring. Julie. She had reached out several times over the months since the funeral, but he had always come up with an excuse not to see her.

"Happy Birthday, Ben," she began. "I'm coming to Austin next week for an arts and crafts show. Can we have lunch?"

Ben hesitated again but decided that he couldn't put it off any longer. They arranged to meet at Eastside Cafe while Julie was in town.

When Ben arrived, he found her waiting for him on the front porch of the restaurant. After they were seated and Ben had ordered his customary half order of artichoke manicotti, Julie unrolled her napkin and placed the silverware meticulously next to her plate. She laid the napkin on her lap and smoothed it over once.

"How are you doing?" she asked.

Ben paused, and then he said, "Things are settling down. I'm taking the Texas Bar in a couple of weeks. After that, I'll need to decide on a firm."

"And your brothers?"

"We're getting there. It hasn't been easy and...." Ben stopped himself. He wanted to paint a secure and stable picture for Julie, but it felt false. "You were right. I wasn't prepared for the task. But I'm doing better. Like I said, we're getting there."

"I did what I had to do, Ben."

He scoffed at the suggestion. "Threatening to sue for custody? That's what you had to do?"

"It worked, didn't it?"

Their waitress brought them a basket of jalapeno cornbread muffins. Ben sliced one open and slathered it with butter while he considered Julie's question.

"What do you mean, it worked?"

Julie smiled. "Men are all alike. You think you're the smartest people in the room, but your psychology is painfully simple."

"Julie, if you came all this way just to insult me, please...."

"I didn't do anything of the sort. When you showed up at the house last Christmas, I could see it on your face plain as day."

"See what?"

"Terror. Ben... I need to tell you something. I never believed that your brothers would be better off with us. I know about Jason. Your mother called me right after she found him with that boy. Grace wanted to call you and ask if you could come home, but Bill talked her out of it. She was afraid that she would fail with Jason the same way she failed with you."

"What are you talking about? She didn't fail with me."

"When your child leaves home and only comes back once a year, and would rather spend his summers sailing in the Hamptons with someone else's family, mothers see that as a failure."

Ben sat, dumbstruck.

"Sam and Nick brought up the custody issue," she continued. "I knew there was no way it would ever go anywhere, but I decided to play along because... well, like I said, you boys are all alike. You're fine doubting yourselves, but if someone else doubts you, it becomes...."

"A challenge," Ben muttered.

"Yes. I knew you didn't want the job, but when I suggested that you couldn't *do* the job, well... you set your heels in and became determined to prove me wrong. Like I said, it worked."

Ben laughed. "Julie, you are full of surprises."

She smiled and took a small bite of her muffin. "I hope you'll come to Dallas one of these days for a visit. You and your brothers still have a family, you know?"

"Do Sam and Nick feel the same way?"

"I don't speak for my brothers, Ben. I'm here on my own. I understand they haven't always been supportive of you."

"Sam called me a pretentious little prick."

"Well, in his defense, you did get a little full of yourself for a while there."

Ben paused and looked at her. "Fair enough."

"I would like my girls to grow up knowing their cousins. *All* their cousins, even the gay ones. Please, consider it."

"Thanks, Julie. Of course we'll come for a visit. I don't know if it will happen before school starts, but definitely by Christmas."

Their lunch arrived and they spent the rest of the time catching up. Ben told her about his misguided idea to move them all to Manhattan, and Julie laughed out loud.

"Sorry," she said, taking a drink of iced tea. "I'm just trying to picture Quentin in New York City."

SOMETIMES at night, driven to distraction by the heat of a Texas summer, Ben would lie in bed and trace Travis's body in his mind. He ran his fingers across the strong pectoral muscles and down the flat stomach with the light coat of fur. He placed a hand on each of Travis's shoulders and felt his way down the slope of his biceps, his cool and pale skin. Ben pulled him into an embrace, allowing his hands to navigate the terrain of Travis's back side. He explored the way his lats tapered into a perfect V, the hollow space at the small of his back, and the round lift of his ass. If he backed up and looked down, he could see Travis's cock jutting out. If he did that, Ben could feel his own erection start to stir. And that was how he jacked off most nights—dreaming of Travis.

CADE played baseball all summer long, both Little League and pickup games at the intramural fields. Like Travis, Cade embraced being a Texan. A typical Austin summer day of 105 degrees barely affected him. Of all his brothers, he seemed to require the least amount of attention. One night in early August, as they drove home from another winning game, Cade told Ben about his plan to play shortstop at UT. "I want it more than anything in the world, but I can't believe it's so far away."

"Don't rush it, squirt. How are you doing these days?"

"I'm good. How are you doing?"

Ben smiled.

"I'm good too. The bar exam is next week. It's...."

"Weird?"

"Yeah. Weird. Feels like a step backward, even though I know it's just a formality."

"You miss Travis?" Cade asked.

Ben made sure to look forward as he continued driving.

"Kind of. I guess. I haven't talked to him, so I'm not sure what's going on exactly. That part isn't much fun."

"Don't worry," Cade said. "I know for a fact it won't be long now."

"Have you talked to him?"

"No. But once the days start to get shorter, he'll head south. Besides, there's no way he would leave for good without saying good-bye to me. And since he didn't say good-bye to me, then he must not be gone for good. And he wrote it on the map. He's coming back, Ben. I'll bet you a hundred dollars."

"What is it with you boys and your gambling? But, okay, you're on. I just wish Labor Day would hurry up and get here."

AND finally, it did. The Walsh brothers began the weekend watching *The Vampire Diaries* on DVD. Quentin, of all people, had gotten them hooked, and by Saturday night, they found themselves fourteen hours into the first season. As the credits rolled on another episode, Ben's phone buzzed in his pocket. He pulled it out and looked at the screen. He didn't recognize the number and thought about letting it go to voice mail, but then decided it might be someone at the new firm.

Ben had taken the Texas Bar Exam in mid-August, and although he wouldn't get the results until late September, no one doubted that he had passed, including Ben himself. Over the summer, once word got around about Ben's move to Austin (the doings of Russ Hardwick), all the top firms started to call him. The Wilson & Mead name cast a long shadow across the country, and every major firm in Austin had made Ben an offer. He planned to give his answer by mid-September, but Ben's mind was pretty much made up.

He stepped into the kitchen and answered the call.

"Ben Walsh."

"Ben, this is Chad Young. My brother tells me you're not returning his calls."

"Hello, Mr. Young."

Chad Young, one of the founding partners of Shackelford, Young, and Young, the number-two law firm in Austin, took his phone off speaker. "Please, call me Chad."

"Okay, Chad. I told your brother I've decided to go with Harrison & Pope." Ben was referring to the number-one law firm in Austin. In the end, Ben wanted to go with the best. Not to mention that Chad Young's brother, Howard, had been put in charge of SY2's recruiting effort, a big mistake on their part. No doubt a capable lawyer, Howard Young specialized in contract law, an area that bored Ben to tears. It didn't help matters that Howard had zero charisma. During a dinner at TRIO inside The Four Seasons, Ben struggled to keep up both sides of the conversation. Still, he'd listen to what Chad had to say. The game, after all, was still on.

"Have you signed any papers yet?" Chad Young asked.

"No, not yet, but...."

"I'll tell you what, Ben. Me and my wife are having a Labor Day picnic on Monday for everyone at the firm. It's at our house in Westlake. We've got a pool, tennis courts, horseback riding, fireworks. Tons of good food. Why don't you bring your brothers out and have a good time? No obligation, except maybe listen to what I have to say. After that, if you still decide to go with the other guys, then you won't hear from us again. What do you say?"

Ben couldn't think of a good reason to say no and figured the boys would probably get a kick out of it. "Okay, sure. Can you text me the address and the time? We'll see you on Monday."

Ben ended the call. He smiled and remembered this from when he finished law school—firms wining and dining him, trying to outdo the competition with their perks. Sounded like Chad Young planned to give it his best shot. He returned to the living room and asked his brothers if they were up for the Labor Day picnic. They displayed varying degrees of enthusiasm over the plan, but all agreed it sounded like a good time.

"Where is it?" Cade asked.

"Westlake."

"Hanging with the rich kids," Quentin said, with more than a little snark.

"Hey," Ben insisted. "There's nothing wrong with learning how to hang with rich kids. Bring a good dose of irony and you'll be fine. And bring Dakota too. She makes us look good." Chad's invitation hadn't included additional guests, but Ben wanted to see his reaction if he showed up with a couple of extra people. "Jason, you should invite Jake as well. He'll fit right in." Ben stopped to think for a moment. "In fact, let's invite all three of the McAlisters. Dan should be there if I decide to take their offer."

"I'll text him right now," Jason replied.

"Does the butt-kissing stop once you take the job?" Quentin asked.

Ben laughed. "You'd better believe it does. So enjoy it now, while it lasts."

They went back to watching the Stefan-Elena-Damon love triangle as Ben did a quick survey of his brothers. He smiled as he realized they had come a long way since the aftermath of that unfortunate trip to New York last spring. Ben had gotten his shit together and was ready for Travis to come home.

When Monday arrived, they all (Dakota included) piled into their dad's enormous pickup truck and headed to Westlake. They stopped by the McAlisters' so Jake and his parents could follow and arrive at the same time. Over the summer, Ben and Dan had lunch together several times, and Ben thought of him as one of those rare finds in the law profession—someone he might be able to trust. When they arrived at the picnic, the guests mingled on the huge green lawn amongst an immense spread of food and fun. If Chad Young had splurged on a real roller coaster it could have rivaled Six Flags.

"Ben!" Chad called, raising his hand and motioning him over. Ben had only met him once before and then only in passing.

"Chad, thanks for the invitation. This is impressive."

"Thank you. I want you to meet my wife, Emily."

Ben introduced his brothers, then Dakota, then Jake and his parents.

"Chad, have you ever met Dan McAlister?"

"No, nice to meet you. How do you know Ben?"

"His brother is dating my son," he answered.

Chad didn't miss a beat. "And that's how we know we're in the twenty-first century. I'm glad you could all make it out here. I told Emily that if I throw a party, I want a lot of people here. So, welcome."

Everyone slowly wandered off and seemed, to Ben, at least, to enjoy the afternoon. Cade headed toward the horseback riding immediately. Quentin and Dakota spent most of the day by the pool, keeping to themselves at first but eventually getting pulled into a conversation with a group of students from Westlake High School. Jason and Jake played a game of tennis and then cooled off next to the pool as well. From where Ben sat, it looked like Jake had introduced Jason to several of his friends from school.

After a couple of hours, Chad asked Ben if they could go into the house and talk. Inside, the place reflected Chad Young's wealth and status, but as Ben had grown accustomed to Mead-style money, this place didn't quite measure up in the details. Emily Young should have opted for an original piece, even a minor work, instead of the copy of *The Starry Night* hanging in the front hallway. Chad led them into a study/library, where Ben immediately recognized Howard Young and another man, who turned out to be Barry Shackelford. The four men sat in plush chairs reminiscent of an old-style gentlemen's club.

Ben began. "Thank you, Chad, for inviting me and my family out here this afternoon. It's been a real treat, I have to say. But I also don't want to waste your time, because—"

Chad Young interrupted him.

"Do you mind if I say something?"

Ben forced a smile. He didn't like people who couldn't take no for an answer.

"Of course."

"I didn't invite you all the way out here to blow smoke up your ass, Ben. And I apologize for not being a part of this process sooner, but our mother has been sick and my dad needed some help, so I had to take some time off. I've done my homework. I know you're used to being the best and working for the best. You're going with Harrison & Pope because they're the best in town. I'm not going to tell you otherwise. But I am going to tell you that they're not the best *fit*. For you. And before you say anything, let me tell you why.

"I know that you and Colin Mead are going to start your own firm in ten years. I may be off on the timeline by a year or two, but I recognize two people who are meant to be partners someday. And I know by that look on your face and lack of denial that I'm right. Now, if I had to guess, I'd say you haven't told anyone at Harrison & Pope about this plan. And I'm not saying you should. But what if I told you that I wanted to help you, as long as you help us take on Harrison & Pope?"

"How?"

"Come practice law with us. We need someone to raise our profile. To win in court. That's what attracts clients."

"But that's not all," added Barry Shackelford.

"No," Chad continued, "it's not. We want you to head up our recruitment next year. We want you to go after the Ivy League and Stanford."

Ben shook his head. "That's unrealistic."

"It isn't if you're doing the talking. Austin has a lot to offer. People want to be where you are, Ben. You're young, good-looking, charismatic—you're a winner. And you're one of them. I'm not expecting an Ivy avalanche. One a year, maybe. You have, what, five or six years before your youngest is out of high school?"

"Six, at least. Cade will probably want to go to UT, so probably more like ten. I'm missing the hook here, though. Sorry to be blunt, Chad, but what's in it for me?"

"Don't apologize, Ben. I like blunt. So here it is—give us ten years and help SY2 become the number-one firm in the city, and I will contribute one million dollars to help get Mead & Walsh off the ground."

Ben sat up in his chair and took a deep breath.

"Walsh & Mead."

Chad smiled. "Of course. We both know your friend Colin will have no problem raising the money, but you don't want to come to the table empty-handed. This way you don't have to."

"Why would you do that for me?"

"I'm not a philanthropist, Ben. What I'm doing for you, I'm doing for us. We're lawyers and we want to win. We're tired of playing second fiddle in this town, and we're willing to pay good money to anyone who can help us change that."

"We do have one condition, though," Barry said.

"What's that?" Ben asked.

"When you leave," Howard explained, "everyone you've recruited for us stays with us. We're cleaning house and rebuilding our firm from the ground up. It's a huge risk for us, so no poaching."

Ben paused.

"My brothers have to come first. You realize that, don't you?"

"We feel the same way about our families. Think about your future, Ben. Think of how much fun you'll have helping us become number one instead of sitting up in the castle being number one. Think about one million dollars for you when it's all over. We all get something we want out of this. We are the best fit for you."

Ben could see that. "I have one more thing."

"Shoot," Chad said.

"I want to bring Dan McAlister with me. He works on his own right now and makes a good living, but I need someone like him, someone I trust, to be successful. And I'm not just saying that because his son is dating my brother. If you're asking me to rebuild your firm, that's where I want to start."

"Consider it done. If you have an assistant you liked in New York, we can relocate him or her as well."

"I might take you up on that. One of the paralegals at Wilson & Mead. She would be a real asset if I could talk her into it, but if I try to poach any of their real talent, I won't get invited to Thanksgiving. And that's something I don't intend to miss."

"I've heard about it," Chad admitted.

They chatted some more and then stood and shook on the deal. They would work out the details later. When Ben returned to the yard for the fireworks, he pulled Dan aside and gave him the news.

"Are you shitting me?" he cried. He wrapped his arms around Ben and hugged him hard. Ben extracted himself as gently as he could, excited to see Dan so happy. "This is absolutely like a dream come true. And I'd be working for you?"

"Technically, yes. But think of it as working with me. And don't thank me yet. This is an opportunity. We both have to deliver now."

"Sarah's going to absolutely flip. Everyone's over here, let's go tell them."

Ben followed him over to a large blanket where his clan had set up camp, waiting for the fireworks to begin. Sarah kissed her husband when she heard the news, and Jake kissed Jason in front of everyone for the first time.

Cade expressed his gratitude that Ben finally had a job. "I was starting to get worried about you, bro."

As the fireworks began to explode over their heads, Ben became increasingly uneasy. The summer had officially ended, and Travis could realistically show up tomorrow. And if not tomorrow, then the next day, or the day after that, until in Ben's mind the future kept rolling out in front of him, still as untamed and uncertain as ever. Ben understood that the wait hadn't ended. On the contrary, Labor Day meant it had only just begun.

SIXTEEN

ON THE first day of October, when Ben started his new job at Shackelford, Young, and Young, Travis still had yet to materialize. At that point, Ben didn't have much time to dwell on it. The addition of work to his family life stretched his time razor-thin. Still, when he lay in bed at night, he sometimes jumped up if he saw headlights flash across the front windows, thinking it might be him pulling up in a taxi he caught from the airport, having nowhere else to go and no one else he wanted to be with. He would come here, and Ben would kiss him, and everything would make sense again. Other times, though, Ben crawled into bed and slept straight through the night without thinking about Travis at all.

One Monday in mid-October, he got a text from Quentin.

He's here.

Ben felt the blood drain from his face. He looked at the time stamp. Four thirty in the afternoon. He and Dan were going over some evidence files at work.

"What's wrong?" Dan asked.

Ben paused for a second, then said, "Nothing. I need to go home. Can you wade through the rest of this?"

"Absolutely. You're not going to tell me what's going on, though?"

"A guy. Someone I dated last spring. He's back."

"Is this a good thing or a bad thing?"

Ben considered the question. "I'll let you know as soon as I find out."

Ben drove home, trying to stay calm along the way. When he pulled up to the house and parked the truck, he prepared himself for whatever waited on the other side of the door. When he went inside, his brothers were sitting in the living room. Ben saw someone with his back to him. His red hair had grown out over the months, falling down and covering his neck. He wore a white, long-sleeved thermal pullover with a black T-shirt over it. He shifted his head and Ben recognized the smile.

Stay cool, he told himself.

"Look who's here!" Cade announced as he walked up to Ben with his hand held out.

"I'll get you your money later, squirt."

Travis stood up and turned around.

"Howdy," he said.

"Hey there," Ben replied.

Quentin and Jason grabbed Cade and tried to hightail it out of the living room.

"Let go of me," Cade protested.

"We're making ourselves scarce, you moron."

"Quentin," Ben warned.

"Sorry. You're not a moron. Now let's go."

They disappeared from the living room. Ben couldn't stop staring at Travis. He looked more mature somehow, and incredibly sexy with his long hair. He looked like a man reborn.

"I lose a lot of money betting against you, Atwood."

"Maybe you should stop, then."

Ben saw something poking out from underneath his shirts. "Is that a nipple ring?"

Travis grinned. "Yep. At first it hurt like hell, but now I think it's kind of hot."

Ben swallowed. His mouth was dry. He took a long pause before he finally said, his voice breaking slightly, "You left."

"Yeah, I… I know. And you didn't go to New York."

"No. It turns out there was a big, twenty-five-year string attached to the check they were writing."

Travis looked him in the eye, his gaze steady.

"I'm sorry I left that way, Ben, but you did call a time-out and I needed some space."

"But now you're back. You came back."

"The boys told me you got my message."

"Yes, I did. Cade had to explain it to me. I can't believe you're actually here."

"For a little while, at least."

Ben felt something break inside. "You're not staying?"

"I don't know yet. I got another job offer. This one's in the South Pacific. Another six months. That takes off from LA in about ten days."

"Oh," Ben said.

He didn't know what else to say. Two minutes into the conversation, and Travis had already disappointed him. Did he want to know any more? Did he want to say, "Have a nice life" and walk away now?

He didn't do that.

"What were you up to in Alaska?"

"I worked for a research team from the Berkeley science department. We were stationed in Barrow. Doing studies of the ice caps. I was their engine man. Three boats and a ship."

"I didn't know you worked with boats."

"I learned on tankers when I was in the Gulf. That's how I got the job. I've worked in a lot of engine rooms. I told you, I can fix anything."

"Do you need a place to stay?" Ben asked, but he regretted it as soon as it came out of his mouth.

"No," Travis answered. "I don't think that would be a good idea. I'm staying with Darrell. He has a house over in the Berkman area with three extra bedrooms. But I would like to see the boys while I'm here. If that's okay with you."

"Of course it's okay. Can you see how much they've grown in just six months? Jason has a boyfriend."

"He told me what you did with the sailing lessons. Nice move, Obi-Wan."

Ben died a little inside when he heard his nickname, but kept it together. "Can you stay for dinner?" he asked.

"Not tonight. I have plans with the boys from the shop. Let me give you my number. You know me and my disposable phones—this one's almost empty." He read out the number to Ben, who programmed it into his iPhone. "I'm free tomorrow night, if that works."

"Yeah," Ben confirmed. "Tomorrow night works great. Just come by anytime after four, they'll be here. I usually get home around seven."

"You work late."

"I have a lot of expectations to live up to."

"I bet. Well, I'll be seeing you tomorrow, then."

Travis walked up to Ben and threw his arms around him, but as Ben started to respond, he pulled away and flew out the front door.

"Shit," Ben muttered. "What in the fuck am I doing wrong?"

THE next day at work, Ben found it difficult to focus. Dan, of course, wanted to know what had happened, and Ben gave him a relatively accurate account of the reunion.

"And then he hugged me and ran out the door. I wasn't sure if I missed something or not. What do you think?"

"I think it sounds like he's here for ten days and then he's gone."

"But he said he had a job offer. He didn't say he'd accepted it."

"Don't dissect the conversation like it's an episode of *CSI*. Besides, it sounds like a good offer. You should absolutely encourage him to take it."

"But…."

"He's the one who left, right?"

"Yeah," Ben grunted, knowing full well that his reply omitted an important detail. He had pushed Travis away. He had no one to blame but himself.

"You've lived without him for how long?"

"Six months."

"Don't sweat it. You're both halfway out the door already. Make a graceful exit and move on."

Ben shook his head, laughing. "Do you know you give the worst relationship advice ever? Halfway out the door? You're supposed to tell people to stay together, not encourage them to send their soul mate halfway across the globe."

Now Dan laughed. "Soul mate? Well, you're probably right. I'm not equipped for this. I'm not equipped for a lot of things. I absolutely did not expect my fifteen-year-old son to tell me he's gay."

"Is that a problem?"

"Of course not. You know better than that. I'm talking about my shortcomings, not his."

"That's crazy."

"What do I know about being gay? What kind of advice will I be able to give him? I'm wishing now I actually had fooled around with a guy in college, just so I'd have something to go on. I'm not equipped, and it scares me sometimes. Another reason I'm glad you came along. But I'll tell you one thing. This guy Travis has you rattled. I'm used to seeing you in control of a situation and, frankly, I like that Ben Walsh better. So send him on his way and let's get back to the real you."

BEN left the office a little early that evening and arrived back at the house a few minutes before seven. He found Travis and his brothers in the living room, finishing up a screening of *50 First Dates* (another Walsh brothers favorite). When the movie ended, they filed into the kitchen to discuss dinner options. Jason wanted to go to Hyde Park Bar & Grill but Cade wanted chicken tacos from Julio's. Ben voted Hyde Park and Quentin voted Julio's. Travis would normally cast the deciding vote, but this time he went for a coin toss instead. Cade won, and they headed out for some Tex-Mex.

Sitting next to Travis only tempted Ben to run his fingers through his long red hair—a temptation he resisted. Cade wanted to hear every detail of his time in Alaska. Travis told them about all the characters on the research team, but especially about Tami and Gretchen, the lesbian couple with whom he spent most of his free time. He talked about the continual daylight as if it were a religious experience.

"And it never went down?" Cade asked. "The sun, I mean."

"Nope. For two and a half months, it was always daylight. I'd sometimes take the smaller boat out by myself at three in the morning, which was the closest you got to dusk."

"How did you sleep?" Quentin asked.

"A good set of blackout curtains."

They stayed and listened to Travis tell his stories until almost ten o'clock. When they finally left and returned to the house, the boys excused themselves and disappeared into their rooms.

"Why don't we go out back?" Travis suggested. "Sit outside on the lawn chairs."

"I don't have a joint on me."

"We don't need that anymore. Come on, I want to hear about your summer."

They went outside and sat under the open sky, like they had on Christmas Eve some ten months ago.

"What happened to you?" Ben asked.

"What do you mean?"

"You're... changed. More sure of yourself. Travis 2.0."

"I had a very productive summer," Travis said, smiling. "I read a lot of books. I found out who James Joyce is. And Manet. And Dan Savage. Gretchen was in charge of my *education des beaux arts*, as she called it, and she butchered the pronunciation even worse than me. She reprogrammed my iPod every day with new music and then we talked about it at dinner. I should show you the flash cards she made for me. You'd get a kick out of 'em."

"What kind of flash cards?"

"All of the one hundred greatest books and who wrote them. Paintings with the artist and period on the back. I even know what baroque music is."

"Why would she do that?"

"Because we got drunk one night, me and Gretchen and Tami, and I told them all about you and my inferiority complex. And the fact that I didn't know a goddamned thing about the world and how pissed off I was about that. I told them about the dinner party at Colin's. Gretchen was like, 'That's hogwash! No one's read everything.' But then the next day she asked if I wanted to fill in some of the large gaps between my ears and I said, yes, please. I've even listened to the original cast recording of *Follies*. I had 'Losing My Mind' on repeat for a solid week. Martin was right. It is the single greatest song about heartache I've ever heard."

Ben paused. "You didn't have to do all that."

"I didn't do it for you."

"Did you meet anyone?"

"You mean dating-wise? No, it wasn't that kind of summer. Did you?"

"No," Ben said, shaking his head emphatically. "I studied for the bar exam, mostly."

"Which I'm sure you passed."

"Yes. I got the results a few days ago."

Neither of them spoke for a minute. Ben looked over and smiled when he saw Travis gazing up at the stars. Travis turned his head and smiled back.

"So," Ben said. "Here we are."

"Here we are," Travis repeated. "You look good."

"So do you. I like the long hair."

"Thanks."

Ben took a breath. "Are we going to talk about it?"

"Us, you mean?" Travis answered.

"Yeah."

"What are you thinking?"

The question left Ben conflicted. On the one hand, of course, he loved Travis and wanted him to stay. But on the other, Dan had a point. This job provided Travis with the opportunity to do something with his life, and Ben should be encouraging that, not standing in the way. After hearing him talk at dinner about his time with the Berkeley crew, Ben knew that was where Travis belonged. He also knew he wouldn't wait another six months. The time had come to move on.

"It sounds like you have an amazing opportunity. Again. I think you should take it. We're not going to be young forever, Travis. This is the time of your life when you should be spending six months in Alaska and six months in the South Pacific. It so obviously agrees with you."

"But what about you and me?"

Ben shook his head.

"Our timing sucks. I'm sorry, but sometimes you can't fix that, no matter how good the sex is."

Travis laughed. "It was good, wasn't it?"

"Spectacular. But you have to do what's best for you, which is something I understand completely. That's what I did."

Travis kept his head facing forward so that Ben couldn't see his reaction.

"Even if it's not what's best for us?"

Ben paused for a moment. "Is there enough of us left to really matter? It's been six months, Travis." Ben felt like he was arguing a case he didn't believe in. Everything about Travis still mattered, but he was determined to stop being selfish.

"I know," Travis said. "I just thought… never mind. I reckon that answers the rest of my questions. It does feel like I'm doing something with my life, even though I'm just fixing engines."

"That's important, don't you think?"

"I guess so."

Out of the corner of his eye, Ben thought he saw Travis wipe a tear away. But he couldn't be sure.

"How was your summer?" asked Travis, changing the subject.

"Hot," Ben answered. "And dry. And long. It never rained. We spent most of our weekends down at the Springs. I've seen a couple of my friends from college. A lot of people come here for school and never leave. I've got everything running pretty smoothly with the boys now, so that's an accomplishment, I guess."

"How is Jason's new school?"

"Like night and day. He loves it. He's getting good grades, he's got a boyfriend. He's more successful than I am."

Travis laughed. "You still crack me up."

"I still crack you up."

"And your new job?"

"I like it. I made the right choice. As it turns out, I think my life may not completely suck after all."

"That's a huge step forward, Ben."

"I love how you see it that way."

He wanted to ask Travis to stay. He wanted to get down on his knees and beg him not to go away again. He wanted to be impulsive and romantic and all the things that had seemed lost to him when Travis disappeared, but then he remembered the last time he'd acted that way and the swollen lip he got for it.

"I do have a question," Ben said.

"What's that?"

"Obviously, you told Mrs. Wright to only give me the map if I was staying. So if we had moved, that would have been it? You never would have said good-bye?"

Travis looked away.

"I was lost, Ben, and saying good-bye wasn't really on my mind. If you were moving to New York and stopping by Mrs. Wright's place to say adios, I sure as hell didn't want her giving you a map that said, 'I'm coming back.' In that case, I wanted you to forget about me and move on."

"Okay. I get it."

"I hope so, because I didn't know what else to do. I just couldn't stay in Austin. I couldn't sit across the street day after day wondering when your time-out was gonna end."

Ben turned to him and tried to smile. "I'm sorry I fucked it up. You did the right thing. I didn't mean to make you feel like it was your... never mind, you did the right thing."

When Travis left that night, Ben almost leaned over to kiss him, but he didn't follow through on the impulse. Travis walked up to Ben and wrapped his arms around him again. This time, though, before he pulled away, Ben quickly caught him in an embrace. Travis didn't struggle, and they stood that way in the backyard for several moments. If Travis had lifted his head, it would have been all over. They would have started kissing and then, well, they both knew the way to the bedroom. But Travis didn't lift his head, and they didn't kiss.

Instead, he went back to Darrell's house like he had the night before.

OVER the next week, Travis came around almost every afternoon and Ben tried to get out of work early. Jason brought Jake over on the weekend to meet 'the mysterious Travis' (Jake's words), and Dakota joined them on Sunday for bowling. It felt like old times, except Travis never spent the night. Ben waited for a sign but Travis kept his distance, like he had become a guest again instead of a member of the family.

On Tuesday, Travis announced he had accepted the new job and had a plane ticket to LA on Thursday evening. Ben continued to steadfastly support his decision to take the offer, even though his heart broke underneath his good intentions. The following night, Travis came over to the house for dinner and to say good-bye. He told Cade he didn't know when he would be back in Austin, but he promised to check in more often by phone. He gave all three boys big hugs and then kept stalling as he stood on the front porch with Ben. They both squirmed, knowing it might be the last time.

"I'll see you later, Atwood."

Travis hesitated, biting down on his lower lip, until there was nothing left to say except, "Good-bye, Ben."

Then he got into his truck and drove away.

Ben felt blood rush from his face and the world receded into the same cavernous silence that had followed that fateful phone call from Father Davenport ten months ago. He went back into the house, where Quentin stood waiting for him, his arms akimbo.

"What's wrong with you, big brother?"

Ben rubbed his forehead. "What are you talking about?"

"Why didn't you ask him to stay?"

"Because. It's a great opportunity for him and I'm done being a selfish prick. I thought you'd approve."

"No, I don't approve. It's a great opportunity for somebody, but not for him. And it's not being selfish if it's what he wants. He was waiting for you to ask him, moron. To stay."

"No, he wasn't."

"*Yes, he was.* You're the one that tagged out, Ben, not him. And I get why you did it. Everyone does, even Travis. Someone slipped Jason some drugs, and in some misguided attempt to fix everything, you told the one person you needed the most to go away. Do you not even recognize when the ball is in your court?"

Ben didn't respond.

"Okay," Quentin said quietly, "I'll give you a little piece of intel. He doesn't want to go to the South Pacific."

"Then why didn't he say that?"

"Because he needs to hear you're ready for him. For real, this time. He needs to hear that you have your shit together and it's time for him to come home. I get it—you think you can't be a boyfriend and a parent at the same time. But that's bullshit. Being a boyfriend makes you a better parent. He's ready, you're ready—the timing is perfect."

"How do you know all this?"

"Because I pay attention. Sometimes you're too wrapped up in *The Ben Show* to notice what's going on right in front of your face. But I have your back."

"There's nothing I can do about it now. He went to Darrell's and tomorrow he'll be gone."

"Call him."

Ben took out his phone and made the call. "It's dead again. He's let it run out of minutes. And I don't know where Darrell lives. It's too late."

"It's not too late. He's going to be at the shop tomorrow afternoon. Darrell is taking him to the airport."

"What time?"

"After lunch. Please, Ben, be there. You're driving me nuts with all your moping around. You've got to fix this."

"Hey, Ben." It was Jason, coming down the stairs holding his phone out.

"What's going on?"

"It's Jake. He wants to talk to you."

Ben took the phone and put it to his ear. "Hello."

"Hi, Ben. It's Jake."

"Hi, Jake. What's up?"

"I heard my dad talking to my mom tonight. He was telling her what he told you, about encouraging Travis to take that job and go away again."

"Yeah?"

"Well, I probably shouldn't say this, but I don't agree with him at all. You could have encouraged Jason to do the same thing. With me, I mean. You could have told him to move on and forget about me, that I had acted like a jerk and didn't deserve another chance. But you didn't tell him that. You helped bring us together. I knew what you were doing with the sailing trip last spring."

"You did?"

"Please, it was so obvious. You think I've never seen *The Sting*? The whole thing was just your way of giving Jason and me another shot. I thought it was really cool that he had a brother who cared so much. Anyway, I think you should follow your own advice and not my dad's. Everyone deserves a second chance, Ben, especially you and Travis. I got a really good vibe from him. I think he's the one for you."

THE next day, Ben took the afternoon off from work and headed over to the shop around one in the afternoon. Darrell was helping another customer when he arrived.

"I'll be right with you, Ben."

Ben looked through the glass window into the shop. While Ed and Royce worked on vehicles hoisted over their heads, Topher looked over and waved at Ben, who waved back. Travis had nothing but good things to say about the men he worked with, and they had always treated Ben like one of the family.

"What can I do for you?" Darrell asked.

"Hi, Darrell," Ben said, offering his hand. "My brother told me you're taking Travis to the airport this afternoon."

"That's right. He's out running some errands but he should be back pretty soon. I think we're heading out around four. Can I give him a message?"

"Would you mind if I waited for him?"

"Not at all. You can call him if you'd like. He got a new phone this morning."

"No, I think this is something I need to do in person."

"I understand. There's coffee and some stale donuts in the back if you care for any. Help yourself."

"Thanks."

Darrell disappeared into the back office, and Ben took a chair in the waiting area. He grabbed the remote and flipped through a few channels on the television. When nothing caught his eye, he did some reading on his phone. Two hours passed. Ben could see into the shop and knew the men were talking about him. He had his head down and his ear buds in when Royce poked his head through the waiting room door.

"Psst! Ben!"

Ben looked up and took his ear buds out.

"He's here."

"Thanks, man."

"No problem," Royce whispered. "Good luck."

Ben stuffed his phone into his pocket and left the shop. He saw Travis standing outside the bays with two duffel bags at his feet. He watched as Travis talked to Ed, waving his hands around about something. Ed, who saw Ben coming up from behind, slapped Travis on the shoulder.

"Have a good trip, buddy. Ben, good to see you."

"You too, Ed."

Travis turned around and looked at him. "Did something happen?" he asked, slightly panicked. "To one of the boys?"

"No, everyone's fine."

Travis paused to process the information.

"Then what are you doing here?"

Ben looked at him.

"I came to ask you not to go."

"What?"

"I can explain, really. When we went to New York last spring and everything fell apart, I know I pulled away. I got swept up in my own forward momentum. But you didn't wait for me like you said you would."

"I did wait for you. I just did it in Alaska."

Ben put his hand to his forehead.

"I'm saying this all wrong. I just realized it sounds like a goddamned closing argument."

Travis laughed. "It's okay, Ben. Start over and say what you have to say. I promise not to interrupt no more."

"Okay," Ben said, taking a breath. "Whatever happened after New York, that was my fault. I got the outcome I asked for. But I said a lot of things on that plane ride back to Austin, things I regretted later, big-time. I thought you were a distraction. I thought I would be able to manage things better on my own. I was wrong about all that." Ben bit down on his lip to keep his emotions in check. He looked into Travis's eyes and saw tears welling up. "So I'm talking to Quentin last night after you left, and he's telling me I'm a moron, as usual. You came back and I never told you that I was wrong to push you away. I never told you that I have my shit together now and I'm ready to be with you. So here it is. *I was wrong and I'm ready.* Please, Travis, stay with me. You once told me there's nothing broken here that can't be fixed. But if you leave, I'll still be broken."

Travis stood in silence, tears streaming down his face.

"Please," Ben repeated. "I'm begging you. Come home and fix me."

Ed, Topher, and Royce watched and waited for him to answer. Darrell caught wind of the scene and came out to investigate. "What's going on here?" he asked. "Travis, everything okay?"

"It sure as hell is, Darrell," he answered, not taking his eyes off Ben. "What do you think I've been waiting for, Obi-Wan?"

"Did I get it right?"

"Fuck yes, you got it right. I didn't want to go to no godforsaken South Pacific. But you kept telling me to—"

"I was trying not to be—"

"Stop," Travis said, smiling. "Let me talk now. I spent most of my time in Alaska thinking about everything we been through, trying to sort it all out. Until I realized it's simple. You're it, Ben. Ever since the knees under the table."

"You mean…?"

"Yes. On New Year's Eve. I didn't mean for it to happen, but my knee just fit there naturally against yours. And that's when I knew. I broke up with Trisha that night."

Ben looked surprised. "But you told me…."

"I'm sorry I lied to you. I was scared, Ben. I didn't know what to say. All I knew was that I—"

"It doesn't matter."

"Are you ready for me to come back? For good this time?"

"I am way past ready. I have missed you so much I can't even begin to—"

Travis ran forward and threw his arms around Ben's neck. Their lips met, and Ben kissed him.

"Hey, Travis," Darrell called, grinning. "You need your old job back?"

SEVENTEEN

AFTER he called and told the Berkeley team that he wouldn't be joining them in the South Pacific, Travis went back to the Walsh house with Ben and they broke the news to the brothers. Everyone expressed their delight, but no one more than Cade, who had missed Travis something fierce.

"Are you gonna move in here?" he asked.

Travis looked at Ben, who did not hesitate.

"This is your home now. With us. Did you put all your stuff into storage?"

"Yeah," Travis answered. "Some place up on North Lamar."

"Then we'll go get everything this weekend."

TWO days later, Travis fell asleep on one of the sofas after a long day of moving boxes. He stretched out on his side in blue jeans and a brown *Keep Austin Weird* T-shirt, his head resting on the sofa's arm. He stretched his right leg out, his left knee bent and tucked toward his body so that he could lie half on his side and half on his stomach, his arms crossed in front of him. His boots and socks sat bundled together on the floor. Ben watched him from the hallway. It was Saturday afternoon and his brothers had left for the day. Ben couldn't hear a sound except the din of freeway traffic that played on a continuous loop in the background. He crossed to the sofa and sat down. Ben lifted

Travis's bare foot and gently laid it down on his lap, nestling it into the crotch of his blue jeans. He put his right hand on Travis's back, circling with his fingers, and with his other hand, he reached up into Travis's jeans to caress his leg. He moved down and rubbed Travis's foot and then worked his hand back up the length of his calf and thigh, bringing it to rest on Travis's denim-covered ass. He ran his fingers up and down Travis's leg and then hooked them into the back pocket of his jeans.

Travis began to stir under his touch, rubbing his foot against Ben's stomach. Ben dipped his head and kissed Travis's ass, moving up kiss by kiss to the small of his back and rubbing his forehead there, inhaling the smell of his shirt. Everything that was good about them returned. His hands moved further up Travis's back, massaging the sore muscles underneath cotton as he went. Travis reached around and pulled Ben closer, grabbing a fistful of his T-shirt.

They had managed to put off sex for two days because Travis wanted to get STD screens. "Look," he told Ben, "I haven't had sex with anyone but you. Not since Trisha and I broke up."

"And I haven't had sex with anyone but you. Not since David and I broke up."

"Then if all our tests come back negative, I want to get rid of the condoms."

"That means you must trust me."

Travis didn't hesitate. "With my life."

That morning, they'd called the special twenty-four-hour number for test results. As expected, everything came back negative.

Ben reached around and rubbed Travis's chest. Travis traced his fingers up Ben's body and along his arm until he joined his own hand with Ben's, intertwining their fingers. Their bodies contracted together into a sinewy embrace. Ben loved the feeling of Travis underneath him as he scooted up, bearing his full weight down. He moved a lock of Travis's hair and nuzzled against the nape of his neck, nibbling on his ear lobe. Travis grunted audibly as Ben started to grind against him. Again, Travis reached back to pull Ben closer, more completely on top of him. He pushed his ass into the air to increase the friction against Ben's hardening cock, still trapped inside his Levi's. Ben touched

Travis's chin and turned his head toward him. God, how he'd missed this. He kissed him—joyful and sorrowful and glorious.

For the first time since his parents' death, Ben saw clear waters.

"I'm glad you're moving in," he said into Travis's ear.

"Are you sure about this?"

"I'm sure. We've earned it, don't you think?"

They kissed again and Travis moved onto his back and ran his fingers through Ben's hair. Ben reached down and undid the fly of Travis's blue jeans. He had to stop kissing Travis for a second so that he could focus on his task. Once Ben got his pants open, he grabbed Travis's thick cock through the moist gray fabric of his briefs. He used rough strokes and returned to Travis's lips. Travis undid Ben's belt and opened up his fly, wrapping his hand around the bulge inside his boxers.

"I missed this."

"And it has missed you too."

Travis laughed.

"Oh," Ben said, "you weren't talking about my dick?"

"Nu-uh, I was. You just crack me up."

"Still?"

"Still."

The head of Travis's dick appeared at the edge of his underwear. Ben pulled the briefs back and revealed his prize in all its rigid glory. He stared at it, mesmerized. Travis pulled Ben's dick through the fly of his boxers. They stroked each other and kissed again, deeper this time. Cocks, lips, hands, tongues, bodies—Ben wanted it all at once. They lay on the sofa and made out for a long time, their jeans pushed open like two teenagers going to second base, their hard cocks jutting out into their hands. Ben pushed Travis's jeans down, cupped his balls, and then ran his fingertips along the inside of his thighs. They continued making out as Ben rose to his knees. Travis reached up and peeled Ben's shirt off before removing his own. Ben slid to the floor, pulling on Travis's jeans and turning them inside out as he ripped them off. Travis sat up on the sofa, completely naked, with Ben kneeling on the floor between his legs. Still in his blue jeans, Ben leaned forward and licked Travis's nut sac, darting his tongue over the smooth skin, then up and down the shaft, up and down again. He looked at Travis as he teased his cock.

"What you grinning at?" Travis asked.

"You."

Ben lifted his balls and licked the musky skin underneath. Up and down, back and forth, shaft then balls. Ben licked the sensitive head, which made Travis thrust his hips into the air. He hooked two fingers around the base of Travis's cock and pulled it down. He put the head into his mouth and shook it back and forth across his open lips. Then he bobbed his head and took the entire cock into his mouth at once. As Ben enthusiastically continued, Travis sat back and closed his eyes, tugging gently on the ring in his right nipple.

After a lengthy blow job, Ben stood up and pushed his jeans and boxers to the floor, discarding them with a toss of his foot. Travis stretched out on the couch, looking up at him.

"Come here."

Ben lay down on top of him, pushing his cock into the space between Travis's legs. Ben kissed his neck and pulled him in close. The heat from their bodies created enough sweat that they slid easily against each other. Ben inched his way forward and up, until he was bent on one knee, straddling Travis's chest. He grabbed Travis by his long hair and fed him his cock. Travis unleashed his hunger. He made no attempt to hide how much he loved sucking Ben's dick as he reached down and stroked his own thick hard-on. Ben withdrew from Travis's mouth and looked down at him.

"I love you, Atwood. You know that, right?"

"I love you too, Obi-Wan. Now lay back and let me suck your cock."

Ben sat back and stretched out against the opposite end of the sofa. Travis flipped around so that Ben could cradle him between his legs. He wrapped his fingers around the base of Ben's cock and started sucking. Ben reached down and ran his fingers through Travis's hair, occasionally taking control and forcing him to bob up and down, sometimes slower, sometimes faster. After sucking furiously for several minutes, Travis lifted up and hovered over Ben, his eyes and smile wild, saying,

"The earth is flat."

Ben looked at him, puzzled.

"Okay...."

"The earth is flat."

"What is this?"

"Come on," Travis teased. "Aren't you Mr. Pad and Pencil? Let's play a game."

Ben considered his options and decided he could handle himself just fine.

"Okay, let's play." He paused. "But in that case, the earth is not flat. It's round."

Travis accepted the response and dropped his head, taking Ben's cock back into his mouth. He sucked and stroked him toward the edge of climax. As Ben started to signal his proximity to orgasm, Travis pulled his mouth away, though he continued to stroke Ben's cock. Once again, he said, "The earth is flat."

"No," Ben responded. "The earth is round."

Travis put Ben's dick into his mouth again, twirling his tongue around as he pushed the head to the back of his throat. It got stuck there for a moment, struggling against Travis's gag reflex, and then finally pushed past like a barreling rod. Ben restrained himself for a few seconds, but eventually he grabbed Travis by the back of the head and started fucking his throat. As he was about to come, Travis pulled away again.

"Fuck!" Ben protested. "This is not fair."

Travis looked up into his eyes, his lips glistening. "The earth is flat."

"What is this game?" Ben yelled. "The earth is fucking round."

Travis went down on him yet again, slowing down this time, teasing, edging, sucking Ben's cock into his mouth in long strokes.

Finally, he pushed it deep into his throat again and kept it there until tears welled up in his eyes. Ben had reached his limit. Six months he'd gone without sex. He rammed his cock against the back of Travis's throat, suppressing his moans so that maybe he could come unannounced. Travis knew all his tells, though, and as Ben got close, Travis pinned his wrists to his side and pulled away a third time. His eyes flashed like a mad man, wet and frantic. Again, he growled, "The earth is flat."

"What do you want from me?" Ben cried in frustration. "Please, just let me come."

"The earth is flat."

A ferocity passed through Ben that started in his stomach, rose up through his throat, and then shot out of his eyes like a laser beam.

"Suck my cock!" he demanded playfully, laughing.

Travis grinned but didn't comply. He continued to stroke the tip of Ben's erection, edging him further into distractedness. "The earth is flat."

"Please," Ben pleaded, trying to retain control of his sanity. But his flesh had reached the breaking point and he gave up, collapsing onto his back. "Okay," he whimpered. "Uncle. The earth is flat. The earth is fucking flat."

"I love you," Travis said.

"Then get me off," Ben begged.

Travis lifted Ben's legs, raising them into the air. He pushed Ben's knees to his ears and licked at his ass crack. Ben moaned as Travis moved up to kiss him.

"So," Travis said. "Here we are."

"Here we are."

"We belong together," Travis continued.

"We belong together," Ben repeated.

"The earth is flat."

"The earth is flat."

"I want you to fuck me."

"I want you to…." Ben hesitated, but only for a moment. "… fuck me. I want you to fuck me."

Travis buried his face in Ben's butt, rimming his hole with enthusiasm. The tongue work sent shivers through Ben's body as he lifted his legs higher. Travis moved up and kissed him again, intertwining their hands and breath, pressing Ben's knees to his chest.

"You promise to never push me out of your life again?"

"Yes," Ben answered.

"No matter what comes our way?"

"I promise. Cross my heart and hope to…."

Ben nuzzled his face against Travis's stubble, knowing full well what he had just agreed to.

Unconditional surrender.

The tip of Travis's cock sat poised at his asshole. Travis spit on his hand and slicked himself up, pushing slightly against Ben's sphincter. At first Ben resisted, but then Travis kissed him again and he opened up.

"Count to eight," Travis instructed.

"One, two…."

As he counted, Ben said good-bye to everything he thought he knew about sex and love. Travis entered him and he allowed it, wanted it, even. Travis had brought him so close to the edge of orgasm that the base of his spine tingled as he inched his cock into Ben's now inviting ass.

"… seven, eight."

"Does it hurt?"

"Nu-uh," answered Ben.

Travis began to fuck him, and once that started, it became clear they weren't going to last long. Ben pulled Travis close and whispered into his ear, "You're the only man to ever fuck me without a condom. To ever come inside me."

The very notion sent a shock wave through their body, considering they now felt more singular than plural. Travis quickened his pace.

"Do it," Ben pleaded, his eyes rolling back into his head.

A few moments later Travis reared up like a mustang as his cock swelled and exploded. He opened his mouth in a silent scream as Ben reached down and stroked his own hard cock, shooting thick sprays of come across his chest and stomach. Travis collapsed on top of him, trembling and gasping. Their lips met and they rubbed their faces together.

"See?" Travis said. "I told you. The earth is flat."

"Yes," Ben agreed, pulling Travis into him. "The earth is definitely flat."

EIGHTEEN

AFTER he moved in, Travis blended seamlessly back into their lives. One night, Ben realized he needed to move fast if he wanted to include Travis in their plans for Thanksgiving. Colin had been urging Ben to bring his brothers back to Manhattan and give it another chance, if for no other reason than to get rid of the stink from the last trip. Since Ben had no intention of missing Thanksgiving with the Meads, he'd bought plane tickets for himself and his brothers back in August.

"Do you want to go?" Ben asked him, chopping vegetables for a salad. Ben enjoyed being Travis's sous-chef.

"Come on, Ben. What do you think?"

"I don't know. You hated it last time."

Travis shook his head. "Things are different now. Do you think I want to stay here and spend Thanksgiving alone when my family is up in New York?"

"But Colin is having another dinner party on Friday night."

"And I'll be fine and dandy," Travis assured him. "Unless you don't want me to—"

"Never mind," Ben said, cutting him off. "I'm calling the airline now to see if they can change our seats around when I add you. And we'll need to get you a tux as well."

"Seriously?"

"The old man hosts Thanksgiving dinner at the St. Regis. It's formal. The boys already have theirs."

"The old man?"

"Joseph Mead, Colin's grandfather. It's a big shindig."

Jason came into the kitchen as Ben got on the phone to the airline. "What's for dinner?" he asked.

"Chicken-fried steak," Travis answered.

"You didn't get the grisly stuff, did you?"

Travis chuckled. "No, Jason, I specifically did not get the grisly stuff."

Ben put his phone on speaker, filling the kitchen with canned elevator music. "I'm on hold."

Quentin and Cade came in from the living room.

"Smells good," Quentin said.

"Who are you on hold with?" asked Jason.

"The airline. I have to get a ticket for Travis. For Thanksgiving."

"If boyfriends are invited, can Jake come too?"

"No," Ben answered.

"Why not?"

"Because, we can't treat the Mead house like our own personal bed and breakfast."

"Mrs. Mead loves it when the house is full," Cade said.

"How do you know that?" Ben asked.

"She told me. She told me lots of stuff when I was sick. Did you know she has nine brothers and sisters? They live in White River, South Dakota. I only remember that because it reminds me of Red River. Did you know their house has fifteen bedrooms? She told me it has that many so that her whole family could come visit at once. But her family never comes to visit. They told her they don't fit into her world. So now it's just the two of them and fifteen bedrooms."

"She doesn't come from money?" Travis asked Ben.

"No," he replied, shaking his head. "She's salt of the earth. She went to USD on scholarship and then moved to Chicago to work at some real-estate firm. That's where she met Carl."

"I'll call and ask her," Cade volunteered.

"No," Ben insisted. "I'm sure Dan and Sarah want Jake at home for Thanksgiving."

"They can go too," Jason said, as if he had a solution to everything.

"Don't be ridiculous," Ben scoffed.

"If Jake goes, I get to invite Dakota."

"Think about it," Jason continued. "Sarah McAlister will think she's died and gone to heaven if you invite her to the Mead Thanksgiving at the St. Regis."

Ben smiled. "She would like it, wouldn't she?"

"They're practically in-laws at this point," conceded Quentin. Which was true. Since Ben and Dan started to work together, the two families had grown quite close.

"Okay, I'll call Mrs. Mead, but I'm dropping your name, Cade."

"SIR, could you put your tray table up, please?"

Travis returned it to the upright and locked position. The flight attendant continued down the aisle.

"You always have to wait until the last possible minute, don't you?"

Travis leaned over and kissed his boyfriend. "I like the tray table down," he insisted. "I don't see why it much matters to them one way or the other."

Ben laughed. On the day before Thanksgiving, they had boarded a plane bound for New York.

All nine of them.

When they landed in Newark, all the bags came through without a hitch. It turned out Cade knew Norma Mead better than Ben did. Ben could feel her smile beaming through the phone when he asked about filling up her house for the holiday. Ben got Travis and Dakota onto their flight, but Jake and his parents were landing at LaGuardia a few hours later. Of course, the McAlisters had visited New York before, but never like this. Dan and Sarah, awestruck by the Mead brownstone, bent over backward to express their gratitude to Mr. and Mrs. Mead for their hospitality.

Jake sighed with relief when he arrived and saw Jason. "I hate flying," he said, taking Jason's hand and pressing their faces together in an Eskimo kiss. It always warmed Ben's heart when he saw them together. If Ben had played any part in turning Jason's life around, it would go down as one of the great accomplishments of his life.

Now that they had one stay under their belt, the brothers, more at ease without the pressure of a prospective move, treated the Meads like extended family. Mr. and Mrs. Mead continued to embrace the role of surrogate grandparents to the boys, especially Cade. Catherine flew home for the holiday and reconnected with Quentin and Jason. She promised Ben no funny business this time and even hooked Dakota up with an original Stella McCartney gown for Thanksgiving dinner.

Most importantly, the temperature held steady and the sky shone a brilliant blue.

ON THURSDAY evening, Ben finished up in the bathroom and headed back to check on Travis. When he entered their room in nothing but a towel, Travis was standing in front of the mirror in his tuxedo.

"Wow," Ben exclaimed.

At Ben's suggestion, Travis had bought himself a classic Armani tux, single button front, with a simple shirt and black bow tie, which Quentin explained, "Is just like tying your shoe."

"Do I look like a penguin?"

Ben grinned and stood behind him, bursting with pride.

"You look amazing," he said to Travis's reflection in the mirror. "Like a young, redheaded James Bond."

"I don't think so. I've seen every James Bond movie—none of them had long hair." He fidgeted from side to side. "The shoes aren't very comfortable."

"They're not supposed to be," Ben explained. "There's a certain amount of discomfort that comes with formal wear. But the way you look makes it all worthwhile."

Ben turned Travis around and kissed him. Travis instinctively reached out and undid Ben's towel, letting it drop to the floor.

"Do we have time for a blow job?" he asked as he massaged Ben's cock to full erection.

"We always have time for a blow job. Just don't get come on your shirt. We didn't bring a spare."

"I promise not to spill a drop," Travis said, grinning.

He pushed Ben back onto the bed and leaned over to swallow his stiff dick. He licked and sucked until Ben shot a substantial load down his throat. Ben never complained that Travis had brought his robust sex drive back with him from Alaska. Although that still meant Travis wanted to get fucked most of the time, Ben enjoyed bottoming more and more, and both of them could always make time for a quick blow job. Afterward, Ben got dressed and they went downstairs to the foyer, where they joined the rest of the group. Mr. Mead had ordered two limos to take them to the party. All the men looked dashing in their tuxedos and the women like they belonged on a red carpet.

"Prepare yourself," Ben said to his brothers as they poured out onto the street. "Your mind is about to be blown."

JOSEPH MEAD always hosted Thanksgiving dinner at the St. Regis hotel, one of the highlights of the year, for his family, friends, and law firm partners. The two-hundred-plus guests even included a few minor celebrities. Ben attended for the first time two years earlier and had never seen anything like it. The St. Regis, one of the finest five-star hotels in New York, dripped with luxury and sophistication. When Ben had called "the old man" to ask about bringing six extra guests, Joseph Mead responded with his usual graciousness.

"You're family, Ben. I always leave room for some last-minute additions. I was sorry to lose you to Texas, but I'm happy to hear you landed on your feet. And I'm looking forward to meeting your brothers. Colin speaks very highly of them."

When the limos arrived at Fifty-Fifth Street, their party made their way through the hotel lobby to the twentieth floor, known as The Roof. The room reminded Ben of something out of Versailles with its vaulted and cloud-dappled ceilings. Six large gilt and crystal chandeliers hung down in spectacular fashion and the drawn gold curtains revealed windows that provided a sweeping view of midtown Manhattan and Central Park. Round tables decorated with autumn-themed floral arrangements and long tapered candles took up much of the main space, while guests drank and mingled in the smaller penthouse before dinner.

As they exited the elevator, Ben saw Colin next to the bar, leaning against David and holding his hand. David spied them first and nudged his boyfriend, who turned around and then headed over to greet them, bringing David along with him.

"Good God, Walsh," he said cheerfully. "You travel with an entourage now?"

"What can I say? I'm a family man."

Jason stepped forward and threw his arms around Colin's waist and trapped him in a hug.

"Now that's what I call a hello," Colin said, wrapping his arms around Jason and kissing the top of his head. "Jake, are you taking good care of my nephew?"

"I think he mostly takes care of me, Colin."

David stepped forward and offered his hand to Travis. "It's good to see you again. I like the long hair."

Travis took his hand but then pulled David into an unexpected hug. "You and Colin, eh? Didn't see that coming."

"Life is full of surprises," David replied. "Cade, how are those Horns doing?"

"They kinda suck this year, but they're rebuilding."

David said hello to the rest of the gang and then turned to Ben. "It's good to see you again."

"You too," Ben agreed. "As always. Let me introduce you to Jake's parents. This is Sarah and Dan McAlister. Colin Mead and his boyfriend, David Foster."

"It's so nice to finally meet you," Sarah said, extending her hand. "I feel like I've stepped into a fairy tale. This hotel is remarkable."

"We absolutely do not have anything like this in Texas," Dan added, shaking hands with Colin and David in the process.

"I'm sorry I didn't get a chance to meet you when I was in Austin for Memorial Day," Colin said. "Your son is a natural with a sailboat. We'll have to get him out on the ocean one of these days."

Catherine grabbed Quentin and Dakota and took them over to meet a few of her cousins. As everyone finished up their greetings, Ben saw Travis staring across the room, his eyes wide with awe and disbelief.

"Good golly," he exclaimed. "Is that the Barefoot Contessa?"

Ben turned around and spotted Ina Garten from the Food Network. She and her husband lived in the Hamptons and were good friends with the Meads.

"You mean Ina," Colin said.

"I love her show," Travis replied. "I use her recipes all the time."

"Well, let's go meet her, then."

"No way."

"Yes way," Colin said, taking Travis by the arm and then escorting him across the room. Cade decided he wanted to meet her too and followed them. Jason and Jake went to check out the view while Dan and Sarah headed for the bar. That left Ben and David facing each other.

"You okay with this?" David asked. "Me and Colin, I mean?"

"Yes. It all came out in the wash, didn't it? I'm happy for you, David, really. I hope you guys will come down and visit us soon. My brothers are crazy about you both."

"We've already talked about a trip the week after Christmas."

"That would be perfect. I'm taking some time off and the boys will be out of school."

"You know that Colin isn't quite the same without you here. He's adapting, of course, but he's always saying, 'Ben would love this' or 'I wish Ben were here.' He misses you."

"I miss him too. I do have my hands full, though."

"How's all that going?"

"Really well. We still have our bad days, of course... me and three teenage boys. Do the math. But the worst is behind us. And now that Travis is back and living with us, it makes a huge difference. Especially with Cade. Travis is really his go-to big brother now. I'm just kind of the backup."

"I noticed he sticks close to his side."

"Yeah. I think he's afraid he'll disappear again if he doesn't keep an eye on him."

"It's a terrible age to lose your parents. Not like there's a good age, of course."

Ben heard a familiar voice call his name. He turned around to greet Joseph Mead. They shook hands, and Joseph patted Ben warmly on the arm.

"Where are those famous look-alike brothers I've heard so much about?"

"Let me gather them up for you, sir."

Ben excused himself and reconstituted his family so that they could all meet their host. Joseph Mead had been a widower for ten years, so he stood alone before the Walsh boys. The old man had the expected reaction when Ben introduced him to Quentin, Jason, and

Cade. "Remarkable resemblance." Joseph Mead had heard about Ben's brothers many times, but it wasn't until he heard their names one after the other that he put two and two together. "Benjy, Quentin, Jason, and Caddy. You're named after the Compson siblings in *The Sound and the Fury*."

"I'm not a girl, though," Cade protested.

"Dad had to do a little fudging there," Ben admitted.

"And I dare you to call him Benjy," Quentin said. "He hates that."

The St. Regis served a lavish traditional Thanksgiving menu with a few modern twists that Travis noticed but Ben didn't pay much attention to. Quentin, Dakota, Jason, and Jake sat at a table with Catherine and her cousins. Ben and Travis sat next to Colin and David, but Travis eventually asked Colin if he wanted to switch seats so he could talk to David about some culinary stuff. That left Ben and Colin to catch up for most of the evening, which Ben enjoyed immensely. He'd missed Colin more than he had realized.

"I didn't tell you about the balloon bonus in my contract with SY2."

Colin raised his eyebrows and looked at Ben over a forkful of turkey. "What kind of balloon bonus?"

"The best kind. My freedom and a million bucks for you and me to start our firm."

Colin choked. "What?"

"Ten years. Then I'll be free. The boys will all have graduated. Travis will be ready for a change of scenery. You can tell he's already starting to like it here."

Colin opened his mouth but no words came out. He put down his fork and threw his arms around Ben. David and Travis turned to look at them. Ben mouthed, *He's okay.*

"I told you New York is never over," Colin said.

"Hey," Travis interrupted, "why is there an empty chair next to your grandfather? Is that for his dead wife?"

"No." Colin looked toward the table where Joseph Mead sat, with a vacant place setting beside him. "It's for Christopher, his youngest son. He died of AIDS back in the '80s. They weren't speaking at the time, and he's never forgiven himself. It's his way of remembering him."

"Good golly," said Travis. "Every rose...."

Mr. and Mrs. Mead had insisted Cade sit between them so that he could keep them entertained. "Some of these old folks are too stuffy for me," Mrs. Mead explained to him. Ben watched how Cade reveled in the lavish attention they poured on him, as if he were the center of their universe. *That's what having grandparents is all about*, Ben thought.

Toward the end of dinner, Joseph Mead rose from his table.

"May I have everyone's attention, please?" he said. The room hushed. "As you know, every year we ask one guest to tell us a story of thanksgiving. This year, after talking to my son, Carl, we decided to ask a young man named Quentin Walsh. I think you will find his story... well, remarkable. Quentin?"

Quentin rose from his chair and unfolded two pieces of paper.

Travis leaned over to Ben. "Did you know anything about this?"

"No," Ben answered. "Did you?"

"Nu-uh."

Quentin cleared his throat and began reading.

"The author Marc Brown once wrote, 'Sometimes being a brother is even better than being a superhero.' That quote means a lot to me, because I have three brothers, and as some of you know, eleven months ago, my parents were killed in a car accident. That was a big change, and the future looked pretty grim at the time. In fact, it was just about the worst possible thing that could happen to a sixteen-year-old. I was pretty pissed off. My older brother Ben came back to Texas, and he was pretty pissed off too. The first couple of days were damn awful, and I said some harsh things to him. I thought he was going to go back to New York and ship me and my two younger brothers off to live with relatives.

"But then something happened. He surprised me and decided to stay and take care of us. He took all his hopes and plans for his life and locked them away somewhere. He went from being a hotshot lawyer in New York City to the guardian of three kids he didn't even know that well. It was a huge sacrifice, and not one I appreciated at the time. I know he thought his life was pretty much over. At least that's how it seemed at first.

"And that's when this other thing happened. In the midst of all the tragedy, Ben met his soul mate, Travis. Because sometimes, and this is really important, the worst possible thing imaginable leads you to the place you were meant to be all along. Even in the most dire of times, life gives you a reason to give thanks.

"So, thank you, Ben, for giving up everything to take care of us. You saved our lives, literally. I'm sorry I said those harsh things to you. I can only hope that someday I'll grow up to be half the man you are. I know you never thought you'd hear me say this, but you really are my superhero."

Ben, Travis, Jason, and Cade all rose at once and walked over to their brother. The five of them huddled together while two hundred onlookers wept at the good fortune of the Walsh clan.

ON THE return trip to Austin, Ben and Travis started laughing when Ben brought up the last time they flew back from New York.

"Let's try to forget about it," Travis said.

"It's all part of what led us here, so I'm not going to forget about any of it."

Ben paused and Travis took his hand.

"Can I ask you about something?"

"Sure," Ben replied.

"What would it take to change my last name? To Walsh?"

"Why would you want to do that?"

"Look, I know we can't get married in Texas...." Travis paused and gestured to Ben, waiting for his two cents.

"Welcome to marriage inequality."

"Thank you," he continued. "But we should all have the same last name. Atwood is my father's name and I never even liked him. You're my family now, and not just you, obviously."

"Okay." Ben nodded. "Well, you have to submit a petition to a district court judge to have your name legally changed. It's all about how the petition is written, and they're decided case by case. We live in the only liberal county in Texas, and I could write your petition, of course. So I don't think it would be a problem."

"Would you be okay with that?"

Ben smiled. "Yes. *Travis Walsh*. My dad would be proud."

"Can we do it when we get home?"

"I'll draft the petition on Monday."

"Thanks."

Ben looked past Travis and out the window. "Hey, do you remember when I was sick with the flu last winter?"

"Now *that* I will never forget."

"Do you remember when I woke up, I told Quentin I had talked to our dad?"

"Kind of."

"I guess it was a dream, but it seemed real at the time. I got out of bed and went into the kitchen. He was making migas for me. My dad. So I sat down and we talked. He was the one who told me to register for the Texas Bar Exam. He told me you and I were going to hit a rough patch. He told me you were the solution to my problem. And he was right."

"I'm glad you listened to him."

"While I was still dreaming, I went back to bed and had—I don't know—I guess you'd call it a dream within a dream. Kind of like *Inception*. It was a vision of this moment, flying home with you, holding your hand. I looked out the window and saw the horizon like you do from a plane. You can't see the earth so there really isn't a horizon anymore. The future was wide open. I remember how happy that made me feel."

Ben pressed the button on his armrest and pushed his seat backward. He closed his eyes and felt Travis follow suit. Before Ben dozed off, he leaned over toward his boyfriend and, in the softest of voices, asked, "Will you put lights on the house this year?"

BRAD BONEY lives in Austin, Texas, the 7th gayest city in America. He likes to tell stories about the hot boys in his neighborhood near the University of Texas. Brand new to M/M fiction, he plans to set all of his books in Austin and hopes to become an ambassador for his city. He grew up in the Midwest and went to school at NYU. He lived in Washington, DC, and Houston before settling in Austin. He blames his background in the theater for his writing style, which he calls "dialogue and stage directions." He believes the greatest romantic comedy of all time is *50 First Dates*. His favorite gay film of the last ten years is *Strapped*. He has never met a boy band he didn't like. And yes, it's true—Emily's season of *The Bachelorette* restored his faith in love. Brad is currently single, and although his heart is open to love, he's not sure his schedule is. All he wants for Christmas is 100 Twitter followers.

Please visit Brad on the web at http://www.bradboney.com or become a part of his Christmas present at http://www.twitter.com/BradBoney.

Also from DREAMSPINNER PRESS

BUTTERFLY'S
CHILD

ALAN CHIN

http://www.dreamspinnerpress.com

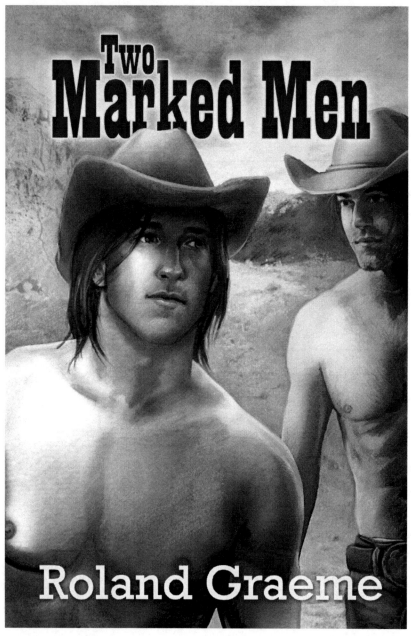

Also from DREAMSPINNER PRESS

http://www.dreamspinnerpress.com

THE LAST SNOW OF WINTER

IAN MUISE

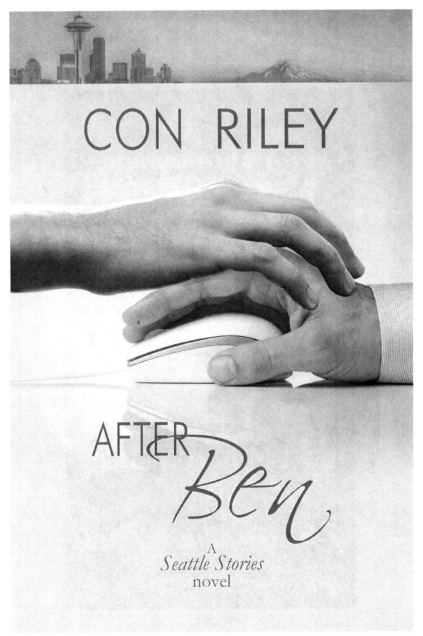

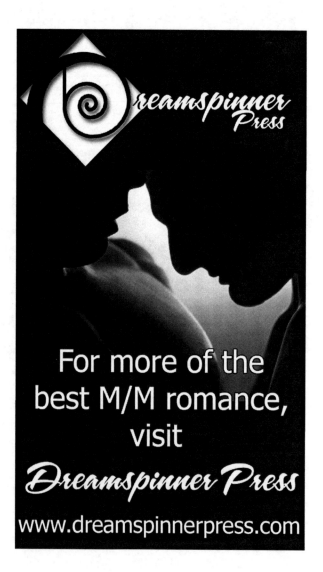

Lightning Source UK Ltd.
Milton Keynes UK
UKOW04f0621120813

215220UK00007B/475/P

9 781623 801380